# Tempered

*A Daughters of the People Novel*

## LUCY VARNA

# Tempered

*A Daughters of the People Novel*

LUCY VARNA

Bone Diggers Press
www.bonediggerspress.com

*For Laura and OhSoon*
*whose strength has seen them through*

Published by Bone Diggers Press, Clayton, Georgia.

ISBN 978-0-9907730-1-6

This story is a work of fiction. Any resemblance between the characters and persons living or dead is coincidental.

## TITLES BY LUCY VARNA

THE DAUGHTERS OF THE PEOPLE SERIES
Book 1: *The Prophecy*
Book 2: *Light's Bane*
Book 3: *The Enemy Within*
Book 3.5: *Tempered*
Book 4: *In All Things, Balance*

THE SONS OF THE PEOPLE SERIES
Book 1: *Say Yes*

THE CULLOWHEE HERITAGE SERIES
Book 1: *A Higher Purpose*
Book 2: *A Wicked Love*

# Notes from the Fab Four

*Notes on the People compiled by Tom Fairfax, Phil Walters, George Howe, and James Terhune, known at the IECS unofficially as the Fab Four.*

**Aenkanien.** A tattoo inked into the left-hand shoulder blade of a Son who becomes the husband of a Daughter. Once approval has been granted by the mothers of both parties and the tattoo is in place, a formal marriage ceremony is unnecessary; the two are considered married in the eyes of the People, though many couples choose to undergo a civil or, less frequently, traditional ceremony.

**Amaetien.** The tattoo Sons receive on their sixteenth birthday (the day they become men under the traditions and laws of the People) to indicate their maternal lineage. Usually inked onto the upper left arm, the *amaetien* is a symbol of the mother's eternal protection and devotion, and a warning to any who would harm the Son.

**Council of Seven.** The People's ruling body, consisting of seven women, one representing the line of each of the Seven Sisters.

**Daughter.** A direct descendant of one of the Seven Sisters, Daughters may be either immortal (if they have not yet broken their own curse) or mortal (if they have broken their own curse or are the daughter of a mortal Daughter).

**Eternal Order**. A supposedly mythical group devoted to undermining the ultimate goal of the People, to break the curse of immortality for every Daughter through the fulfillment of the Prophecy of Light.

**High Guard**. Seven Daughters devoted to eradicating the Eternal Order. A highly secret and deadly group.

**Institute of Early Cultural Studies (IECS)**. Located in Tellowee, Georgia, USA, the IECS is the main historical research branch of the People and serves as a repository for much of its history.

**Kaetyrm**. Sister, usually used in a formal situation, though not always.

**Maetyrm**. Mother, usually used as a term of respect for an elder Daughter and not necessarily as a reference to one's own mother. Teachers, for example, are referred to as Maetyrm.

**People, The**. The name used by the descendants of the Seven Sisters to describe themselves. The People include all immortal and mortal Daughters, Sons, and the mortal descendants of all submitted Daughters to the second degree (i.e. through the grandchildren of Daughters who have submitted their wills and become mortal). Other descendants are not counted among the numbers of the People.

**Prophecy of Light**. Issued by an unknown person at some distant point in the past, the Prophecy of Light portends a way for the curse of immortality to be lifted from all of the People, and not solely the Daughters who submit their wills and become mortal. (See the Daughters of the People website.)

**Seven Sisters**. The progenitors of the modern People. The seven women, all sisters, avenged the deaths of their parents by killing the men of the People (the original band) and were cursed by the god An to live immortal lives without the ability to bear sons. The curse was tempered by the goddess Ki, who decreed that the curse could be broken by each one if she would submit her will, in whatever way (except sexually), to the man she loved. (See the Legend of Beginnings on the Daughters of the People website.)

**Shadow Enemy**. The traditional enemy of the People.

**Son**. Usually refers to the child of a Daughter who has broken the curse and become mortal, but may also reference the child of a Son or another male descendant of a Daughter.

**Tellowee, Georgia, USA**. One of the centers of the People, located in rural northeast Georgia.

# ONE

THE NOISE in the main conference room of the Hyatt Regency Atlanta grew as fans flocked in to watch the stick fighting exhibition and the wrestling matches that would follow. Hawthorne stretched slowly and observed the people milling about. Across the ring, Levi Ewart, her opponent, bent over at the waist and touched his palms to the floor in a straight-legged stretch. He was tall and solid with the sturdy bone structure of his Scottish father and the innate grace of his musician mother. His vivid personality matched the copper hair capping his even features.

Women were drawn to him, moths to a living flame, handsome young man that he was. Behind him, a mother seated with her young son patted her chest, her wide eyes fixed intently on Levi. Near her, two younger women tittered and sighed trying to catch his eye, then slumped when he ignored their efforts.

Silly women. What temerity these modern women had, to think they could catch the attention of a Son, this one in particular. Hawthorne had plans for her great-grandson, not one of which included mating him to a mundane mortal.

Levi walked his hands forward along the mat, held a plank, and moved smoothly into a cobra pose. He pushed into a stand

and winked at Hawthorne, as if he knew exactly what effect he had on the women in the audience.

Incorrigible lad.

Three rows away from the fighting ring and to Hawthorne's right, a tall, dark-headed man in his early thirties took a seat next to a shorter, pudgy man with the sallow skin of one who seldom saw the sun. She shifted subtly to include them in her view. The tall man slouched in his chair, arms crossed over a broad chest, knees spread wide. His hair fell in disheveled waves to curl over his collar, framing a tanned rectangular face. This one was not afraid of the sun. From his appearance, he dwelt in it regularly. Heavy thighs under worn jeans, muscled forearms, flat stomach; possibly gained through bicycling and swimming, perhaps hiking.

Aaron Kesselman, a graphic artist and native of San Francisco, presented a stark but pleasant contrast to his bloated friend. This was the man Rebecca Upton had asked Hawthorne to investigate during DragonCon. Apparently, his last creation had mimicked the world of the People a shade too closely to be a coincidence. Rebecca had requested information on Kesselman's sources, and Hawthorne had acquiesced as a favor to the other warrior.

She would resent the intrusion on her time if not for her sense of duty to the People. The Con was the one time each year when she exposed herself to the mortal public as precisely herself. There was no need to hide her apparent lack of aging or to assume a polite expression, no need to navigate the intricate and often tedious politics inherent in being an elder, no pressure to reproduce or lead or do anything aside from protecting and caring for her family. At the Con, no one asked her to be anything other than what she was, a storyteller. It was a blessed relief to have the favorite part of herself outweigh her other obligations, if only for four days.

It would be no hardship to investigate a man as handsome and fit as Kesselman. Perhaps she could persuade him to share a brief sexual interlude. She indulged herself so rarely, it seemed shameful to waste the opportunity now. If his work derived from an innocent source, she would seduce him into her bed, thereby fulfilling two needs, her duty to the People and her need for intimacy. Sensible, efficient, and all without having to bother herself with the social niceties.

A referee stepped into the ring, signaling the beginning of the exhibition. Hawthorne shut everything out of her mind save her opponent. They swung their hanbō in unison, Levi wearing a cheeky smirk. Her muscles flexed and pulled, stretching deliciously in a sinewy motion so ingrained it was nearly automated. A bell rang, the crowd hushed as if collectively holding a breath. Levi circled lazily to her left, his hanbō lowered in a deliberate taunt.

Hawthorne's lips twitched. Boy was getting cocky. Perhaps a set-down was in order. Nothing that would wound him or his pride, simply a reminder that he should be careful when dealing with a warrior nearly two millennia his elder. She lowered her own guard, coaxing him to come closer, and set out to give their audience a show they would remember for a very long time to come.

AARON KESSELMAN divided his attention between the banter of his agent, Jason Truman, and the exhibition in the center of the room where a man and a woman, each dressed in form-fitting athletic wear and carrying a hefty, yard-long stick, circled one another preparing to fight. The man was tall and rangy, his red hair shades lighter than the woman's. Hers was cut short and gelled so that it stuck out in irregular intervals, making her look like a demented pixie. A tall demented pixie, but still. Her face was completely expressionless, her toned form relaxed, loose. The man struck a testing blow to her waist. She deflected it with a casual downswing, using no more effort than if she'd been swatting a fly.

Interesting.

Aaron sat straighter in his chair, angling for a better view around the two gossiping women in front of him. His mind automatically formatted the fight, breaking it into panels on an imaginary storyboard.

Thrust, parry, evasion. *You're no match for me!* in a dialogue balloon above the woman's head.

Leg sweep, thump. Aaron winced as the man hit the mat with a thud and bounded back up into an attack so swift, his stick hand was a blur.

Man: *Ha, I've got you now.*

Woman: *In your dreams.*

They moved around the ring in a graceful dance of swings and lunges, their muscles bunching and stretching as they fought, the action so smooth it could've been choreographed.

He should be filming this to use as a reference for his next book.

Aaron patted his jean pockets absent-mindedly. Right. He'd left his camera in the hotel room so it wouldn't be in the way. He dug a scrap of paper and the nub of a pencil out of his pocket and made a quick sketch of the woman's face. Oval with high cheek bones, tilted almond-shaped eyes. Too far away to see the color. He glanced at her, lined in the bow of her mouth, the delicate line of her nose. How old was she? Twenty-five, thirty? Older than the man she fought, but not by much.

He stuffed the sketch and pencil back into his pocket in time to see the woman tap the man three times in succession, once each on his back, stomach, and butt as she twirled around him, completely eluding his defenses. The man laughed and held his hands up in surrender, and the referee called the match as the audience burst into applause. The man snatched the woman up in a ground-clearing bear hug and kissed her firmly on the mouth.

Aaron scowled and slumped into his chair. Figured she'd be taken.

Jason nudged him with an elbow. "She's something, isn't

she?"

Aaron grunted. "Good fight."

"What crawled up your butt?" Jason shook his head. "I thought you'd enjoy seeing the famous Al C. Hawthorne in action."

"That's Hawthorne?" Aaron studied her again. She spoke quietly to her opponent, who listened as if she were reciting the divine law. "I thought she was a he."

"You really need to get out more, man. She's hot property right now. A dozen novels out in half that time, all released under her pen name. Epic fantasies. Complex shit. Her agent's Dana Goldburg."

"We've met."

"That's right. The Con in San Diego last year."

"See? I get out."

Jason snorted. "Right. Anyway, Dana loves her. Thinks she's the best thing since sliced bread, even if she is a hermit. Only event she'll attend is this one. I got an earful of Hawthorne on the flight over."

Aaron slid a glance to his agent. "Told you to fly out with me."

"Then I woulda missed out on some great gossip." Jason waggled his eyebrows. "Also, flirting. It's that thing you do with women where you laugh and make gaga eyes at each other. You remember that?"

"Ha. Funny. I get out."

"Only when I make you. Come on." Jason slapped Aaron on the shoulder. "Time to meet the fabulous Al C. Hawthorne."

"Who says I want to meet her?"

"The sketch in your pocket says so," Jason said bluntly. "Last time you drew a woman, you married her."

"That's not true." And it wasn't. He drew women all the time, sometimes even from live models. It was merely a coincidence that Jeanne had been one of those women. "Besides, looks like Hawthorne's taken."

"Then it won't kill you to make nice."

They stood and edged their way through the crowd. A handful of women had cornered Hawthorne's boyfriend, twirling their hair and batting their eyelashes at the handsome young man, who graciously autographed whatever was placed in front of him, including one woman's arm.

Hawthorne stuffed her bare feet into unlaced tennis shoes, gathered her stick, and stepped gracefully through the ropes and off the edge of the ring. She caught Aaron's gaze as she slipped through clusters of fans, politely deflecting requests for autographs until she stood in front of him. She was half a head shorter than him, if that. Her pearlescent skin gleamed under the harsh lighting, bare of makeup.

If she'd broken a sweat during the fight, it didn't show.

Jason held out his hand. "Jason Truman and this is Aaron Kesselman."

Hawthorne shook Jason's hand then Aaron's, her grip firm but brief. "I am Hawthorne. You work with Dana," she said to Jason, her voice as accentless as her expression was empty. "She is here?"

"At the Con, yeah," Jason said. "Don't know where, though."

"I shall find her later." Hawthorne turned piercing gray eyes on Aaron. "Mr. Kesselman. You are interested in my form?"

Aaron choked on an indrawn breath. "What?"

"My fighting form. You were sketching." She blinked, the only change in her expression. "Or were you more interested in Levi? I shall fetch him, should you like."

"No, that's ok. Your, uh, form is fine." He stuffed his hands into the back pockets of his jeans. "You must have quick eyes to've caught me drawing."

"Observation. It is a simple skill, though much neglected among modern humans."

Aaron exchanged a puzzled glance with Jason. *Modern* humans?

"We shall talk," she continued. "I must bid Levi adieu and then you will accompany me to my hotel suite where we shall drink to our acquaintance."

"That's my cue." Jason waggled his eyebrows. "People to see, places to go."

He slipped away, leaving Aaron alone with a woman who, unless he was sorely mistaken, had just propositioned him.

On the other hand, she seemed completely straight-forward. Maybe to her, a drink was just a drink.

Levi appeared behind her and rested his right hand on her left shoulder. "Stirring up trouble again, Nana?"

"Interacting with my professional peers. Mr. Kesselman, this is my relative, Levi Ewart."

Aaron nodded at the young man, who eyed him with a steady gaze eerily reminiscent of Hawthorne's. "Great demonstration."

"Thanks. Don't get a chance to fight Nana often." Levi's mouth twisted into a smirk. "She usually kicks my arse, though. Says it builds character."

"Character and fortitude. I cannot have you defenseless to the world." She turned to face Levi and cupped his face in her hands. "Mr. Kesselman and I are going to my rooms for a drink. Please tell your mother I said hello."

"I will." Levi grasped her elbows and bowed until their foreheads touched. "Be good, Nana."

"Am I not always?" She kissed him lightly on the mouth and forehead, and released his face. "Well met, child."

"Well met, Maetyrm." Levi nodded solemnly to Hawthorne and Aaron, then slid past them toward the entrance.

Aaron followed the young man's progress with his gaze. "Maetyrm?"

"A term of respect." She moved to stand beside him. "Shall we go?"

He hesitated, not because he didn't want to. She was the first woman to catch his interest in months. It had been a long time

7

since he'd had a date, let alone sex, and he didn't quite trust himself to behave, especially considering the venue. *Professional image*, he reminded himself. *No touching*.

Looking, on the other hand, was perfectly acceptable. One drink with an attractive woman wouldn't kill him, and he could enjoy the view while they talked.

"Sure," he said. "Lead the way."

He followed her to a private elevator, waited while she swiped a keycard to open it. They were silent on the way up. Aaron leaned against the back wall and studied her. She held herself the same way she had during the fight. No tension, no fidgeting. He'd never seen a woman with such economy of motion before. He eyed the graceful set of her shoulders, the curve of her hips, the firm length of her legs. Desire stirred in his gut, surprising him, and he eyed her again. That skin-hugging outfit was better than her being naked.

The elevator dinged and its doors slid open. They stepped out into a short hallway with two doors on the facing wall and two on the elevator's side, spaced widely. Hawthorne led him to the right and flicked her keycard along the lock of the door on the left. It opened into a large living room with a sitting area between the entrance and the opposite wall of windows, a kitchen and dining area to the right, and two doors beyond that. What looked like a well-stocked bar occupied the left corner of the room. A row of bookcases occupied part of the wall near the bar. Portraits in various sizes were strategically placed around the room. It seemed more like a permanent residence than a hotel suite, and was much homier than his own room two floors below.

Aaron stepped through the door and closed it behind himself. Hawthorne whirled and pressed one blunt end of her stick against his sternum. She leaned into it, forcing him backwards. His back thudded against the door. He held his hands up and eyed her warily. What the hell was she doing?

Her eyes were flat, uncompromising in her otherwise neutral expression. "Now, Mr. Kesselman, you will tell me how you obtained information about the People and their activities."

There was no *or else*, but there didn't need to be. He'd seen her fight and was pretty sure she'd checked herself to keep from hurting her *relative*. He scrambled through his mind. Who were the people, and what activities was he supposed to know about?

She trailed the end of the stick down his abdomen, resting it in the juncture between his legs, exerting just enough force behind her stance for the end to press up through his jeans.

"I have no idea what you're talking about," he said. "Honest. Who are these People?"

The stick eased upward a fraction. He inhaled sharply. It didn't hurt, but a tad higher and it would. Oddly, he wasn't scared. A strange woman had a stick between his legs, a woman who'd used that stick to take down a man half a head taller and fifty pounds heavier than herself, and he wasn't scared.

When he got back to San Francisco, he really needed to have a long chat with a psychiatrist.

"Look." He glanced at her helplessly. "What's your first name?"

"Hawthorne."

"Your first name is Hawthorne? What's your last name?"

"Hawthorne. Do not attempt to distract me with trivialities."

"Knowing the name of the woman who's backed you against a door doesn't seem too trivial to me."

Her expression didn't change, though the pressure on his groin eased slightly. He had the feeling he'd amused her.

"Can't we sit down and talk about this like rational adults?" He nodded toward her hand. "I'll tell you what you want to know without the stick."

"It is called a hanbō." A phone rang nearby. Hawthorne stepped back, dropping the hanbō as she did. "Please excuse me. I am expecting this call."

She turned and walked toward the coffee table, putting her back to him. He eased his hand down and behind him, searching for the doorknob.

9

"Do not attempt to leave unless you wish me to chase you down," she said without turning around. "I *will* catch you, Mr. Kesselman. Should you run, there is nowhere you can hide that will spare you from my questions, or my wrath."

She picked up a cell phone and spoke into it in rapid Spanish, only half of which he caught. Something about a lolly and bedtime. She perched on the arm of the sofa, her eyes glued to him as she spoke. During a lull in the conversation, she lifted the hanbō and gestured from him to the bar.

He scrubbed a hand across his nape. A drink would at least distract him, even if it did put him farther away from a possible escape route. Not that he believed he had much chance of escaping. She seemed determined to have him there for some reason.

"Lali," Hawthorne said in precise English. "It is past your bedtime."

So, Lali was a child. Hawthorne's?

He ambled to the bar, sorted through the liquor bottles, and selected a bottle of Johnnie Walker Blue Label. He raised an eyebrow and wiggled the liquor at her. She nodded once, so he found two glasses and openly eavesdropped on her conversation. Apparently, Lali wouldn't take her evening bath and go to bed without Nana reading her a story. Levi had called Hawthorne Nana, too. Aaron tucked that tidbit away for later thought and poured a scant finger of scotch in each glass.

Hawthorne finished her call and dropped her phone onto the coffee table. She stalked toward him with a loose-limbed roll of her hips that grabbed at his gut and wouldn't let go. He'd never met a woman as relaxed and confident and sure of herself as Hawthorne was.

It was sexy as hell.

She slid onto the seat of a barstool and pinned a piercing gaze on him. "Now, Mr. Kesselman. Tell me what you know of the People."

# TWO

HAWTHORNE ACCEPTED the drink Aaron handed her. A spark of attraction passed between them as their fingers brushed. He sipped his drink and met her gaze evenly. This pleased her. A man who whined and begged held no appeal, but a man who demonstrated his strength was to be treasured.

"I have no idea who the People are," he said. "Honest."

"So you have said. Yet, your last graphic novel detailed the life of Rebecca the Blade and her kin." She leaned the hanbō against the side of the bar within easy reach and cupped the glass he'd given her between her hands. "Explain."

His laugh held enough incredulity to draw a sharp glance from her. "That's what this is about?"

"Where did you obtain your information?"

"Single-minded." He blew out a breath. "From the Bancroft Library at UC Berkeley. I have a friend who works there and happened to be in town a few days after she found this great collection of historical documents in the vault, some dating back to the middle ages. There were two volumes written by an author known only as the Chronicler, a historian who lived during the early Renaissance. Apparently, his works are rare."

The Chronicler. Rebecca would not be pleased.

Hawthorne raised her glass and drained it in one swallow.

Liquid fire burned its way down her esophagus. "Where are the volumes now?"

"Still in the vault, far as I know." He eyed her with what might have been concern. "That's supposed to be sipped."

"I am well aware. Another, please." She slid the glass to him and waited while he poured a scant finger of scotch into it, his large hands gentle and elegant. Those hands would be on her tonight, if she could persuade him. Her skin tingled with possibilities. "You read through these volumes?"

"Yeah. Great stuff. Epic battles between good and evil, a young warrior overcoming adversity against staggering odds. I took one of the characters, this Rebecca the Blade, and gave her story a new setting, a couple of twists. Couldn't let a story like that go untold." He leaned his forearms on the top of the bar. "So, what's your interest in the Chronicler's tales?"

"Personal." She threw back her drink, consuming it in one swallow. Its heat shuddered through her. "I shall verify your story. If this is, indeed, where you obtained your information, then we shall never have to speak on it again."

"So that's it? I'm free to go?" He pushed away from the bar and shot her a sour look, his brows furrowing over sinfully dark chocolate eyes. "Next time you need to know something, try asking."

"I shall remember that," she murmured and rose from the barstool. "You may go unless you wish to converse or copulate."

"Copulate," he said in a strangled voice, his eyes wide. "As in, have sex?"

"If that is your wish, I am amenable. The attraction is mutual." She pivoted and pulled off her athletic top as she walked toward the bedroom. He wheezed out a cough, and she almost smiled. "I wish to shower first. The exhibition with Levi left me sticky."

She glanced over her shoulder. He had braced his elbows on the bar and was rubbing his eyes with the fingers of one hand. Satisfaction purred through her. Yes, he found her attractive and he would stay. Their interaction would be a pleasant diversion, perhaps enough to temporarily assuage her worries over the discovery of the Chronicler's tales in a location far beyond where they should have been.

"Come, Aaron Kesselman. You may watch me bathe."

He gaped at her, then snapped his jaw shut. "Just like that, you're ready to strip down in front of me? Don't you want to get to know me first, maybe have dinner, catch a movie?"

"If you are hungry, I shall call room service. Otherwise, I should like to copulate." She held out her hand. "Come along, now."

He muttered under his breath as he came around the side of the bar, but took her hand and allowed her to lead him into her bedroom.

"I had no idea modern men could be so shy," she said. "Is this typical among your social set?"

"You have a strange way of putting things."

"That is not an answer." She stepped into the bathroom and turned the water on, adjusting the knobs and testing until the temperature felt right. Even after decades of having access to it, nearly instantaneous hot water was a blissful luxury. She stripped off her yoga tights and stepped into the shower. "A young man of your age should be ready to copulate at a moment's notice. Is this not evolution's way of ensuring the survival of our species?"

At his continued silence, she turned. He was leaning against the bathroom's counter, his long legs crossed in front of him at the ankles, his hands gripping the edge. His gaze was fixed firmly on her body. Even over the chemical scent of the water and from across the room, she could smell his arousal in the pheromones he exuded, observe it in the growing hardness beneath the zipper of his trousers.

She slid the shower curtain open, catching his attention. "Have you never seen a nude woman before?"

He closed his eyes and pinched the bridge of his nose. "Sorry."

"If I did not wish you to look, I would not have undressed in front of you." She closed the curtain and began to bathe, reveling in the warm water sliding across her skin. "I am puzzled by your reluctance to perform a natural act. Such modesty is unnecessary."

"I can honestly say I've never met a woman quite like you before."

"The women of your era are soft, weak." Hawthorne washed her hair quickly, rubbing her fingertips briskly across her scalp as she lathered and rinsed. "They would not endure three minutes on a battlefield."

He grunted out a laugh. "Not a lot of battlefields in America."

"There are more than you can know, Aaron Kesselman."

"Maybe you should call me Aaron. Now that I've seen you naked, using my whole name seems a little too formal."

She turned off the water and stepped out of the shower. He handed her a towel. She handed it back to him. "I wish for you to dry me."

"Ah." He eyed the towel, glanced down her dripping form. "Are you sure about that?"

"I would not ask if I did not wish it so."

"I'm beginning to believe that," he murmured. He draped the towel over her head and chafed gently. "Never met a woman who says exactly what she means."

"You have not met many Daughters, then." She sighed as he slid the towel down, drying her shoulders and arms, her breasts and torso. The towel was rough against her skin in spite of the softness of his touch. She would speak with housekeeping concerning that on the morrow. "You are very gentle for such a large man."

"Don't want to hurt you."

"You cannot," she assured him.

He knelt in front of her, rubbed the towel up and down her legs in quick, brisk motions. She shifted, allowing him better

14

access, and combed her fingers through the curls of his hair, watching him. He hesitated, holding the towel near the juncture of her thighs. She tightened her fingers in his hair and gently tugged, pulling his head back until their gazes met.

"Why do you hesitate? This is where I wish you to be."

His eyes went molten and his breath hitched. "You are the oddest woman."

She released her grip on his hair. "Is it odd for a woman to speak her mind, to direct a man to her pleasure?"

"In my experience? Yeah."

He slid the towel upward, dried her in soft dabs, denying her the friction of the fabric against her clitoris. When he finished, he continued kneeling in front of her, as if uncertain. She urged him forward with a hand to the back of his head. He pushed back, resisting her silent plea for his touch. Such recalcitrance, from a man who clearly wished to be with her. It would amuse her if his arousal were not obvious, in the erection visible beneath his pants, in the musky smell of it drifting to her.

She stepped forward, straddling his thighs in a wide-legged stance. "Touch me."

"I really think we should move this to the bedroom," he said, his voice thick and low. "And then, if you still want me to, I'll touch you all you want."

"Then that is what we shall do." She stepped back and took the towel from him, hanging it on the metal bar above the toilet while he rolled back onto his heels and into a stand. When he reached for the buttons of his shirt, she placed her hands over his. "I shall do that, if you please."

He dropped his hands and followed her into the bedroom where he slipped off the boating shoes he wore and placed them neatly in front of the dresser. He sat on the edge of the bed and scrubbed his hands down his thighs in a gesture that tugged at her sympathy.

"Have you never known a woman?" she asked gently.

"Seriously? At my age?" His eyes widened and he wheezed

out a breath. "Yeah, I've had sex before."

"You seem nervous. Scoot back, please." She knelt on the bed, straddling his thighs, and unfastened the buttons of his shirt before pulling it off and folding it. He wore a t-shirt underneath, so she pulled it off as well, working it over his head and raised arms, and placed it with his outer shirt. She ran her hands over his chest in admiring sweeps, memorizing the silky smoothness of his muscled physique, not overly so, but enough to indicate the care he took with his body. "You are well-formed."

"Thanks." He rested his hands on her hips and squeezed. "You, too."

She trailed her hands up over his firm pectorals, across his shoulders, and twined her hands behind his neck. "I shall kiss you now, if you are amenable."

"I'm amenable," he murmured, and slid his arms around her as their mouths met.

She darted her tongue out, tasting him, and he opened for her, taking control of the kiss, melding his mouth to hers with a passion that took her breath. Need climbed in her, sending a deliciously melting heat through her veins. His hands skimmed over her back, one finding her ass and the other the back of her head, and he pressed her forward, molding their bodies together, her breasts brushing his chest, their stomachs aligned. He tightened his grip and twisted until her back was on the bed with him above her, resting between her thighs.

The need chilled within her and she cursed inwardly. Two millennia and she still hadn't conquered this fear.

Aaron drew away, crawling backward off the bed, and stood by its side. His eyes were dark pools of heat as he stared at her, full of possession and need and want. He unfastened his trousers and pushed them down, and his erection sprang free, a thick, hard length that jutted from his body, begging to be tasted. She levered herself up, intending to do just that. It had been too long since she had pleased a man in that fashion, and the urge to do so with this one came inexplicably.

"Stay there." He kicked away his trousers, his expression taut and greedy. "I have plans for you."

Her amusement dissipated under the tickling touch of his mouth along her instep. He nibbled her ankle, slid his hands up her calves and licked behind her knees, pressed light, teasing kisses to her inner thighs. Each touch lifted the desire within her, sending it coursing through her limbs, melting her fear and resistance at having a man holding her down. He pressed an open-mouthed kiss to her clitoris and suckled her there, igniting the heat into a raging flame. She clasped his head in her hands, holding him against her sex while his mouth explored her, writhing under his touch.

"That is very pleasing." She gasped the words out, her voice breathy, needy. This man, a near stranger, was mastering her. It could not be so. She, a Daughter who never submitted to anyone, could barely control the desire he raised in her.

Aaron's tongue dipped into her core and then he licked, a long, slow caress. Her hips shot off the bed and her fingers tangled in his hair and her breath left her as he teased her, tonguing her clitoris in hard strokes that gentled until they were a feather-light torture against her need.

She tugged at his hair. "I would like to copulate now."

His teeth flashed, white and even against his tanned skin. "Let me get a condom."

"No condom. My needing time is months hence and neither of us carries diseases that would harm the other."

"Don't get me wrong. I'd love to be in you without a condom getting in the way, love to feel your heat without that barrier, but I don't think it's a good idea."

She tugged at his hair again. "Do you trust me?"

He considered her for a long moment. "Yeah, I do."

"Then you will do as I say. We shall copulate now."

He shook his head and scooted up, bracing himself over her. "Why am I giving in to you, again?"

"That is simple. You wish to be with me. It is, therefore,

easy for you to accede to my wishes."

She flipped him onto his back. He landed with a startled *oomph*, his hands scrambling for purchase on her body. She straddled him quickly, taking him into herself in one smooth stroke. He closed his eyes on a low groan and grasped her hips with his hands.

"That is..." He exhaled slowly and fastened his gaze on hers. "Beautiful."

"I find you beautiful as well," she said, and he chuckled and tightened his grip on her flesh.

She moved over him slowly, watching the pleasure build in his expression, in the heat gathering in his eyes and the flush of passion on his skin. He rocked with her, gentle, exciting counterpoints, building her own need to a fevered pitch. She clamped down on it, struggling for control, struggling to contain the need to submit to the desire raging between them. His fingers found her clitoris and rubbed, sending her soaring as he thrust up into her and spilled his seed into her body in long, rolling throbs of pleasure.

AARON'S HEART pounded hard, threatening to break through his ribs and escape. Hawthorne straddled him, her own chest heaving with shuddering breaths. Even after the completely out-of-this-world sex they'd just had, she seemed tightly controlled. For a moment near the end, he'd thought she might pull back, and then he'd touched her and she'd thrown her head back and come on a low cry, sending him over the edge with her.

He pulled her down onto him and nestled her close as their breaths calmed and their skin cooled in the air-conditioned room. He nuzzled the side of her neck, tasting the salt on her skin. She shifted above him, murmuring softly as he stroked her back, found her mouth with his.

When he found his voice, he said, "You ok?"

"I am well. You?"

"Peachy." He shifted her to his side, facing her on the mattress, and wedged his thigh between hers. "So, do you have sex with strangers a lot?"

"That is a question you should have asked before we copulated." She traced idle circles on his chest, grazed a fingernail along his nipple. "I discarded my last lover in 2009."

"Discarded, huh." He dropped a tender kiss to her mouth. "What happened?"

"He was a man. Easily distracted, unfaithful." She shrugged. "I let him live, which is more than he deserved."

Her answer stunned him into silence. Did she go around killing her lovers willy-nilly? She'd been willing enough to use her stick on him earlier, and all he'd done was write the wrong story. What would she do to him after tonight?

"I would not let him bring me to an orgasm. He thought me cold, unfeeling."

So, her holding back hadn't been his imagination. He shifted against her, drawing her close. "Why not?"

"That is personal," she said, her voice glacial.

He eyed her, puzzled by her reluctance. She seemed so straight-forward, almost tactlessly blunt in her honesty. "You came for me."

"You took what you wanted." She wiggled away from him, easily evading his hands as he reached for her. "I shall order sustenance. While we are waiting for its arrival, I shall pleasure you as you pleasured me."

He flopped onto the bed with a groaning laugh and watched her stroll through the hotel suite, so comfortable in her own skin she might as well have been fully clothed. A moment later, her voice drifted through the doorway from the living room, giving rapid instructions in harsh, guttural tones. What was she speaking? He propped up onto his elbows and tried to follow the patterns. Russian, maybe? Ukrainian?

It didn't take him long to abandon his efforts. Languages had never been his forte. Spanish was a necessity in California and he spoke it well enough to be understood. Other than that and the occasional Yiddish sentiment, he was hopeless at anything outside of English.

He pushed himself off the bed, stretched, forcing energy into pleasantly languid limbs, and padded across the carpeted floor into the bathroom.

He'd never met a woman like Hawthorne before, not in thirty-three years of travelling. That they hadn't met since she'd become a published author astounded him. So he illustrated comics and she wrote fantasy. There was a lot of overlap between the two, professionally and otherwise. He'd attended DragonCon two years earlier and didn't recall hearing her name spoken not once. Her appearance was so striking, her demeanor so self-contained. Surely he would've noticed her.

He relieved himself and washed his hands, then went to find Hawthorne. She was curled into a loose ball on the bed, propped on one elbow with a book open in front of her. While he'd been in the bathroom, she'd flipped the overhead light off and cut on the bedside lamp. It bathed her in an intimate glow that muted the fire in her hair and cast shadows over her lean curves.

He eased into the bed behind her, spooning her nude body with his. They fit so well together, better than he would've imagined given their relative heights. She marked her spot in the book and closed it, then shifted onto her back beside him. Her face seemed softer, relaxed. She traced her fingers over his cheek and down his neck, her eyelids fluttering to hide her nearly ice-gray eyes as they followed her fingers downward.

"Piotr will have a meal for us soon." Her breasts shifted as she sat up.

He had yet to taste her there, had yet to explore her in full. He would, though, if she wanted, as much as he could.

"I should like to take you in my mouth, if you are amenable," she said.

"I'm amenable to pretty much anything you want, so if you want to put your mouth on me, by all means, do." He pressed her back against the bed and moved over her, burying his face in her neck, his body hardening with need. Under the light scent of her sweat, she smelled of roses and soap. The floral undertones were unexpected, a stark contrast to her candor. How could a woman as blunt as Hawthorne be comfortable in such a feminine scent? "But later. You rushed me before."

"I do not rush." She hooked a leg over his thighs and levered him onto his back, straddling him. "Then, it was time to copulate. Now, it is time to play."

He threaded his hands behind his head and considered her. "That's the second time you've done that. What do you have against being on the bottom?"

Her forthright gaze met his evenly. "It is unpleasant."

"Why?"

"That is personal. Do you not derive pleasure from this position?"

"Oh, yeah, but that isn't what we're talking about here. Define unpleasant."

"Unpleasant," she said flatly.

"That's not really helpful." He inhaled, easing his impatience. If she didn't want to talk about it, fine, but he needed her to open up. "Do you think I'll hurt you?"

"Do not concern yourself. Though you are a large man, you fit well within me."

"That's not what I'm talking about and you know it. I'm asking if you think I'll abuse you."

She blinked owlishly. "You are a gentle man."

"But you don't trust me." He sighed and scrubbed the heels of his hands across his face. "Why did you have sex with me?"

"You ask questions that will lead to nothing but more questions. Is it not enough that I have taken you to my bed?"

"No, it's really not." He tapped her hip. "Come on. Time to build some trust."

She stayed stubbornly in place above him. "It is my turn to pleasure you."

"You can. Later. When you trust me. Where's the remote?"

He cajoled her into sliding beneath the covers while he slipped on his boxers and found a monster movie marathon playing on a local station. He set the remote on the nightstand and turned off the lamp, slid into bed and curled up behind her under the covers.

She jerked her chin at the TV. "What is this?"

"*Godzilla vs. Mothra*. A classic. You haven't seen it?"

"I do not watch moving pictures."

"Really? You don't know what you're missing."

She twisted and speared him with her gray-eyed stare. "What does Godzilla have to do with building trust?"

"You'll see." He dropped a kiss on the end of her pert nose before nudging her. "Hush now. You're missing the good part."

As soon as she relaxed against him, he slipped his hand from her hip to her stomach, caressing her silky skin gently, learning her shape. Her self-control was tight, but eventually he began to understand the minute signs she made when she enjoyed a particular touch. The subtle shift of her legs when his fingers brushed the curls at the juncture of her thighs. A slight intake of breath when he thumbed the crease beneath her breast. The infinitesimal tightening of her fingers against the bedspread when his breath caressed the nape of her neck. He suspected an untapped well of passion lay hidden beneath her cool exterior.

A knock sounded on the door. He padded into the living room, signed for the meal Hawthorne had ordered, and peeked into the covered dishes. They contained individual-sized pepperoni pizzas, crisp home-made potato chips, and New York style cheesecake topped with fresh strawberries. As if on cue, his stomach growled. Sex and food, he thought, and grinned. God, he was such a man.

He coaxed Hawthorne into eating in bed. After they'd polished off the pizzas and chips, he persuaded her to straddle him and fed her cheesecake one creamy spoonful at a time while Godzilla stomped and roared in the background.

Later, he put the dishes away and stripped off his boxers, cuddling behind her on the bed, exploring her. When his touch had her breaths coming in silent pants, he eased her onto her back, pulled her leg over his, exposing her core to his touch, and slid his fingers over the nub of her sex as he kissed her.

He waited until she was ready, until she was writhing under his hand and her mouth clung to his in a desperate kiss, then shifted over her and nudged her core with his erection. He slid inside inch by agonizing inch, gritting his teeth as he fought not to seat himself fully within her in the first thrust. *Building trust,* he thought around the haze of molten need welling up in his gut, and then he was there, sheathed inside her slick heat in a satisfying pleasure that engulfed him, pushing everything else aside. He managed one gentle thrust before she slid a leg over his thigh. The next thing he knew, he was on his back and she was moving over him, her hips undulating in steady circles, pulling him into a sharp peak, their cries mingling as waves of intense pleasure crashed over them.

# THREE

OURS AFTER Hawthorne brought him to her suite, Aaron slipped from her bed. She inched over into the space he had vacated, surrounding herself with the remnants of his warmth, and watched him dress. A sigh of contentment rolled through her. They had pleasured one another three times that evening. Even the raucous noise of Godzilla had not been enough to dampen the need. Building trust, he had called it. These modern humans and their euphemisms.

He sat on the edge of the bed and toyed with the ends of her hair. "I'll see you tomorrow?"

"I shall find you when my schedule permits."

"I'm amenable to that." He pressed a light kiss to her mouth, ending it far too quickly. "I don't carry my phone with me or I'd give you the number."

"I would rather speak with you in person."

"Me, too." He considered her for a long moment, his chocolate eyes intense. "I can't believe I want you again."

She sat, allowing the sheet to fall to her waist, baring her breasts to his gaze. "You may stay, should you wish."

His laugh was shaky and low. "Tempting, but it wouldn't look good for me to come out of your room in the morning."

"Think you I care?"

"No, but I do. You deserve better than having people gossip about you."

"They already do. If you are not comfortable staying, I shall not harangue you."

"Good. Don't think I could handle any more haranguing, not after the hanbō incident." He kissed her again and rose from the bed, and muttered a curse under his breath. "Those breasts should be registered as lethal weapons." His hands went to the buttons of his shirt, unfastening them in rapid twists of his fingers. "One more time and then I really have to go."

She held her hand out to him and welcomed him into her bed and body, and when he left, held his pillow close and breathed in his scent as she fell into a deep, peaceful sleep.

Her morning errands ran longer than she would have liked, eating into the time she had set aside to find Aaron and perhaps break her fast with him. She called her assistant and had her begin checking Aaron's story, spoke with housekeeping about the roughness of the towels, and called Lali to wish her a good morning. Her granddaughter chattered aimlessly, her soft voice punctuated by giggles and squeals. Hawthorne snagged an apple from the kitchen and ate it in delicate bites as she listened to Lali and wove her way through the hectic hustle and bustle of the hotel. Upon entering the dining room, she spotted a familiar dark head bracketed between Dana Goldburg's pudgy coworker and a woman whose fingers trailed along Aaron's forearm with more familiarity than was healthy or wise.

"Lali, darling," Hawthorne said. "I must attend to business now."

After disconnecting the call, she found a trash can and threw the remainder of her apple away, her gaze fixed on the tableau containing Aaron. He had left her bed less than six hours before and already allowed another woman to claim him with inappropriate intimacy. Hawthorne licked the apple's juices from her fingers as she strode through the half empty room and contemplated her options. Fairness dictated that he have one opportunity to explain his actions, and then? She shrugged, testing the harness holding her sword across her back. He would not be the first man she had beheaded for infidelity, nor was he likely to be the last.

She hated killing a man who built trust the way Aaron did. A man with such skills should be nurtured, cultivated. Infidelity, however, could not be tolerated.

The moment Aaron spotted her, his eyes went heavy with need. Gratifying, but not enough to stay his impending punishment.

She stalked toward his table and halted beside it. "Good morrow."

"Hawthorne." Aaron rose politely. "We were about to eat. Join us?"

"No, thank you." She met his bemused stare levelly. "I have only a moment to spare."

"Ah." Aaron stuffed his fingers into the pockets of his jeans. "You remember Jason, and this is Jeanne Cho."

The woman speared Hawthorne with a condescending gaze, her dark, slanted eyes contemptuous in her round face. "His wife."

Hawthorne's eyes narrowed subtly.

"Ex-wife. Very, very ex," Aaron said. "We've been divorced for years."

Jeanne slid a coy glance to Aaron. "Only because you're stubborn."

"More because you walked out." Aaron shifted his gaze to Hawthorne. "Jeanne writes fantasy, too. The two of you have a lot in common."

"I do not share," Hawthorne said. "It is therefore unlikely that she and I have anything in common."

Aaron dropped into his chair as an awkward silence fell over the group. Levi approached the table wearing an apron and carrying a tray laden with steaming plates of food. He distributed them with an easy grace, then slid the tray under his arm. "Can I get y'all anything else?"

"We're fine, thanks," Jason said.

"Great. Let me know if you need me." Levi came around the table and bussed Hawthorne's cheek. "Morning, Nana."

"Nana?" Jeanne said. "You know this woman?"

"Hawthorne is my relative," Levi said.

"My great-grandson, to be precise." Hawthorne stared down her nose at the offensive woman. "He is not to be trifled with."

"Nana." Levi breathed out the warning. At the same time, Aaron said, "Your *what?*"

Jeanne raked a narrow-eyed gaze down Hawthorne's form. "You don't look *mature* enough to have children, and I know you're not old enough to have greats."

"The women of my people age gracefully," Hawthorne said evenly. "Unlike the women of your people."

"Cougar," Jeanne muttered.

"Sloth."

Jeanne leaned forward and hissed, "Ice queen."

Hawthorne shifted her attention to the woman.

"Oh, shite." Levi clunked the tray onto a table and put himself between Hawthorne and Jeanne, his arms spread wide. "Don't do anything rash, Nana. Remember what happened the last time."

"Last time?" Jason sat up straight, his gaze avid. "Eh, what last time?"

Aaron pinched the bridge of his nose. "I'd like to know that, too."

"The woman shall not come to harm by my hand," Hawthorne said, more to placate her kin than anything. If Jeanne laid another finger on Aaron, Hawthorne would use the point of her sword to inflict damage. Technically, that was not her hand. "However, one would think a writer could do better than to recycle a hackneyed insult. Do you not agree, Levi?"

He dropped his hands and smirked. "Good one, Nana."

"Exactly how old are you, Hawthorne?" Aaron asked.

Hawthorne opened her mouth to give him an honest answer. He had asked, after all, and should he not know the truth

27

since they were building trust?

Levi interrupted. "Older than she looks."

Aaron's gaze drifted quickly over her unlined face and athletic build. His eyes lingered on her midriff, bare between the bottom of her leather halter top and the low-slung waistband of her leather pants. "How *much* older?"

"You know how you shouldn't ask questions you don't want to know the answer to?" Levi said. "This is one of those times."

Aaron slumped back into his seat, appearing dazed. Jason's gaze bounced between him and Hawthorne.

"I have to get back to work." Levi picked his tray up off the floor and dropped his voice to a low mutter. "Behave, Nana. Remember how good this Con is for business and try not to cut anyone's head off, ok?"

"You worry unnecessarily." Hawthorne gave him the customary farewell, touching her lips to his mouth and forehead. "All will be well."

He shot her a skeptical look as he left. She watched him for a moment, ascertaining his safety before turning her attention back to Aaron.

"Your food chills, so I shall be brief." She pulled a spare keycard out of her back pocket and held it out. "I wished you to have this, should you desire to build trust with me this evening."

A flush crept up Aaron's cheek under his tan. Jason raised an eyebrow at her. Even the indomitable Jeanne looked puzzled.

"Is 'building trust' not a euphemism for sex?" Hawthorne asked.

Aaron covered his face with his hands and groaned.

Jason snickered. "That's one way to put it. I wondered what you were up to last night."

"Cut it out," Aaron muttered. "She has trust issues, ok?"

Hawthorne dropped her hand and stepped away from the table. "I have embarrassed you in front of your friends. My apologies."

She pivoted away, ignoring the ping of hurt in her chest.

Men. Rational talk failed and beheading was frowned upon by her kin. What was a Daughter to do?

Behind her, Aaron scrambled from his chair. "Hawthorne, wait. I want to build trust with you."

She peered at him over her shoulder. "Truly?"

"Honest." He came around the table and placed his warm hands on her shoulders, rubbing gently. "I can come up around nine, if that's ok."

She toyed with his shirt, another button-down, this one a deep red and gold plaid. "I shall be there."

"Yeah?" He pressed a kiss to her forehead, then one to her mouth in a lingering kiss. "How's that?"

"It is the other way around," she said gently.

"I know. This way, though, I get to kiss you as much as I want."

She cupped his face in her hands, absorbing the smooth texture of his skin. "You please me, Aaron Kesselman."

"You please me, too." His mouth brushed across hers twice more before he stepped back. "Maybe I'll see you around today."

"Perhaps." She slid the keycard into the front pocket of his denim trousers and ignored the satisfaction she gained when Jeanne squawked. If Aaron's ex-wife minded the intimacy, she should have cared for him better, a mistake Hawthorne had no intention of emulating. "Try to keep other women's hands off of your person."

He grinned. "I'll do my best."

Hawthorne observed him reseating himself, admiring the long legs and firm bottom encased in worn jeans, then turned to leave. Her departure was interrupted by Jeanne's hissed question.

"What are you doing whoring around with that bitch?" Jeanne asked

Dead silence descended on the area around Aaron's table. In two seconds flat, Hawthorne reached it and grasped the top of the other woman's chair, tilting it back at a dangerously steep angle. She placed her face close to Jeanne's pale one and allowed the deadly intent in her own eyes to seep into her expression. When Hawthorne was certain the woman understood, she shifted, speaking into Jeanne's ear in a voice that carried no farther than the table's occupants. "Let us be clear, child. I allow you to live because Aaron is my lover and his affection for you lingers. Otherwise, my sword would have already cleaved your pretty little head from your slovenly body. Do not mistake my mercy for anything other than what it is."

She released the chair, letting it drop onto its legs with a thud.

Jeanne reared away from Hawthorne, her expression twisted with fear and loathing. "You're insane."

"Believe that if you must." Hawthorne nodded at Aaron and Jason, who gaped at her. "Gentlemen."

She strolled away, confident her warning would be heeded.

Behind her, Jason said, "So, you're building trust with Hawthorne, eh?"

Aaron snorted out a laugh. "In more ways than one."

Hawthorne allowed a small smile to lift the corners of her mouth. Yes, Aaron Kesselman pleased her. Perhaps when DragonCon had run its course, she would invite him to attend her in Tellowee. He would come, of this she was certain, and he would not think of another woman during his residence in her home.

Her smile faded abruptly. Aaron's ex-wife had fumbled her bid for his heart. That the woman could not accept the loss graciously spoke ill of her character, particularly when considered in tandem with what Hawthorne already knew of her. A woman such as that was unworthy of a man of Aaron's talent and stature, but it was of little consequence now. Hawthorne would see to that.

She put the matter out of her head and focused on the day ahead, ignoring the mounting melodramatic hysteria issuing from the frightened Jeanne.

THE DAY DRAGGED BY as Aaron made the rounds, moderating one panel, sitting in on another one, answering questions from aspiring comic book artists as patiently as he could. His final panel of the day was on publishing. The illustrator on his left droned on and on about traditional media versus drawing software. Aaron checked his watch discretely and stifled a groan. How much more of this did he have to sit through before he could be with Hawthorne again?

He'd caught glimpses of her throughout the day. After his first obligatory appearance, he'd caught the tail end of her reading from her latest novel to an enthralled group. She'd changed her accent for each character, breathing life into them with an ease that had surprised him. Occasionally, she interpreted gestures, too, making the audience laugh.

Who knew the somber woman had a sense of humor?

Once, he'd passed by her in the hallway as she knelt beside a group of young girls dressed similarly to her, gently correcting their holds on sword-like weapons made of balsa wood and tinfoil. Her eyes had shifted to his as he passed and drifted down his body with a proprietary gleam, heating him through and through. Hawthorne had murmured something to her fans too low for him to hear, making them giggle, and then said plainly, "Someday, when you are great warriors, perhaps you will win the hand of a handsome man."

He hadn't known what to think about that.

She'd slipped into the back of the room during one of his panels, her attention seemingly riveted on their discussion of creating realistic characters. Not long after, an officious little man had bustled up to her and all but dragged her out of the room. Later, Aaron had caught sight of her listening to the same man, her arms crossed under her breasts as she nodded solemnly. She'd looked up, her eyes meeting his as if she'd known he was there the whole time. Another gaggle of girls had surrounded her as the officious man stepped back, then Jason had pulled Aaron away, effectively ending the seductive pull of her gaze.

31

It amazed him that they'd seen each other at all. DragonCon's events were spread over five venues and there were so many people in attendance, it was entirely possible to go a whole day without seeing the same face twice.

Some faces he'd rather not see at all.

Jeanne had given him hell after Hawthorne's demonstration at breakfast, lighting into him for sleeping with a *misogynistic heteronormative libertarian* to the point that she'd put his teeth on edge. He'd set her straight about the misogyny. As far as he could tell, the only woman Hawthorne despised was Jeanne, and he honestly couldn't blame her for that, especially after the cattiness his ex-wife had resorted to. Honest to God, what had she been thinking? Hawthorne carried a sword, a real-life, genuine sword, and knew how to use it. Hadn't the rumor mill circulated that around to Jeanne after the stick-fighting exhibition the night before?

But no. Jeanne had never been one to bow to reason, not if she could twist a situation to suit her own ends.

She'd left him for being insensitive to her needs as a woman. That's what she called his wanting to have sex, which he'd always believed was a natural part of any relationship. It had been a devastating blow to his manhood. For a long time, he'd blamed himself for marrying her right out of college, for working two jobs while they each established careers as artists, for not spending enough time with her. His belief that they belonged together had carried him through those years. He'd wanted a family, wanted to grow old with her, and looked forward to the day when they'd both be successful in their respective fields and could laugh at the trials they'd endured to get there.

After she'd cleared out, her views on children as parasites and men as a necessary evil had come to light. It had put a whole new perspective on their marriage. Instead of the guilt he'd felt for not working hard enough, he'd gradually understood that his part in their marriage's failure had been small in comparison to hers. She'd never wanted marriage, not really, and if she'd been honest about that, they could've parted more amicably without the mess of a legal union. Instead, she'd all but dragged him down the aisle and he, believing his love was enough to carry them through, had given everything he had to her. It had never been enough.

Over time, she'd created a revisionist history of their marriage, bragging about the good times, glossing over the bad ones, and completely ignoring her own role in its failure. Her hints that she wanted to reconcile with him had grown heavier over the past couple of years, but he was content with the casual friendship they'd built on top of the ruins of their marriage.

Now that he'd met Hawthorne, he damn sure wouldn't take Jeanne back, even if he never saw Hawthorne again. Her blunt honesty was a pleasant change from the cutthroat social scene in San Francisco. Ok, so she was a tad volatile. Then again, Jeanne had goaded her. The other women in his ex-wife's circle of friends would've resorted to infantile name-calling and bitchy conversations on Twitter. After overhearing Levi's comment about beheadings, he had a feeling they were all lucky Hawthorne had made do with a quiet threat. And though he didn't believe Hawthorne would really kill anyone, he damn sure knew she had the skill for it.

He shifted his attention back to the audience and answered a question from a neophyte illustrator, expanding on an answer another panelist gave. The event wound down gradually, slower than Aaron would've liked, until only a few stragglers remained. He slipped away as soon as he could, grabbed a snack on his way to his room. Showered quickly then checked his phone messages while he dressed in a clean t-shirt and running shorts. At the last minute, he packed a bag with toiletries and a change of clothes and, as an afterthought, dropped in his sketchpad and some pencils. It never hurt to be prepared.

He took the private elevator to her floor and tapped his fingers on his thigh as the floor numbers lit up above his head. Inhaled slowly, calming the rapid patter of his heart. The doors slid open. He stepped through them and dug her keycard out, rapped on the door before he opened it.

Hawthorne was lounging on the sofa, fully dressed, talking to Lali on her cell phone.

The door swung shut behind him and their eyes met across the room. She ended the call and dropped the phone on the coffee table, and then she was on him, wrapping herself around him and claiming his mouth in a passionate kiss that stole his breath and sent heat skittering through him, all cockeyed and nimble. Their hands fumbled, sending their clothes flying as they were yanked off and discarded. When they were nude, he lifted her up and pressed her back against the door, and slid into her with a relief quickly overwhelmed by need. He took her hard, urged on by her nails digging into his skin and the breathless gasps she made with each thrust of his hips. He never wanted it to end, never wanted to leave her tight, wet heat.

She tangled a hand in his hair and arched her back. "Harder," she whispered against his throat. He flexed into her, lifting her up, up, up. She groaned and her body jerked and she came, spasming around him, pushing him over the edge into a release that went on and on and on.

He touched his forehead to hers and tried to catch his breath and the happiness zinging through him on the tail end of passion's ebbing beauty. Happiness, so much. Too much for how long he'd known her. He reined it in, tried to, but it lingered and waxed and filled him from stem to stern.

Later, he persuaded her to pose for him and drew her nude body illuminated in the soft glow of the bedside lamp with the sheet pulled over her breasts. They talked while he drew, about her writing and his drawings, and about Lali, who turned out to be Hawthorne's granddaughter.

No matter what Levi said about Hawthorne's age, Aaron had a hard time believing her to be old enough to have children let alone grandchildren or, as she'd claimed Levi was, a great-grandson. The only reasonable explanation he could muster was that she was an honorary relative. That accounted for the Nana nickname and the odd, almost ritualistic farewells, but it didn't jibe with what he knew of her. When a woman as literal as Hawthorne told him something, he had a hard time not taking her at her word.

He finished her portrait and turned his sketchpad around to her.

She blinked up at him, her huge gray eyes guileless. "This is how you see me?"

"Yeah." He started to put it away. Her hand shot out, startling him into handing it over. "What?"

"You must think me beautiful."

"You are beautiful," he said softly.

"Perhaps your vision is colored by pleasure." She sat up slowly and took his sketchbook, laying it on the nightstand. "I shall thank you properly for your time now."

"Drawing is its own reward." He grinned as she pushed him back onto the bed and straddled him. "On the other hand, it's been at least an hour since you had your wicked way with me."

"Sex is not wicked, Aaron Kesselman," she chided gently. "Unless you wish it to be."

"Oh, yeah. I do," he breathed, and lost himself in the wicked feel of her mouth on his.

# FOUR

ARON MET JASON for brunch the next day. Hawthorne had kept him up late the night before, talking and *building trust*, late enough that he'd fallen asleep wrapped around her, waking only when the sun shone brightly through the cracks between the drapes. In Atlanta, that was pretty damn late. She'd already been gone, though she'd left a note inviting him to "use the suite as if it were yours" and reminding him that she'd be an hour later getting in that night if he wanted to spend time with her.

He was of two minds there. On the one hand, he enjoyed being with her. For the sex, yes, *God yes*, but also for her company. She was easy to be with and, for the most part, open and tolerant. For the first time in his life, he felt like he could be himself with a woman. While she never hesitated to express her opinion or call him out on his, she also never judged. It wasn't just refreshing; it was downright seductive, and therein lay the problem. He didn't know anything about her, not where she lived or where she was from or even what her full name was. Every time he tried to ease the conversation around to her past, she deftly sidestepped him by changing the subject or, if he was especially persistent, drew him into another bout of sex.

She was brutally up front about everything else. Why not her past?

There were other problems, though. She was a hardcore libertarian, and while he saw her point on a lot of things (people *should* take more responsibility for themselves), he disagreed with enough of the finer points that he knew it would drive a wedge between them sooner or later. By then, it would be too late. He'd already taken the first teetering step into love with her, what anyone else would call infatuation, but he knew better. His heart was tender and ready for it, and she was so close to the kind of woman he'd hoped to meet. Beautiful and fiercely independent, intelligent and, underneath it all, kind. Any closer to love and the damage would be irrevocable. She'd break his heart and after all the crap he'd gone through with Jeanne, he wasn't sure it could take another hit. Love he was willing to sacrifice for. Certain heartbreak? Not so much.

A waiter came by and took their order. Not Levi this time, thank God. Aaron didn't need one of Hawthorne's relatives spying on him.

"I know that look," Jason said. "You've got woman on the brain."

"Doesn't take a genius to figure that out."

"Not with the scorchin' hot looks passing between you and the ever-sexy Hawthorne." Jason propped his forearms against the edge of the table. "So what gives?"

"What gives about what?"

"The chemistry's there, you seem to like her. What are you worried about?"

Aaron sat back in his chair. "I don't even know where she lives."

"Somewhere near here, I think." Jason shrugged. "What does that matter?"

"Don't be dense, Jase. She lives in Atlanta, I live in San Francisco, and ne'er the twain shall meet."

Jason waggled a finger. "I might have a solution to that, old son. Seems Dana talked Hawthorne into submitting a proposal for a graphic novel based on one of the characters in her Black

Queen quadrilogy. Her publisher wants to move on it, but the editor's dicking around on the illustrator, especially since Hawthorne insists on collaborating in person."

Interest stirred. "Yeah?"

"I could put in a word, maybe rub a few elbows. You'd have to go to her for a couple of months to finalize the proposal, do your drawing magic, maybe build a little trust."

Aaron scrubbed his hands down his thighs. Two or three months would give him enough time with Hawthorne to figure out if sex was all they had in common. On the other hand, it would be hell if the physical side of their relationship fizzled while they were still under contract. Mixing business and pleasure wasn't such a hot idea.

"Take some time to think about it," Jason said. "But not too long. Word is, the publisher's pushing to get the project underway. You snooze on this one, man, I may not be able to get you in."

The waiter brought their brunch by, steaming plates of eggs and grits with piping hot biscuits on the side. A good Southern breakfast, minus the ham. Aaron cracked his biscuit in half and spread butter on one side. Had Hawthorne eaten anything or had she started work on an empty stomach? They'd worked off so many calories over the past two nights, it was a wonder she had the energy to move. She was already on the skinny side, muscled, sure, but lean with it. A couple of missed meals couldn't be good for her.

He blew out an exasperated breath. Man, was he a goner.

"So, are you going to the catfight?" Jason asked.

Aaron paused with the biscuit halfway to his mouth. "What catfight?"

"Hawthorne and Jeanne." Jason knifed out a packet of butter into his grits and dumped in an unhealthy dose of salt. "First Ladies of Fantasy Fiction panel at eleven thirty."

Aaron dropped the biscuit and checked his watch. Alarm shot through him. "That's in forty five minutes."

"Relax, man. It's being held here in the Hyatt. We've got plenty of time."

"Tell me other people will be there."

"Sure." Jason rattled off the names of four other high profile female authors. "But the big show will be your two ladies. Word's already spread about their little showdown yesterday over you."

"That wasn't about me." Much. "You better not be spreading that rumor."

"Hell, man, it came back to me, not the other way around. Besides, it's a pretty accurate recap. If Jeanne had opened her mouth one more time, I bet Hawthorne would've wiped the floor with her." Jason sighed dreamily. "God, I'd love to see that."

"Stick around," Aaron muttered. "It might happen."

They finished their meal and paid the bill, then headed to the room where the panel would be held. Jason protested the speed of their march through the hotel the whole way. Aaron slowed marginally, trying to give the other man's stubby legs time to catch up. Hawthorne and Jeanne on a panel that would likely touch on the role of women in SciFi and Fantasy. No good could come of that.

They slipped into an already packed room. Other con attendees poured in behind them, taking places around the walls. Aaron's gut sank like a stone. He'd hoped Jason had exaggerated the rumor mill. Apparently not. The fist-sized anxiety in his stomach punched and jabbed. Hawthorne was seated at the end of the panel's table with Jeanne on her left. Great. Why hadn't someone sat between those two or at least had the foresight to seat them at opposite ends of the table?

Levi's lithe brawn sure would come in handy right about now.

Dana waved to them from near the front of the room. Aaron pushed his way to her, Jason in tow, and plopped into one of the two seats she'd saved.

She leaned around Jason and caught Aaron's eye. "I hear you and Hawthorne are an item."

Aaron shot a glare at Jason and ignored the other man's attempt at an innocent shrug. "We just met."

"That doesn't mean you're not an item." Dana's smile was just shy of knowing. "She asked me to recommend you as a collaborator on a graphic novel she's writing."

"I told him." Jason shifted in his seat and crossed his arms together on top of his round belly. "He's thinking about it."

"Think quickly," Dana urged. "The editor needs to find someone by the end of October at the latest or we'll miss a chance to release the graphic novel in conjunction with one of her other projects."

The panel moderator tested her microphone and the room went silent. Aaron tried not to focus too much on Hawthorne, though it was hard. Dana had seated them on the first row but to the side, not far from Hawthorne's seat at the front. His gaze was drawn to her again and again, to the quiet stillness of her posture and the even tones of her voice. Unlike the other women, she sat back, away from the microphone, and spoke only when addressed directly. She never looked straight at him, but she didn't have to. Every time he moved, her hand tightened imperceptibly on her leather-clad thigh. No one else would notice such a slight gesture. He only did because he'd made such a careful study of her, trying to figure out what made her tick, trying to understand what unpleasant event had happened to make her so leery of having a man above her.

He'd deliberately pushed his suspicions out of his mind. Hawthorne wasn't a victim. He couldn't imagine anybody getting a jump on her and forcing her into anything she didn't want to do. That wasn't her. She was controlled, aware of her surroundings, and a fighter. There's no way some man could've slipped under her guard and hurt her. No way.

Half an hour into the discussion, Aaron relaxed. So far, the questions had been innocuous. How did you become a writer? Why did you choose fantasy? How did you find an agent? Where do you get your ideas? Typical fare for a con, nothing controversial or overly personal, especially when spread out over six women.

The conversation turned to sexism in the field. Hawthorne remained silent, though the other panelists had plenty to say. One went into a diatribe on systemic sexual harassment and another remarked snidely on how hard it was for a woman to break into the genre thanks to the oppressive patriarchy demonstrated by publishers.

Aaron agreed, to a degree. There were injustices in the field and those needed to be addressed. On the other hand, he was always stunned by the vitriol with which many women approached the topic, attacking anybody who even called for a calmer dialogue, often leaving no middle ground for a rational discussion, let alone a just resolution.

Jeanne jumped into the fray. "All of this is nothing but violence perpetuated on women, a kind of rape of our minds and bodies by capitalist fascists bent on domination and repression of our art, of our very *beings.*"

A throb set up residence in Aaron's temple.

Hawthorne turned a glacial stare on Jeanne.

"Uh oh," Jason muttered.

"Have you ever been raped?" Hawthorne's voice was quiet over the hush of the crowd. "Have you ever had a man touch you in a way that you did not wish?"

Jeanne blinked, her expression blank. "Well, no, but..."

"Then you have no leave to use that word in conjunction with the actions of men in your presence."

"I've had plenty of men sexually harass me," Jeanne shot back hotly.

"That is not rape," Hawthorne said flatly. "Conflating one with the other is a disingenuous effort on your part to turn all women into victims and all men into criminals, simply because of their sex."

"All women *are* victims," Jeanne snapped. "Haven't you been paying attention?"

"Being female makes no one a victim." Hawthorne leaned forward, her gray eyes intent. "I am a woman. Do you truly think I would allow another to perpetuate harm upon my person?"

Jeanne drew back. "Yeah, but you're a walking poster child for a woman who hates her femininity."

"I do not parade my vagina around for all to see, it is true, nor would I. That is only one part of who I am, not the whole of me. It is sad that you do not recognize this in yourself."

"You dare pity me?" Jeanne laid her hand on her chest "You, with your boyish haircut and your manly attitude. You're nothing but a misogynistic whore for this country's rape culture."

Hawthorne faked a yawn and patted her mouth. "Sticks and stones."

It was the most expressive Aaron had ever seen her outside of sex. His gut knotted and he glanced around the room, searching for Levi.

The moderator leaned over the table toward Hawthorne and Jeanne. "Ladies, could we get back on subject here?"

"Gladly," Hawthorne said, while Jeanne hissed, "Home wrecker."

Aaron dropped his head into his hands.

Hawthorne covered her microphone with her hand and spoke quietly to Jeanne, whose responses echoed clearly around the room, to the delight of the audience and the despair of the other women on the panel. "He was mine first," she said, followed closely by, "Building trust my ass. You're fucking him," and then, "You nearly killed me, you moron."

By this time, Levi and three burly men had ranged themselves into a semicircle around the two women, not ten feet from where Aaron sat.

"Is there a problem, Nana?" Levi said quietly.

Hawthorne turned to him and said evenly, "This woman is being disruptive. Please remove her until such time as she is calm."

"I'm not the one being disruptive," Jeanne squawked.

"Nevertheless, you will leave quietly and with a dignity that will not embarrass yourself or your peers."

Jeanne stood with a huff. "This isn't over."

Hawthorne rested an unblinking stare on the other woman. After a tense moment, Jeanne wilted under it and allowed one of the men to escort her out of the room. The moderator jumped in gratefully with a call for more questions, and though the other women on the panel continued to look askance at Hawthorne, she relaxed into her seat as if nothing out of the ordinary had happened.

Aaron sighed out his relief. Thank God for Levi.

Jason whispered, "I'll pay you to take the job with Hawthorne if you promise to let me hold it over Jeanne's head."

Aaron shot him a sour look. Like he needed more guff on that front. As soon as his ex-wife had a chance to rewrite the scene in her head, he was certain he'd hear all about it. *That woman you're sleeping with assaulted me*, or some such nonsense. Honestly. Where did she get that stuff?

The panel ended without further incidence. Jason whisked Aaron away before he could talk to Hawthorne, who was besieged by fans. Their eyes met and held over the heads of the people between them. He could've sworn he saw warm humor in her expressionless gaze.


THE CALL from her assistant came near the end of her day, catching Hawthorne on her way to the elevator after a long meeting with the hotel's manager on daily operations during the Con. Hawthorne preferred to allow the corporation she'd set up to manage the hotel and the other businesses she owned. Once in a while, though, it was more prudent to check on the businesses herself rather than relying on the reports of others, if only to ascertain their veracity. If not for her family, she would sequester herself in her home and devote herself to the written word, but needs must.

She opened her cell on the second ring. "Hello, Yvette."

"I have news, Maetyrm," Yvette said. "There are indeed two volumes attributed to the Chronicler held at the University of California, Berkeley's Bancroft Library. Would you like for me to arrange their retrieval?"

"I shall see to that." It would be no hardship to fly cross country and remove the volumes herself, and while she was there, perhaps she and Aaron could see one another.

"I've been able to confirm Mr. Kesselman's acquaintance with one of the archivists," Yvette continued. "But, I've not been able to completely ascertain whether or not he's been in touch with other members of the People."

"Contact a private investigator allied with the People and initiate a check. We must eliminate the possibility of such connections prior to meeting with Rebecca Upton."

"Yes, Maetyrm."

Hawthorne closed her cell phone, satisfied that her assistant would take care of the matter. The young Daughter had come highly recommended and had served well during her short tenure in Hawthorne's employ.

She put the matter from her mind. Aaron would leave the following evening after fulfilling his duties during DragonCon's last day. She had only this night left with him, and though she hoped to persuade him to return to Georgia for a long visit, she would not squander their time based solely on that hope.

When she entered the suite, he sat on the sofa, his fingers moving rapidly over the keyboard of his laptop. He glanced up and smiled as he closed the device and set it aside. "Hey, you. I was beginning to get worried."

"Do not fear, Aaron. I am capable of defending myself."

His eyes crinkled at the corners with a smile. "Don't I know it. That was some show earlier today."

Annoyance rippled through her and was just as quickly suppressed. "Jeanne Cho is not a nice person. Whyever did you marry one such as her?"

"A weak heart and raging hormones," he said wryly. "We were young and foolish and thought we were in love. Don't tell me you've never felt that way."

"My youth was far different from your own."

He patted the cushion next to him. "Come tell me about it."

She shrugged off the sword's harness and placed the weapon on the coffee table. "Our acquaintance is too short for such a tale."

"You'll have to tell me sooner or later."

"Not today. This is our last night together." She curled up beside him and rested her head on his firm shoulder. "I would not spend it in talk."

"Eh, you've got a point." He brushed a kiss over the top of her head. "So, your side of the bed or mine?"

She trailed a hand down his chest. The muscles of his stomach bunched under her touch. "Would you be amenable to showering with me?"

"If you let me wash you." He tilted her chin up and kissed her, a lingering exploration of her mouth that fanned the first sparks of desire within her. "Maybe we could try out the couch first."

They eventually made it to the shower, then to bed. In the dark of the night, Hawthorne nestled within his comforting embrace, languid under the lazy stroke of his hand on her hip. It was good, what they had. When the time came for his departure, she would tell him so and invite him to visit Tellowee. Surely after all that had passed between them, he would welcome the chance to see her again. Perhaps if her editor so desired, they could even work together on the graphic novel Dana Goldburg had insisted Hawthorne write.

"Are you asleep?" Aaron said in a quiet voice.

Hawthorne shifted on the bed, facing him. "I am not."

"I'm leaving tomorrow."

"I know." She slid her fingers along his chest, memorizing the hard plane of firm muscle under taut skin. "I shall miss you."

"Me, too." His breath feathered across her forehead as he pulled her close. "Before I go, tell me something about your past. Anything."

"Why is this so important? The past is..." She inhaled a careful breath, afraid of what would spill out if she grew incautious. "It is of no consequence."

"It's what made you who you are, and I don't know anything about it. Give me something to remember you by."

"Has our time together been so meager?"

"I want more." His hand squeezed her hip. "Please."

"Very well, Aaron Kesselman. I shall tell you what I can." She sat up and cut on the bedside lamp. "My name is Hawthorne."

He rubbed a hand across his eyes. "That's it? Just Hawthorne?"

"It is a good name, a solid name, but not the name of my birth."

He propped up onto an elbow, his dark eyes solemn.

"My mother was a great warrior, my father a leader of some renown." She drew in a breath, using the time to gather her thoughts. It had been so long since she had told the tale, so long since she had had to remember it. "My father died when I was twelve."

His hand found her thigh in a comforting squeeze. "I'm sorry."

"He was old. My mother was not. At least, not in the same way. He expected us to continue living the life we had had before his death, if we so chose, and to this end, he willed his leadership to be divided between my sister and I on the one part, and the people who owned his land for the other."

"It feels like you're leaving out a lot of important details."

"Nonetheless, the story remains." She clasped his hand in her own, needing his comfort. "The land owners were not satisfied with this arrangement. They beat my mother severely and raped my sister and I, leaving us all for dead."

He sat up abruptly, horror etching itself into his expression. "My God, Hawthorne. Why didn't you tell me?"

"It was a long time ago, Aaron."

He snorted. "Not so long that it doesn't affect you. You still have a problem with sex and God only knows what else."

"Occasionally, yes, sex is a problem. There were many men that day," she explained gently.

"Many..." His face paled under his tan and his hand tightened painfully on her thigh. "You were gang raped."

"We did not think of it thusly. I was strong, as were my sister and my mother. We survived and rose up against those who hurt us. Eventually we lost, but not before we avenged our honor and rendered justice upon our enemies. My mother is still remembered for her bravery."

He blew out a shaky breath. "It's a wonder you survived."

"It is what Daughters do."

Questions swirled in his eyes, questions she could not answer until she was certain of his trustworthiness. To forestall them, she continued her tale. "We limped from our last conflict, my mother and sister and I, and hid in the countryside, well away from the ones who sought us. My mother's strength failed not long after and she died. We buried her in a grove of hawthorns."

"Hawthorne," he murmured.

"That is the day I found my strength, my purpose. I determined then that I would never allow another to lay harm to me or mine. My sister and I swore to this. We hunted down the men who had destroyed our lives and avenged our mother's death. After that, my sister and I took separate paths. She eventually found love and became..." *Mortal.* Hawthorne cut the word off before it could be uttered. "Happy."

"And what about you?" He smoothed the hair from her forehead, his touch tender and sweet. "Did you find happiness?"

"As much as I could." She cupped his face in her hands and kissed his soft lips. "You must not mourn for the girl that was, Aaron. She died a long time ago. I have made my peace with that part of my life."

"You made your peace quickly. How long ago was this? A couple of decades, maybe?" He shook his head. "You can't be much more than thirty."

"Yes, Aaron, I can be." She pushed away from him. "I am much, much older."

He regarded her with a narrow-eyed stare. "How much older?"

"Older," she said flatly. "Did Levi not warn you on this?"

"Just tell me already, Hawthorne." He huffed out an angry breath. "Do you know what it's like to not know your lover's real name, to not even know how old she is or where she was born?"

This much, at least, she could honestly share. "In what is now Great Britain."

"God." He bunched his fingers in his hair. "What's that supposed to mean?"

"Great Britain. It is a..."

"I know what it is." He dropped his hands, his gaze flat. "What I want to know is what you meant by the 'now' part. What was it called when you were born?"

She hesitated, long enough that he flipped the covers off of his nude body and scooted to the edge of the bed. Her heart burst into a panicked beat. "Iceni," she said in a rush. "North of Londinium, when it was held by the Romans."

He froze with his back to her.

"That is all I shall tell you, for the non."

He glanced at her over his shoulder. "You're kidding, right?"

"This is the information you wished me to impart." She lifted her hands in a helpless shrug. "Why do you now doubt me?"

"Because that's impossible. Londinium? Christ, Hawthorne. London hasn't been called that in..." He compressed his lips into a thin line.

"Centuries," she finished for him.

He turned away from her and scrubbed his hands through his hair. "I'm supposed to believe you're centuries old."

"Nearly two millennia," she said softly. "I have been alone a long time, save for my progeny. They bring me great comfort."

"So you're saying Levi really is your great-grandson."

"He is. I am proud of the man he has become."

He shifted to face her. "And Lali is your granddaughter."

"They are but two of my kin. There are many others." She held the covers up for him, a silent plea for his return there. "It is late and tomorrow will be a hard day."

He hesitated so long, her breath froze in her chest. "I have more questions."

"Should we continue our acquaintance after the con's end, you will have your answers. This I vow."

"I'm gonna hold you to that. Two millennia." He slid between the sheets. "Jeanne was right. You are a cougar."

"Do not bring that woman into my bed," Hawthorne warned.

"Merely an observation," he said with a wry twist of his mouth. "Let's get some sleep."

She switched the lamp off and curled up beside him, and breathed a relieved sigh when he accepted her touch. Tomorrow, she would help him to better understand, perhaps even persuade him to stay another night and view proof of her veracity for himself, held in her vault in Tellowee. He would listen. He had to.

She fell asleep with this certainty, secure in the belief that Aaron would give her time to explain.

# FIVE

ARON SLOUCHED against the Hyatt Regency's bar, nursing his second whiskey sour. After the incredible tale Hawthorne had spun the night before, he'd had a hard time getting any sleep. He'd ended up slipping out of her bed in the wee hours of the morning and going back to his hotel room, where he'd paced for hours thinking over what she'd said. Her story had nagged at him enough that he'd done some research into it. What he'd found had killed any hope he had of building a relationship with her.

Jason plopped down on the barstool next to him. "You're one hard man to find."

Aaron grunted. "Don't you have other clients to harass?"

"Sure, but they're all where they're supposed to be." Jason caught the eye of the bartender, a pretty blonde with huge gray eyes whose nametag read *Ruby,* and motioned for her to bring him a whiskey sour, too. "Speaking of, you have a book signing in half an hour."

Aaron cursed under his breath. "Sorry, man. I forgot."

"That's what women do to you." Jason accepted the drink Ruby set in front of him with a friendly nod. "They suck out your brains and offer them up to the goddess of love."

The bartender winked at Jason, who grinned back.

Aaron hunched his shoulders.

"You made a decision on whether or not to work with

Hawthorne yet?"

"You could say the decision was made for me," Aaron said bitterly. "She'll have to find another illustrator."

"What did you do to piss her off?"

Aaron rounded on him. "This isn't on me, Jase."

"So what did *she* do?"

"You wouldn't believe me if I told you," Aaron muttered. Ruby moved a couple of feet away, polishing glasses with a clean, white towel. Aaron lowered his voice. "Remember how I said she had trust issues? Turns out she had a really rough childhood."

"Yeah?" Jason leaned closer. "So what's the big deal?"

"It did things to her."

Aaron gave a half laugh and downed the rest of his drink. Ruby took his glass with an oddly familiar smirk. His memory of where he'd seen that look disappeared into the fog of too much alcohol. She lifted the decanter of whiskey, and he waved her away. He'd had more than enough if he couldn't remember a simple thing like a smile.

"Twisted her up on the inside. I know, she looks normal, acts normal. Ish," he amended. "But her mind is... Let's just say Jeanne was right about Hawthorne. She's crazy as a loon."

Ruby's eyes went huge and round in her face. "Uh oh."

Aaron's heart sank into his gut. "She's standing behind us, isn't she?"

"Yup," Ruby said.

Jason glanced over his shoulder and flinched. "Uh oh."

Aaron rubbed tired fingers over his eyes. "How much did she hear?"

"Pretty much the whole thing." Ruby's expression twisted into sympathy. "I'm pretty sure you're toast."

"Yeah, that's what I thought." He wished briefly for the courage of one more drink, took a fortifying breath, and swiveled around, facing Hawthorne. She stood still as a statue a few feet away, expressionless except for a slight tightening around her eyes.

"You think me insane, Aaron Kesselman?"

"You told me you were Boudica's daughter, Hawthorne."

Her gaze held his steadily. "Those were not my words."

"They might as well have been," Aaron said flatly. "It didn't take a lot of research for me to put two and two together and come up with Boudica. I mean, the Iceni? Seriously? It's not like they produced a lot of warrior queens."

"Eh, who's Boudica?" Jason said.

Ruby shushed him.

"You asked me to tell you something of my life," Hawthorne said.

"Yeah, something truthful, not a story borrowed from history."

"It is true. I did not wish to tell you of my past, Aaron Kesselman, and would not have if you had not threatened to leave."

Hawthorne's voice broke on the last word. Guilt hit him hard and he lashed out.

"So you made up some bullshit story to placate me?" He laughed, a harsh, bitter sound. "Atta way to keep me around."

Her already pale face leached of color. "You will allow me to show you proof."

Even through the placid tone of her voice, he could hear the plea. He hardened his heart against it. "I don't think so. I've already been dragged through one woman's delusions. Sure as hell, I won't do that again."

Hawthorne's hand twitched.

"Crap." Ruby vaulted the bar and fell into a defensive stance in front of him, facing Hawthorne. "No beheadings, Nana. He's just a man. Plus, think of the trouble it would cause. The police will be drawn into it, I'll have to find somebody to clean the carpet. Really, he's not worth it."

"Thanks a lot," Aaron muttered.

"She's got a point," Jason said.

Aaron glared at his agent.

"Did I mean nothing to you?" Hawthorne said.

Aaron's gut churned with *might have beens* and the beginnings of an emotion she'd nipped in the bud with her ridiculous evasion of simple questions. Why couldn't she be honest with him? How hard could telling the truth possibly be?

"I see." A tear slipped down Hawthorne's cheek. She touched her face and looked impassively at the wet spot on her fingers. "It seems there is nothing left to say."

"Nana." Ruby hurried to her and turned her gently away. "Come on. Let's get you home."

"He did not care for me," Hawthorne said. "I thought to claim him."

"I know, Nana, I know," Ruby murmured as she led Hawthorne away. She shot a glare over her shoulder. "Did it never occur to you that she was telling the truth?"

He stared after them, cut to the bone by the quiet despair in Hawthorne's voice, by the slump of her proud shoulders and the tears on her beautiful face. She'd wanted to claim him. He dropped his head into his hands and scrubbed hard. What a mess he'd made of it.

"I hate to break up this happy party, but you've got a book signing in fifteen." Jason thumped him on the back. "Don't even try to wiggle out of it. We've already got the room set up. Everybody else that's signing is probably already there, along with a lot of your fans."

"God in Heaven, Jase, give me a minute."

"I would if we had one." Jason slid off the stool and tugged at Aaron's arm. "You can catch up with her later, make it right if she'll let you."

Aaron stood slowly. "I don't think this can be made right."

"I were you, I'd try. She might be crazy, but she floated your boat. Anyway, I like her." Jason shrugged at the incredulous look Aaron turned on him. "What? She took Jeanne down a notch or two, she put a smile on your face. How bad can she be?"

Aaron snorted. "Let's leave aside the fact that she claims to be nearly two thousand years old."

"We're at DragonCon. Anything goes here."

Aaron let Jason lead him away, though his gut told him to go after Hawthorne with an urgency that grew during the hour he signed books and chatted with fans and other authors and illustrators. He slipped away as soon as he could and took the private elevator to Hawthorne's suite. His heart pounded in his chest as he swiped the keycard over the lock and entered.

"Hawthorne," he called. He stepped inside and his heart sank in his chest. The rooms were empty. He wandered through the suite anyway. No toiletries in the bathroom, no clothes anywhere. His eye caught on a wad of paper resting in the bottom of a trash can stationed next to the chest of drawers. He retrieved it with fingers that weren't quite steady and flattened it out. The drawing he'd made of Hawthorne. He'd given it to her to commemorate their time together. His heart twisted as he gazed at her, at the beauty of her features, the honesty in her expression, the gentle warmth no one else would've seen.

*Shit.*

What did it matter if she was telling the truth? It was what she believed, maybe what she *had* to believe in order to deal with the trauma of her childhood. How could he have missed that? How could he have made light of her need when she'd tried so hard to reach out to him?

*Stupid, stupid.*

He rushed out of the room and took the elevator down to the lobby, tapping his fingers in an impatient rhythm on his thigh as the numbers slowly decreased until it hit bottom. At the reception desk, he snagged a clerk and handed him the keycard to Hawthorne's suite along with the drawing of her. "This woman invited me to her room, but now she's gone."

"Hawthorne?" The young man handed the drawing back. "I know her."

"You're not another relative, are you?"

The man laughed, his tanned face creasing with humor.

"Afraid not."

"Is there any way you can help me track her down?"

"It's against our policy to hand out that kind of information." The man tapped the keycard against his palm, then glanced subtly around. His voice dropped to a near-whisper. "Especially about the owner."

Aaron dropped back on his heels. "The owner?"

"Ssh. Nobody's supposed to know outside of family and employees." The man eyed Aaron speculatively. "You don't look like family and I know you don't work here."

"I'm attending the con," Aaron admitted.

The clerk leveled a pointed stare at Aaron. "I've never heard of her giving a keycard out to anyone who wasn't a relative, not in the three years I've been here."

"Look, that's the thing. We met here, we hit it off, but since we were both busy with the con, she never gave me her phone number." Aaron tried not to look desperate. "I don't even know where she lives."

"I can't help you." The clerk's expression tipped into sympathy. "Wish I could, but if anyone found out, I'd lose my job."

"I understand. Thanks."

Aaron pushed away from the counter with a heavy heart. How the hell did you go about tracking down a woman with only one name, and likely a false one at that? He took the stairs to his room, using the time to sort through his options. Halfway up, he stopped in midstride. What an *idiot* he was. Jason worked with Hawthorne's agent, who would know exactly where he could find the elusive Hawthorne. And if that didn't work, he could always lean on Jason to lean on whoever so he and Hawthorne could work together on her graphic novel.

He yanked out his cell phone and dialed. "Hey Jase, ol' buddy, ol' pal. I need a favor."

He jogged up the remaining stairs to his floor, planning out a strategy for apologizing to Hawthorne and finding a way to help her deal with the reality of her past, whatever that might be.


A WEEK LATER, Hawthorne met Rebecca Upton at the other Daughter's office on the campus of the Institute for Early Cultural Studies. Rebecca was half Hawthorne's age, a warrior of great skill who had earned the nickname of the Blade, after her primary weapon, and now served in the coveted position as director of the IECS, the People's leading branch of historical research and preservation. Word had it that when her aunt abdicated her seat on the Council of Seven, Rebecca would be the one tapped to fill the vacancy.

Hawthorne slouched in her chair and stared at the mortal Daughter, waiting for her to finish reading the report Yvette had compiled. A twinge of hurt pricked at Hawthorne's heart. Rebecca had found love with her kindly husband after only a thousand years of waiting. She'd submitted her will to his and had a beloved son, Bobby, who had become a great warrior in his own right, following in the footsteps of Rebecca's several daughters, all much older than her son, and all fierce Daughters.

Hawthorne waited still.

After three nights with Aaron Kesselman, she had thought herself close to finding her own mortality. Of all the men she had known in her endless life, he had had the most power over her. He had tempted her heart the most, beckoning it into love.

Instead of nurturing her nascent feelings, he had driven her to tears, something she had not indulged in for centuries, not even upon the death of her youngest daughter nearly four years before. She had almost trusted him, had even shared one of her most precious secrets with him, only to have him value the opinion of his former wife over Hawthorne's word.

She hardened her heart against him, as she had done every moment since leaving DragonCon. Had she not learned long ago that men could not be trusted?

"Thank you for taking care of this for me." Rebecca flipped

the last page of the report and raised her gaze to Hawthorne's. "I know it was an imposition, but I appreciate the help."

"It was little bother," Hawthorne said, though that was a slight stretch of the truth. It had been no bother to investigate. Having Aaron trample her heart, however, had been a painful reminder of the reality of a Daughter's life. "You need not worry any longer that your past will be discovered."

Rebecca leaned back in her chair and smiled. "You've added those two volumes to your vault, I take it."

"They were mine to begin with. Reclaiming them was a small matter."

"The Chronicler," Rebecca murmured. "Did you ever think all those years ago that someone else would take your histories and develop them into fictional tales?"

"It was never a glimmer in my mind." Hawthorne rose and waited politely while Rebecca did the same. "If you should have need of my aid in the future, please do not hesitate to call upon me."

"I shall." Rebecca smoothed back the wispy blonde strands of her hair. "Has your PI found any connection between this Kesselman and the People?"

"I have directed him to report to you." Hawthorne turned away, weary of hiding her pain from those around her. "I have no wish to discuss this matter again."

"Of course. Thank you for your help."

Hawthorne ignored the curious note in Rebecca's voice. "You are welcome. Well met, Director."

"Well met, my friend."

Hawthorne strode out without looking back. She did not need to. The Blade's regretful tone had etched itself into Hawthorne's mind, drawing upon the centuries of their acquaintance to supply the head tilted with concern, the tired slump of the other woman's shoulders. A great weight rested on Rebecca, as it did upon all of the Daughters who had assumed leadership positions among the People.

As it did upon Hawthorne, even in her nominal role as a respected elder.

The weight of years alone could drive anyone beyond repair. Such is what Aaron suspected in her, though it was not true. Her mind was strong and capable enough, well able to deal with the blows her long life had dealt. Her heart weakened her resolve, that wretched organ of emotion and need, and drove her to actions she could hardly credit, all on behalf of a man who had scorned her.

While in California reclaiming her volumes, her heart had pleaded with her until she had given in and sought him out, watching him from afar as he had gone about his day. She had snuck closer when he had claimed a table at a little café and brought out his work, his stylus moving rapidly over the surface of a computerized tablet. Though she had been across the street, well out of range to draw his attention, he had peered around, as if sensing her observation, and nearly caught her spying on him.

She had melted into the crowd and retraced her steps to his apartment. It had been a simple matter to break into the flat and explore the well-appointed space, her booted heels echoing in the spacious rooms as they struck the hardwood floors. She had been drawn to the open shelves of framed photographs, made of friends and family, she presumed, and some of Aaron in various stages of life from childhood to the near present. Such a handsome child, with chubby cheeks and wildly curling mink-brown locks, who had grown into a handsome man with a kind heart and skillful hands.

Her heart had twinged painfully at the reminder of his betrayal, snapping her out of her curiosity. She had made to leave when her eye caught on a framed drawing, hung among a series of others, stealing her breath. The drawing he had made of her. In her haste to remove him entirely from her life, she had thrown it away. He had retrieved it and given it a place of honor on his wall. Her hands had itched to reclaim it in much the same way as she had reclaimed the Chronicler's volumes. Instead, she had eased out of his flat and secured the door behind herself, letting him go as she did.

Eventually, his heart would fall to another woman and he would forget about Hawthorne.

She rubbed at the ache in her chest, unable to contain the action or the hurt. The curse that kept her immortal also strengthened her memory and guarded against its failure. She would never forget Aaron Kesselman, not until death struck her low and the Lady Goddess reclaimed her soul.

AARON YAWNED and rubbed tired fingers over bleary eyes. Since coming home from DragonCon, he'd put in horrifically long hours, pushing himself to finish the illustrations for his third solo graphic novel. He slept when he could, often during the day, ignored everybody's calls except Jason's, the bastard, and ate so infrequently his clothes sagged off of his ever leaner frame.

His dreams were haunted by stricken gray eyes and a tear sliding down a pale cheek.

In every spare moment, he tried his damnedest to track Hawthorne down, pushing Jason to find her address ("I can't, man, those are fucking confidential.") and hitting a dead-end on address searches on the 'net. Knowing she owned the Hyatt Regency Atlanta hadn't done him any good. Turned out it was held by a corporation with an Atlanta address, but that was as far as he'd gotten. Researching finances or anything related was beyond him. That's why he had an accountant, so he wouldn't have to deal with money.

Every day, he called Jason and left a message on his agent's voice mail. *Any word from the editor? Am I still up for the illustrator job with Hawthorne?* Every day, he hung up, discouraged. Jason had stopped answering his calls, and hadn't bothered to return them either.

Work carried Aaron through. It was the only time he could push her from his mind, and even then, it didn't always work. A week and a half before, he'd been sitting at a café working when his neck had tingled, as if he were being watched. He'd glanced up and thought he'd seen Hawthorne standing across the street, her gaze fixed on him. A blink of his eyes and she was gone. He'd laughed it away even as longing and the thrill of her presence had clashed within him. Her face pinned itself to the front of his mind, leaving room for nothing else, including work.

A few hours later, he'd walked into his flat and been hit by her smell, the gentle perfume of roses and woman that had surrounded him when they'd made love. He'd rushed through the flat looking for her and eventually dropped onto his bed, heartsore on finding the apartment empty.

He'd crashed where he'd dropped and slept for twelve hours straight, oddly comforted by her scent.

It was the only time his mind had gone that far into delusion, and it had shamed him. How could he have judged her so harshly after everything she'd been through, especially when his own mind hadn't held up to something as benign as her leaving?

Unless she'd been lying about everything, and he didn't think so. That part, the rape, at least, made all too much sense. It was the one part of the tale he wished with all his heart was false. What he wouldn't give to make it so.

He saved his work, set his stylus down, and rose into a bone popping stretch, ignoring the hunger clawing at his gut. He'd eat. Later. Coffee first. He stared into his cup and grimaced at the mold clinging to the bottom. How long had he been working?

He glanced at the wall calendar pinned above his desk and scowled. The August section was still up, which couldn't be right. DragonCon had started in August and bled into September. He pulled the calendar down and ripped off the offending page, wadded it up, and threw it into his trash can, where it bounced off the overflowing mess and landed in the floor.

He left it where it fell and padded into the kitchen, coffee cup in hand. Cups and plates were piled high in the sink, overflowing onto the counter. Pizza and take-out boxes filled the other side of that counter. He pushed past them, pulled the pot out of the coffee maker, and stared at the dried up mess in its bottom with a frown.

A knock sounded on his front door. He grunted and trudged back into his office, ignoring the increasingly frantic beats and Jeanne's strident voice as she called to him through the solid wood. She was the last person he wanted to talk to, the very last one. As far as he was concerned, her idiotic conflicts with Hawthorne had been the last straw, his own guilt notwithstanding. He could've kept his trap shut. Instead, he'd thrown Jeanne up in Hawthorne's face, not once but twice. He'd meant nothing by it, not the first time anyway. That didn't make the words right.

What had driven him to do something so utterly insensitive?

Right. Hawthorne's delusions.

Was he doomed to gravitate toward women whose heads weren't quite on straight?

The knocking at his door ceased. Aaron picked up his stylus and meticulously outlined a character centered in his tablet's screen. His cell buzzed as he finished the last stroke. He scrambled for it, checked the number, and scowled. Jeanne. No way in hell did he want to hear her squawks.

He dropped the phone and focused on the character's background, switching to a finer digital point, creating a shadow with strategically positioned dots. This was the part he loved, creating the nuances that would deepen the colors applied to the illustrations at a later stage. For this project, he'd pass that step on to another artist for efficiency's sake, though if he worked on Hawthorne's job, he'd try to do each step himself, depending on how long she'd tolerate him.

Likely not long, judging from the way her hand had twitched the last time he'd seen her. Apparently, she had a habit of beheading people. Whether she really did or not was immaterial. She carried a sword and she knew how to use it.

*Note to self: Hide Hawthorne's sword. Also, anything*

*pointy, sharp, or weapon-like.*

No need to take chances she'd swing something at him.

The phone buzzed again, startling him into streaking a line across the illustration. He cursed himself roundly. He usually put the damn thing away while he was working. A glance at the number had his heart hammering in his chest. *Jason.* At last.

He fumbled to answer the call and barked, "Hello."

"Don't say a word," Jason warned. "I can't tell you where Hawthorne is, but I have news."

"Yeah?" Aaron hit the undo feature, erasing the unwelcome streak he'd made. "It better be good."

"Good enough." A chair creaked. The rush of Denver's traffic drifted through the connection. "Hawthorne's editor wants to see samples of your work. I've already sent them."

Panic spiked through Aaron. He'd spent hours carefully selecting his best work to send in. "Dammit, Jase, you should've talked to me first."

"Not likely, not after the way you've hounded me about Hawthorne," Jason said. "Relax, man. I've got your back. You think I didn't send her your best work?"

"I had something better," Aaron groused.

"Hunh. Well, this'll do well enough. Word is, you're at the top of the list."

Aaron straightened in his seat. "So I've got the job?"

"Not officially," Jason cautioned. "We'll know within the week."

"Great." Another week without Hawthorne, another week with his conscience pricking at him and memories of her gentle voice haunting him. "Only a week."

"Look, I know you're hung up on her, but this is ridiculous. Jeanne called, hysterical because you wouldn't answer your door. She said your mother hasn't seen you either. That's not like you, man."

Aaron ran a hand over his hair, and grimaced at the gritty, greasy feel. When was the last time he'd showered? He searched his memory and came up empty. "I know. I'll see her. Ma," he amended. Jeanne could rot, for all he cared. "I promise."

"Do that. Otherwise, I'll have to mail Jeanne my key to your apartment."

"Christ, Jase. Don't be cruel."

"Hey, if it gets you back to being you." The chair creaked again, a door squeaked opened. "Listen, man, I gotta go. I'll let you know as soon as I hear anything."

"Thanks."

Aaron hung up and dropped the phone onto his work table. His gaze fell on the overflowing trash can. When had that happened? He glanced around. Cups were stacked in a teetering pile on the end table next to his chair. Half a dozen pairs of shoes and at least that many socks were scattered under his desk, one of them matching the sock he wore on his right foot.

His left foot was bare, his boxers were turned inside out, and the button-down shirt he wore was buttoned wrong.

God in Heaven, he had it bad. He needed to get his act together before Jason called in the hellhound that was his ex-wife. Shower first to wash off the accumulated grime, and then he'd clean his flat. After that, food and a walk around the block, and then a good night's rest. Tomorrow was soon enough for work, this time with an alarm set to remind him to take care of himself.

He brushed his teeth twice for good measure and focused on the hope Jason had offered. One week and he'd know, just one more week. Maybe then he'd have an opportunity to at least apologize to Hawthorne, even if she refused to renew their budding friendship.

# SIX

*Late October*

**H**AWTHORNE OBSERVED Lali's gentle stretches as they readied for their morning on the mats. The young girl balanced carefully on one foot, mimicking Hawthorne's tree pose. She teetered and fell, giggling on the way down.

A child's laughter was a treasure Hawthorne never tired of hearing.

"When are we gonna go to the park, Nana?"

"After you practice somersaulting." Hawthorne shifted smoothly, reversing her pose to balance on the other leg. "This we do each day. Why do you continue to ask?"

"Because." Lali dragged the last syllable out into two distinct sounds as she flopped over onto her back. "I wanna go now."

"Somersaults first."

Lali hefted a sigh, her chest rising and falling sharply with her breath. "You're a hard woman, Nana."

"I am, indeed." Hawthorne dropped to the floor beside her granddaughter and smoothed the wispy blonde hair from her forehead. "Who told you that?"

"Levi," Lali said cheerfully. She pointed her toes at the ceiling, staring at them with one eye open and one squeezed tightly shut. "I asked him to marry me."

"And did he say yes?"

"No." Lali dropped her legs onto the mat with a thud. "He said I was too young and we was cushions and it was wrong and how one day my prince would come along and then I'd be sorry I'd married him."

Hawthorne bit back amusement at the child's sing-songy recital. "Did he, now. I suppose he was right."

"But I'm a Daughter. I'm s'posed to take what I want, not wait for it." Lali flopped onto her belly with another heavy sigh. "This growin' up business is hard on a body, Nana."

"It is indeed." Hawthorne patted Lali's back and shook her gently, eliciting another giggle. "Come now. Time for somersaults."

They worked on the mat for half an hour, the most Lali's young mind would tolerate before giving in to restlessness. Hawthorne allowed her own mind to wander as she adjusted Lali's form, correcting her gently, helping her learn how to roll into a somersault from a handstand.

The illustrator her editor had chosen would arrive that week. Hawthorne had not inquired as to the identity. As long as it was not Aaron Kesselman, and there was no chance of that, she did not care whom she worked with. Her heart was no longer quite as sore from Aaron's words at DragonCon, but she had no wish to see him again. One encounter had been enough.

She closed her mind off to his memory, still vividly fixed into her mind, focusing instead on Lali's chatter and the many items that needed her attention that week. Maria had taken the week off for a well-deserved vacation, leaving the house sparkling and the kitchen well-stocked. A shipment of Hawthorne's latest novels should arrive on any day. Lali would need to be reminded of the rules for opening the door, though there was little fear of her letting in a stranger. Still, good habits were easier to build than bad ones were to break.

After completing their exercise, they retired to the kitchen for a mid-morning snack of fruit and cheese. Lali climbed onto the chair Hawthorne brought to the sink and carefully washed grapes. Hawthorne stood beside her, preparing kiwi while Lali chatted happily. The doorbell rang as they were sitting down to their snack.

Lali slid off her chair. "I gots it."

"Think before you act," Hawthorne reminded her.

Lali nodded solemnly. "Yes, Nana."

"What are the rules for opening the door?"

"Always peek through the hole first to see who it is," Lali recited dutifully. "Never open the door to a stranger. Come get you instead."

"And when you are past the age of decision?"

"Never open the door to a stranger without a weapon in my hand." Lali shifted excitedly from one foot to the other. "Can I open it now, Nana?"

"You may."

Lali skidded off, her bare feet pattering rapidly along the wood floor as she scampered through the house. Hawthorne listened carefully, heard the pause between footsteps and the squeak of the door, and was satisfied that Lali had obeyed her instructions. A moment later, booted feet thudded into the hallway accompanied by the bright voice of her granddaughter.

Hawthorne sighed. That was not the UPS man.

She rose and made her way to the front door. Bobby Upton stood just inside it, holding an enraptured Lali in the crook of his arm. He was a handsome man in his own way, with his father's dark hair, and hazel eyes lit by his mother's ruthless determination. He was also a warrior, a worthy Son of the People with a successful business he and two of his friends had built from the ground up. Hawthorne had quietly made inquiries into his availability as a mate on behalf of her unmarried progeny, and had been just as quietly turned away. Young Bobby had given his heart away long ago.

In this, Hawthorne envied him.

"Lali, darling, when a stranger appears at the door, you must fetch me."

"Strangers are ugly and mean." Lali leaned her head against Bobby's chest and blinked up at him with wide, gray eyes. "He's very pretty, like a puppy. Can I keep him?"

Only in the mind of a four-year-old could such logic be reasonable, Hawthorne thought.

"This one's asked me to marry her." Bobby goosed Lali's ribs, earning a giggle. "I suppose we'll have to arrange a contract now."

"I shall not hold you to her word. She has proposed to a string of young men," Hawthorne said drily.

"That's a Daughter for you." Bobby set Lali on the floor and ruffled her hair with one calloused hand. "You have a minute?" he asked Hawthorne.

"For the son of the Blade, always." Hawthorne turned a stern look on Lali. "You will eat your snack and consider the dangers of opening the door to the wrong person."

Lali wilted and heaved a heartfelt sigh. "Yes, ma'am." She trudged through the doorway, her steps dragging as if she were preparing to face a firing squad.

Hawthorne stopped Bobby from following after her, amused by his concerned expression. Such tender sentiment from a man who had spent a good portion of his life eradicating the enemies of his country. "It is an act," Hawthorne said softly. "She attempts to stir your sympathy."

Bobby grinned ruefully and shook his head. "She had me there, too."

"You are too soft," Hawthorne chided. "Someday, you will have children and will learn the value of a firm hand."

A shadow crossed his face and the grin dropped away. "Let's hope. Is there someplace we can talk?"

Hawthorne led him to her office, a large room situated in the left wing of house. It doubled as space for her personal library, the part of it others were allowed to see. She had always been proud of this room, with its sturdy décor and cozy atmosphere. When Lali had come to live with her, Hawthorne had installed a wood heater in the fireplace and made room for a collection of children's books. Occasionally, she replaced the furniture. More frequently, she added books to the shelves, moved others to her vault, and culled still others as donations to the local library. For the past two decades, this space had been her sanctuary, a refuge from the world where she could create her beloved stories in peace.

She took a seat behind her desk, pleased when Bobby waited for her to sit, then took his own. Such lovely manners. Another treasure to be cultivated. "You have business to discuss."

"Mom's asked me to track down a group of Daughters who are believed to have betrayed the People, possibly by working with the Shadow Enemy."

Hawthorne inclined her head once. "There are always those who stray from the fold."

"In this case, the straying hits pretty close to home. A few months ago, Mom came across a list of names." Bobby leaned forward, his gaze steady on hers. "Isolde was on that list."

"The daughter of my sister," Hawthorne murmured. "Have you proof of her betrayal?"

"Only suspicion." His shrugged, his muscled shoulders stretching the knit fabric of his black shirt. "Since she's a member of the Council of Seven, I figured the situation called for a bit of tact."

"You came to me for tact?"

Bobby grinned, an irreverent gleam in his eyes. "You're her elder."

"And the rightful heir to her seat on the Council." Hawthorne considered him carefully. "With her gone, I would have to claim it, thus realigning the political leanings of the Council. Is this your mother's purpose?"

"Far as I know, her only purpose is to uncover those who might be undermining our common goals," Bobby said in a hard voice. "Eliminating the threat posed by the Shadow Enemy, ensuring the fulfillment of the Prophecy of Light. Who sits on the Council doesn't enter into it."

"The arrangement of the Council should always be well considered, young Upton."

"Not this time," he insisted.

"At all times." Hawthorne inhaled a slow breath, exhaling it on a regretful sigh. "I cannot assist your efforts, though I shall not hinder your progress."

The doorbell rang, chiming through the hallway outside Hawthorne's office. Bobby stood and bowed. "Fair enough. Thank you for your time, Maetyrm."

"It is always a pleasure to have such company." The bell rang again. A chair skidded in the kitchen a moment before Lali's feet beat a rapid tattoo on the floor. "I shall see you to the door, else Lali is likely to allow the world to enter."

"Only if it has a handsome face."

The low murmur of a familiar male voice drifted through the hallway. Hawthorne's heart tripped in her chest and her breath hitched. *It could not be.*

Bobby's hand came to her elbow, steadying her. "You ok? You look like you've seen a ghost."

"Not a ghost, merely the ghost of a memory."

"You, too, huh." Bobby snorted. "Love's a bitch, ain't it."

"Just so," Hawthorne agreed. She led her guest to the door, half hoping she had heard wrong, half afraid she had not.


IT WAS A LONG DRIVE from Hartsfield International, south of Atlanta, to the snug community of Tellowee in northeast Georgia. Aaron sat in the back of a hired car, pencil moving swiftly over paper as he sketched, and chatted with Hank, the sixty-something cabbie with a lean, wrinkled face and the shambling, cocksure walk of a man half his age. He was only too happy to give the low down on the best restaurants, where to get tickets at a good price, and a hundred other things only a local would know. Aaron figured Hank's well of knowledge would come in handy if Hawthorne didn't behead him on arrival.

Nearly two hours after leaving the airport, Hank turned off the interstate and followed a series of roads through ever more sparsely populated areas. The land narrowed as they drove, from the wide, rolling cityscape of Atlanta's suburbs into rift valleys where houses clung to the sides of mountains and cattle grazed on thin strips of land along the roadside, bracketed between the elevated roadway and swiftly flowing creeks. Lush, verdant forests dressed in autumn's colors covered the mountaintops and hawks soared overhead. Aaron pressed his face against the window, watching one circling lazily overhead and another sitting placidly on a nearby utility line, its head cocked at the car speeding by.

Half an hour outside of the small town of Clayton, they drove past two small green signs, one posted above the other, that read *Tellowee, Unincorporated.* The cab topped a hill and the land widened out again. Houses reappeared, stationed at irregular intervals along the side of the road while side streets of varying sizes shot randomly at odd angles off of the main road. A few minutes later, they entered downtown Tellowee, a thriving, well-maintained area exactly two blocks long and one block deep on each side of Main Street. Jagged rows of stores lined the streets, their windows displaying witches and ghosts and goblins.

Men and women, more of the latter than the former, jogged up and down the sidewalks, pushed baby carriages into and out of stores, or gossiped in the tiny cafés and doorways. Several women marked the cab's progress as it passed by. Aaron glanced back. All of them had pulled out phones and were texting or calling someone.

He turned around to enjoy the view. They passed a huge gated complex on their left, circled by a high, solid fence and honest-to-God guard towers. Aaron tried to read the small sign imbedded in the wall next to a guardhouse, and lost his view when a guard stepped in front of it, phone to ear as her eyes followed the cab's progress.

Strange. Either everyone in Tellowee was paranoid or the residents really liked talking on their phones.

Not long after, Hank executed a gentle stop on the side of the street behind a late '80s model Chevy pickup. "Here we is," he said cheerfully. "Safe and sound, or my name ain't Hank Wilder."

Aaron opened the cab door and stepped onto the curb outlining a lush, well-kempt yard surrounding a rambling Craftsman. Wide wooden steps led to the ubiquitous Southern porch. Large rock columns supported the porch's cedar shingled roof, their square bases tapering as they rose. The house itself rested on a rock foundation and had wood siding painted a deep gray with forest green trim around the doorways and windows. Dark brown, curved shingles graced the gables under the roof's angles. It was a massive structure, stretching out in even wings to either side of the yard.

Hank opened the trunk and Aaron helped him unload the two suitcases he'd brought on the cross-country flight from San Francisco. He'd shipped his bicycle and a box of art supplies by UPS in the hopes that he'd actually need them. Hawthorne could still change her mind.

Or draw her sword.

He rubbed his temples with one hand and stifled a sigh. Chances were good she'd do one or the other.

He helped Hank drag the suitcases up the steps to the wide front porch, gathered his overnight bag and the bag holding his tablet and sketchpad from the back seat, and exchanged business cards with Hank.

"You want me to stick around, make sure somebody's at home?" Hank glanced furtively around the neighborhood. "We was getting some mighty strange looks coming through town."

"Probably just checking out your handsome mug."

Hank cackled and smacked Aaron's arm. "Probably checking out yours. You get bored, you call. I'll hook you up with some fine entertainment."

Aaron slipped the cab fare into the old man's hand as they shook. "I'll do that. Thanks, Hank."

"Anytime, son, anytime. Get you a receipt for this."

A few minutes later, Hank pulled away from the curb with a cheerful wave of his arthritic hand. Aaron studied the house. What if Hawthorne wasn't home? He eyed the truck parked at the curb, the closed door of the garage. She must have company, a guy by the looks of it. Had she already found somebody else? Or did the vehicle belong to one of her innumerable relatives?

He gathered his courage and walked down the rock sidewalk and up the carefully crafted wooden steps to the front porch. He set his bags next to his suitcase. A few more steps put him at the door. Before he could lose his nerve, he jabbed at the doorbell. It echoed inside the house before dying off, leaving silence in its wake.

Maybe she was out back. All of the houses in this section of Tellowee seemed to have large back yards. He eyed what he could see of the side yard. If he went around there, he'd probably get in trouble. Already, a neighbor in a nearby house had moved to the edge of her porch, peering at him intently with a phone to her ear. He couldn't catch her quiet conversation, the houses were spaced too far apart for that, but he could imagine who she was calling. Hawthorne, the police. Maybe the mean-looking guard at the complex they'd passed. She'd appeared more than eager to use the gun slung over her shoulder, the really big gun that looked like it could do a lot of damage in a short amount of time.

He rang the doorbell again. Footsteps beat out a rapid patter inside, and a moment later, the door opened on a pretty blonde girl who stared up at him from waist height. She wore the same kind of athletic wear Hawthorne and Levi had worn at DragonCon and stood eerily still in the doorway.

He squatted down in front of her. "You must be Lali. Is Hawthorne home?"

She stuck a finger in her mouth and blinked at him with

huge gray eyes.

"I'm Aaron, a friend of your Nana's." Which was true. Sort of. They'd been friendly enough for nearly four days. Surely that counted for something. "Can I see her?"

The finger dropped away from Lali's mouth. "She gots comp'ny."

"Oh." Aaron's heart sank. So, she'd already moved on. *Dammit.* "She's expecting me to come by so we can work on a book."

"I like books." Lali tucked her hands behind her back and peered at him from eyes gone suddenly shy. "You're pretty."

"Ah, thanks. So are you."

"Are you married?"

"No. You?"

"Nunh-unh." She sighed deeply and smiled. "You could marry me and then we could live happily ever after."

"Um." How did a man even go about turning down a proposal from a little girl? "Don't you think I'm a little old for you?"

Lali scowled, her bow mouth curving down into a frown. "That's what Levi said."

"Well, it's kind of a practical question."

"I don't know what that means, but I don't like it." She crossed her arms over her chest and stared him down with a look that was pure Hawthorne. "Not one bit, mister."

"Aaron," he corrected. "Look, we could compromise here. How about we try friendship first and see how it goes?"

Her bow mouth twisted into a skeptical frown. "Really?"

"Sure." He stuck out his hand. "Shake on it."

She remained stubbornly in place.

Yup, she was definitely related to Hawthorne.

"I likes hugs better," Lali said.

"Oh, well, that's probably not appropriate..." He *oomphed* as she leapt into his arms and wrapped herself around him, nearly knocking him over. "Ok, then. Hugs it is."

She buried her face in his collar, muffling her voice. "You smell good. Will you be my puppy?"

He stood carefully, steadying her with one arm under her bottom and a hand on her back. "Make up your mind, Lali. You want to marry me or keep me as a pet?"

"Both," she said cheerfully. "I like puppies, too."

Two sets of footsteps approached the open doorway, one the heavy thuds of a man's boots on wood, and the other a nearly silent swish of bare feet. A well-built man of about Aaron's age appeared on the threshold, his hazel eyes hard in a handsome enough face. He stepped out onto the porch, his expression softening when his eyes fell on Lali. "Thought you were my girl."

Lali leaned away from Aaron, twisting to wrap her arms around the man's neck while her legs clung to Aaron's waist. "You can be my other husband."

"Spoken like a true Daughter." He eyed Aaron from head to toe. "Bobby Upton."

"Aaron Kesselman." Aaron juggled Lali as she let go of Upton and wrapped herself around him again. "I'm a friend of Hawthorne's."

Bobby raised an eyebrow at Hawthorne, who stood quietly in the doorway, her fit body clothed in athletic wear that left little to the imagination. "Yeah?"

"Aaron is a co-worker," Hawthorne explained. "Lali, please release Aaron. You must dress now for our trip to the park."

Lali's hands squeezed tighter around Aaron's neck. "Can Airn come with us?"

"Perhaps," Hawthorne murmured.

"Gotta run." Bobby lifted Hawthorne's chin with one work-roughened hand and pressed a lingering kiss to her mouth, then speared Aaron with a hard stare. "Kesselman."

Aaron's mouth dried up and his heart dropped through the floor. She hadn't pulled away. Bobby's boots thudded heavily on the wooden porch as he walked by. Aaron nodded, the only polite gesture he could manage while his tongue cleaved to the top of his mouth and his hope of at least rekindling his friendship with Hawthorne withered on the vine.

"Lali, to your room now. Mr. Kesselman and I must talk."

Lali scrambled obediently down and raced past Hawthorne into the house, where she skidded to a stop. She turned and said, "Are you gonna go to the park with us, Airn?"

The truck roared to life behind him, its engine settling into a low rumble as it moved away. Aaron stuffed his fingers into the back pockets of his jeans. "If Hawthorne says it's ok."

"Ok." Lali waved cheerfully, then scampered up a set of steps just visible from where he stood, her footsteps diminishing into silence.

Hawthorne speared him with a glare not much different from the one Upton had directed at him. "Why are you here, Mr. Kesselman?"

He sighed and rubbed the nape of his neck. "So we're back to that, are we?"

"That was not an answer."

Aaron dropped his hand. Her expression hadn't so much as flickered since she'd appeared in the doorway. His heart dropped another notch. He was pretty sure it was close to hitting bedrock. "I'm here to collaborate on your graphic novel."

Hawthorne blinked. "That is not possible."

"So you don't want to work with me." Dammit. Hadn't he expected as much? "Look, it's already been arranged. You can find somebody else if you want, but you know what kind of delays that'll cause."

"I am not concerned with delays, merely with your appearance on my porch," she said evenly.

"I'm here to work."

"So you say. Yet, I have found you to be not quite trustworthy."

He winced. "C'mon, Hawthorne. That's not fair."

"Nothing is," she murmured. Rapid, skipping footsteps sounded on the stairs. "You may bring your bags in and visit the park with us."

Some of the hope rebounded, right into Aaron's throat, squeezing it tight. "So I can stay?"

"You may accompany us to the park, only because my granddaughter has taken a shine to you."

"She thinks I'm a puppy."

"She is lonely for a father," Hawthorne corrected gently. "Come. I must change and then we shall discuss your visit while Lali plays with her friends."

Aaron gathered his luggage and followed Hawthorne inside. A visit to the park wasn't a kick to the curb, though on top of that kiss between her and Upton, it wasn't exactly a sign of welcome. He dropped his things and held Lali's hand when she offered it, and chatted with the young girl in the foyer while Hawthorne changed into street clothes.

# SEVEN

T HE CRISP AUTUMN AIR was filled with the smell of leaves floating to the earth, coating the ground in shades of orange, yellow, and red. Hawthorne stuffed her hands into the pockets of her denim jacket and observed Lali interacting with her playmates. The little girl dangled upside down on the monkey bars, her legs threaded through the metal rungs as she swung back and forth, chattering with a friend who hung the same way a few rungs away, facing Lali.

Aaron set his sketchpad aside and shifted on the bench. Hawthorne placed a light hand on his forearm. He tensed beneath her fingers, and she allowed them to slide away.

"Aren't you worried she'll fall?"

"She will not." Hawthorne nodded to the monkey bars, where Lali had already wiggled free and righted herself. "The children here learn how to handle themselves at a young age."

He exhaled noisily and slumped against the back of the bench where they sat. "I've never seen so many laid-back parents in my life."

Hawthorne glanced around the park, reimagining it through his eyes. Fathers and a few mothers occupied the other benches surrounding the play area, chatting with one another or tending to other children. A few bent diligently over handiwork, knitting or the like, their eyes sharp as they glanced from their work to the playing children.

"Is it not normal for parents and children to visit playgrounds in California?"

"You're kidding, right? In the land of litigation and helicopter parents?"

"What is a helicopter parent?"

He shook his head with a mild *hmph.* "Never mind. Forgot who I was talking to."

Hawthorne turned her attention back to Lali. "No need to be dismissive, Mr. Kesselman."

He shoved his hands through his hair. "Look, can't you call me Aaron?"

"I would rather not." Doing so would only remind her of their prior relationship and the harsh words he had uttered during their last meeting. She ignored the pang in her chest. "How did your name come to be drawn as my collaborator?"

"Ah, well, about that." Aaron rubbed his hands down his jean-clad thighs. "I asked my agent to put my name in the hat."

"And the publisher chose you among the many illustrators available." Hawthorne stifled a sigh. Perhaps that would not have happened if she had not offered his name as well, but there was no help for it now, unless Dana Goldburg could intercede. "I am not surprised. You are a good illustrator."

"Thanks."

"You sound surprised. Did you think I would not study your work when we became involved?"

"Ah, I..." He crossed his arms over his chest. "Not really."

"I was aware of it before, of course." Lali did a series of somersaults across the grass, racing through them with two of her friends. Hawthorne watched them flip, their little bodies lithe as they tucked and rolled. "Why would you wish to work with me after our last parting? You made your contempt of my personage rather clear."

"Look, about that." He rubbed his nape, cleared his throat. "I'm really sorry. I swear, I didn't mean to hurt you like that."

"Then you should have given me the chance to prove my words to you, Aaron Kesselman." Hawthorne stood, suddenly restless. "That does not explain why you are here today."

He stood slowly, his long body ranging out to its full height next to her. "I wanted to apologize, see if we couldn't work things out. I guess you're seeing somebody else now, huh?"

She eyed him curiously. "I am?"

"Don't pretend you didn't just kiss another man."

His apparent jealousy amused her, though she was careful to mask it. "Young Upton was being mischievous, nothing more."

"That didn't look like mischief to me."

"I assure you, it was. In any case, it is of no consequence. Bobby's heart lies elsewhere."

Aaron's expression turned skeptical. He turned his gaze upon Lali as she took a turn at the seesaw. "Yeah, right."

"You should not concern yourself with my affairs," Hawthorne chided. "It was your choice to quit our relationship."

"You told me you were Boudica's daughter. What else was I supposed to do?"

"Believe me," she said flatly.

Lali came running toward them, her face wreathed in grins, and held her hands up. "Did you see me, Airn, huh? Did you see me? I did four somersaults in a row."

Aaron hefted Lali up and settled her on his waist. "I saw, kiddo. You've got some talent there."

"One day, I'm gonna be a great warrior, just like Nana. You'll see." Lali rested her head on Aaron's chest and closed her eyes on a sleepy yawn. "You're gonna be there when I do, right, Airn?"

Aaron's gaze met Hawthorne's over Lali's head. "I don't know, Nana. Will I?"

Hawthorne shut her heart off from the child's plea, and from Aaron's. He had already abused her heart enough for one lifetime. She could not imagine allowing him close enough to have another chance, not for something as simple as collaborating on a book, not even for Lali, who had never known her father and longed fiercely for one.

They walked from the park to Hawthorne's house with Lali between them, each holding one of her hands. Occasionally, Lali lifted her feet and they swung her out and back by her hands as her laughter rang out. Aaron's laughter mingled with hers, a deep harmony to the girl's high-pitched giggles.

Hawthorne kept her own counsel. While he did not appear to be the kind of man who would use a young girl's feelings to his own ends, it would be wise to nip Lali's affection in the bud before it had a chance to grow into attachment.

Hawthorne knew only too well how harsh Aaron could be with a woman's heart.

Lali dropped their hands and raced ahead of them, her earlier fatigue forgotten.

"Wow," Aaron said. "She's a bundle of energy."

"As children of that age should be."

"Yeah? Hunh." He kicked a piece of gravel off the sidewalk into the gutter. "Look, I know me showing up out of the blue is awkward."

"You never said why you have." She stopped in the middle of the sidewalk and peered up at him. "Why would you wish to work with me?"

"It seems like an interesting project." He fixed his eyes on Lali and shrugged. "Plus, I hated the way we left things. I'd kinda hoped we could at least be friends."

"I would rather not." She ignored his wince. His regret would not soften her resolve. "You may apologize, if you feel the need to, and then you should go."

He rubbed a hand over his mouth. "Ok, then. Well."

She nodded and set out to chase down Lali, stopping when he grasped her arm.

"Hawthorne, wait." He dropped his hand at her icy stare, his own gaze helpless. "I *am* sorry about what I said. I could've at least been a bit more tactful."

"Is there a tactful way to tell a woman you think she is insane?" She shrugged the hurt away, refusing to let it linger. "I offered you proof. You rejected it."

His voice dropped to a soft, low pitch. "Could you show me now?"

"No," she said flatly. After everything that had passed between them, how could he even ask? "There is no further need for you to believe me, not when you will depart shortly."

She walked away, quashing the words clogging her throat, staunching the hurt rising in her chest. Tears pricked at her eyes. She, who never shed them, was on the verge of crying a second time over the same man. Such would not be tolerated.

She followed Lali into the house, leaving Aaron to enter or not. Lali snagged a book from the coffee table and climbed onto the couch with it, calling for Aaron as she did. Hawthorne kissed Lali, reminded her granddaughter to behave, and slipped past Aaron into her office to call her agent.

Fifteen minutes later, after a marginally calm discussion with Dana Goldburg, Hawthorne terminated the call and bit back an exasperated sigh. Aaron had not been exaggerating about the severity of the delays losing his assistance would cause to the project. If they wished to release the graphic novel in conjunction with the final book in the Black Queen quadrilogy, then work would have to begin now. As Dana had gently pointed out, the graphic novel complemented the quadrilogy perfectly, as it followed the life of a minor character that played an important role in the main series.

Hawthorne dropped her head against the cushioned back of her chair. She would have to work with him. Joy sprang immediately into her heart. She ruthlessly stamped it out. Aaron Kesselman could not be trusted. If he stayed, and on this she hesitated still, he would have to be put on a tight and short leash. No touching, no friendly chats, and absolutely no sex.

She rose from her chair and followed the sound of his voice into the living room. Lali sat on his lap, book in hand while

Aaron read to her, his finger underlining each of the words in turn. Hawthorne pressed a hand over her heart. It flipped and raced in an unacceptable manner. *Aaron is not to be trusted*, she told it.

Her heart ignored her caution, unwisely.

Aaron glanced up and smiled, his chocolate eyes gentle in his handsome face.

No, he could not be trusted. He was up to something, something other than work and rebuilding the ruins of their budding friendship. He was a man, after all, and men always wanted more than a Daughter was willing to offer.

HOURS LATER, Aaron wandered aimlessly around Hawthorne's office while she tucked Lali into bed for an after-lunch nap. After their trip to the park, Lali had pulled him into the living room for a story while Hawthorne had retreated here to make a phone call. She hadn't said who she was calling, but he could guess: Anyone who would ok finding another illustrator. A few minutes later, she'd come out and stared down at him, her eyes hot in her otherwise blank expression, the fingers of one hand curled into a fist.

Strangely enough, he'd been more satisfied than scared. Hawthorne losing control? Maybe not such a bad thing after all, especially if it gave him an edge in their battle of wills. He wanted to stay, she wanted him to go. As long as she stayed away from her sword, he might have a chance of gaining the upper hand.

He examined her office, circling it in slow strides while he waited. It was a large room, more library than anything, with row upon row of books lining every wall. A fireplace with an inset wood heater broke the pattern of shelving on one wall, though no fire burned in it now. The day had been too warm. Two distinct sitting areas occupied the open interior of the room, each defined by a large, antique rug. One held a sturdy wooden desk with a comfortable chair behind it and two in front. The other held a dark brown leather sofa, a twin to the one in her living room, a mission style coffee table, and matching end tables. Tiffany lamps were placed on the end tables, shedding soft light into the cozy room.

He explored the books, occasionally sliding one off its shelf for a closer inspection. A lower shelf was packed with children's literature, Lali's he presumed, but the rest covered a broad range of non-fiction and fiction alike. Two entire sections, from floor to ceiling, were devoted to histories. Classic science fiction occupied another section. He thumbed through an Edgar Rice Burroughs, raised an eyebrow at the first edition signed copy of *The Moon Is a Harsh Mistress*.

One shelf held the works of Al C. Hawthorne. In the week before coming to Tellowee, he'd finally found the time to read *The Dawn of Time*, the first book in the Black Queen quadrilogy, released a few weeks before DragonCon. The carefully layered story had fascinated him, drawing him into a world woven by a woman who outwardly seemed so simple. The mind behind that story had to be so much more complex. Reading Hawthorne's work, coming to know the part of herself she'd chosen to share within those pages, had stiffened his resolve to repair the fragile pieces of their friendship.

She came in not long after he discovered a shelf of westerns. He replaced *A Lonesome Dove* in its spot and rose. "Is she asleep?"

"Yes." She swept a graceful hand toward her desk. "Please have a seat. We shall discuss your arrival here now."

"I'd rather sit on the couch," he said mildly.

She stared at him, her gray eyes implacable.

"Don't pretend it's just business." He made his way to the couch and sat at one end, deliberately slouching into the plush leather. "Comfortable, casual. Just right for a meeting between friends."

"We are not friends." She took the other end, sitting stiffly on the edge, her spine so rigid, he thought it might snap. "The desk is perfectly appropriate."

"I know that's not how you sit in here. C'mon, relax. Get comfortable."

"I do not wish to become comfortable with you again."

"Tough," he said cheerfully. "We're gonna be working together for a long time. Might as well get used to me being here."

"I have not decided to allow you to stay."

"Yes, you have."

Her gaze turned cold. "You presume much."

"Cut the b.s., Hawthorne." He leaned forward, pinning her with a hard, even stare. "We both know I'm staying."

She held his gaze for long moments, then murmured softly, "I do not wish it. Why do you persist?"

"Because what we had was good and I want it back. I want to earn your forgiveness, see if there's something between us besides sex, at least try to build a friendship. Look, I know your past was hard and it did things to you."

She rose slowly and stared down at him. "What do you think it did to me?"

He stood and edged closer to her, gradually closing the distance between them. "It hurt you, inside and out. I want to help you find a way to put it behind you."

"You think what happened made me insane, and perhaps it did," she said flatly. "For a while, a very long time ago. I purged it by avenging my mother's death and the honor stolen from me by vicious, greedy men."

"I don't doubt that." He held his hands out, eased them toward her, cupped her shoulders. Her skin was warm through the thin sweater she wore and her scent, an intriguing combination of roses and autumn, drifted up, teasing him. "I don't doubt you did everything you could to find yourself again."

"You do not believe I achieved this finding, and so you would like to help me in order to copulate with me again." She shrugged her shoulders, wiggled them when he wouldn't let go.

"Such manipulative arrogance."

"No," he said. "Ok, maybe a little. Can't I worry about you?"

"You lost that right when you discarded me." She stepped back, effectively dislodging his grip. "I shall not trust you again."

"I guess I can understand that."

"While you are here..."

Hope pricked at him. "I'm staying?"

"Only as long as I wish it," she said, her voice sharp. "While you are here, you will not touch me in any way. We shall maintain a relationship appropriate for business associates, nothing more."

"I've got a lot of good friends who are business associates."

Her eyebrows lowered so slightly, he would've missed it if he hadn't been paying attention. "You will find a way to occupy your free time other than with my granddaughter."

"Hey, I'm Lali's puppy, not the other way around," he pointed out.

"Nonetheless."

"Forget it. I'm not ignoring her while I'm here."

She went rigid, though her voice remained calm, controlled. "I need not tell you the consequences of harming Lali."

"If I stay away from her, it'll hurt her feelings and you know it." He blew out an exasperated breath. "She won't understand why I keep pushing her away, and I don't want to. She's a sweet little girl and, dammit, maybe I want to get to know her."

"That is not your..."

"You tell me I don't have a say in it and I'm gonna get pissed." He shoved his hands into his pockets and glared at her. "Christ, Hawthorne. I'm not a damn monster."

"No," she said in a voice as cold as the winter wind. "You are a man."

He bit back a curse. "You know, in your mind, I don't think there's much difference."

"In my experience, there is not."

"If that's the way you feel, why did you even bother to have sex with me?"

She blinked once. "The hour grows late. Lali will awaken soon and I have much to do."

He whipped a hand out of his pocket, catching her forearm as she brushed by him. "Oh, no, you don't. You're not getting off that easy."

She twisted her arm, breaking his hold, and shoved his hand away, all in one smooth motion. "I have asked you not to touch me."

"Ok. Fine." He held his hand up in surrender. "I'm not trying to hurt you. All I want is a straight answer, just this once."

Her expression went flat. "You are here by the grace of Dana Goldburg. Were it my decision, you would now be on your way back to San Francisco. Best you remember that."

"I will. As long as you remember that we have to talk about this sometime."

"No," she said. The word held a finality that cut him to the quick. "I am of no mind to discuss the past with you, Aaron Kesselman."

In other words, he'd had his chance and blown it. He was beginning to think there wasn't anything he could do to persuade her to give him another shot, but damned if he wouldn't keep trying. "You're a hard woman, Hawthorne."

She nodded solemnly. "So I have been told. Come. I shall show you to your bed chamber."

They left his luggage in the foyer and went quietly up the wide staircase to the second floor. The stairs ended in a half-circle landing with a second set of stairs carved into the arc. Beyond, a carpeted floor stretched toward a curved wall holding a single portrait of a woman driving a horse-drawn chariot, her flaming red hair trailing behind her in long, winding curls. Two young girls stood in the chariot behind her. The black-haired girl held a bow strung with an arrow aimed at a man on horseback reaching for the reins held by the woman. The red-headed girl gripped the chariot's edge with one hand. The other held a sword at the ready, its point inches away from slicing through another man's neck.

Aaron drew to a stop and examined the painting. It was painted in the style of the Romantic era and seemed achingly familiar. He rifled through his memories, searching for where he'd seen it before, and came up blank. "Wow. That's a really great painting. Where did you find it?"

"It is a family heirloom." Hawthorne pointed to the left. "My room is beyond the double doors at the end of the hallway, should you need me."

Need her? Hell, yeah. He pressed his lips together, holding the comment back. She probably wouldn't appreciate it right then.

"Lali's room is the first door on the left." She turned to the right and led him up the second set of stairs into the hallway beyond. "Your room is at the end of this wing. It should be adequate for your needs. Once you have settled in, you may choose a space in which to work."

The right wing turned out to be a mirror image of the one housing Hawthorne and Lali's rooms. Two doors were spaced at even distances on each side of the hallway, the walls between them decorated with more portraits and paintings, spots of random color against the ivory walls. At the end, a set of double doors stood open.

He stepped into the room and whistled, low and long. The bedroom spanned the width of the upper story. Windows lined each of the eggplant colored walls. Opposite the entrance, a queen-sized sleigh bed covered in a sage green duvet was stationed with its head against the wall, surrounded by windows. Matching night stands stood on either side in front of the curtained windows, both holding simply styled lamps with curved wooden bases and off-white lampshades. A love seat and a recliner were arranged into a seating area around a coffee table near the right wall. A drafting table, a plain wooden table, and an office chair occupied the left wall. Two chests of drawers, one with a mirror, bracketed the entrance, with a door set into the wall beyond each.

"Some digs," he said.

"I wished my coworker to be comfortable during our collaboration."

"I guess so." He poked his head into the door to the left and found a cedar-lined, walk-in closet with enough space for two people's clothes. A cursory examination of the other door's contents revealed a bathroom with a garden tub, a shower stall, a toilet, and a long counter holding two sinks set into cabinets below a large, lighted mirror. "I've lived in apartments with less square footage."

"Have not we all." She cocked her head toward the door, as if listening. "Lali has awakened and I must tend to her. Please make yourself to home."

She brushed past him, leaving him alone in the room that would be his home for the next few months.

"Wait," he said.

She peered at him over her shoulder. "Yes?"

"Thanks for letting me stay. You won't regret it, I swear."

"I already do," she murmured, and then she was gone, her long, confident strides eating up the distance between his room and Lali's. He watched her go, admiring the graceful way she carried herself and the shift of her lean body beneath the jeans and sweater she wore. He pinched the bridge of his nose, stemming the tide of memories. Hawthorne with water streaming over her skin. Hawthorne moving above him, her head thrown back in ecstasy. Hawthorne turning from him, one tear marring the perfection of her cheek as Ruby led her away.

Even knowing that her past had twisted her mind, she was still the most beautiful woman he'd ever met, and in every way but that one, the most sane, rational woman he'd ever known. He'd been a fool to let her go without at least looking at the proof she claimed to have. What would it have hurt? Not a damn thing.

Instead, he'd hurt her deeply and maybe even ruined his chance at something more, something good and strong and unique with a woman who hadn't bowed to conformity or twisted under time's steadfast hand.

She had to forgive him. It was that simple, and he would do everything in his power to see that she did.

Lali's bright voice echoed to him from the other side of the house. A moment later, she and Hawthorne walked out of her bedroom, hand in hand.

Here was another problem he intended to tackle head on. He'd never been around a lot of children, not since he was a kid himself. This kid he could see spending time with, and not because she was Hawthorne's relative, of an unknown kinship. He had a feeling it would only take Lali a few days to wrap him around one of her delicate fingers. Already, her sweet smile and sassy attitude had wormed their way into his heart. He had no clue how to convince the overprotective *Nana* that he wouldn't hurt the little girl, but he had to try, and not solely for the sake of peace.

When Lali spotted him, her face lit up. She dropped Hawthorne's hand and raced down the hallway. He met her halfway and lifted her into a hug.

She patted his cheeks playfully. "There were big people in my dreams, Airn."

"Yeah? How big?"

"As big as a house," she said, her gray eyes round.

His gaze met Hawthorne's over Lali's head. For a moment, he thought he saw something akin to fear cross her face before her expression turned impassive. That look stole the breath from him. Surely she didn't honestly believe he would deliberately hurt her or Lali, no matter what she'd said about monsters and men.

Surely not.

# EIGHT

**H**AWTHORNE ROLLED out of bed an hour earlier than usual, well before the sun topped the horizon. During the night, she had slept little. Aaron's presence in her home disturbed her. His motives for coming to Tellowee remained suspect, though that did not interfere with her sleep as much as the fierce need clamoring through her for him.

Even after what had passed between them, she still wanted him, wanted his kiss and his touch, wanted to feel him moving within her, bringing her pleasure while finding his own.

Perhaps she was insane after all.

She shrugged out of her night clothes and pulled on an athletic tank top and running shorts. If Maria were home, Hawthorne would slip out into the morning's chill and run through the streets of Tellowee until her mind cleared and her body zinged with fatigue. Instead, she would ease her frustrations on the treadmill.

She pulled on socks and running shoes, then shut her bedroom door quietly behind herself. A quick check confirmed that Lali slept on. Hawthorne tucked the bed linens around her granddaughter's shoulders, smoothed her hair back from her forehead, and pressed a gentle kiss there.

She left Lali's door open and crossed to the stairs, her footsteps silent on the carpeted floor. Her eyes were drawn to

Aaron's room. After Lali's nap the day before, Hawthorne had given him a tour of her home and pointed out the extra office space she had cleared for him. She had invited him to use the other areas of her home at his will, the dining room and kitchen, the living and workout rooms. Other than agreeing to begin work the next day, she had spoken to him only when politeness deemed it necessary.

He had not seemed to mind.

Lali had taken up much of his time, chattering avidly to him, holding his hand whenever he would allow, and generally treating him as if he were an established member of the household. He had drawn the line at Lali's request to help her bathe, much to Hawthorne's relief. When he had explained that, "Big guys don't help little girls take a bath," Lali had sulled up like a mule and glared at him. "I'm a big girl," she had said. Aaron had laughed, shot a knowing grin at Hawthorne, and said, "Not big enough for that."

Her blood burned with the memories his words had stirred, memories she had tried to bury since their time together at DragonCon.

She hesitated at the top of the stairs, her eyes caught by the doors leading to his room. One stood ajar, open wide enough that it could only have been arranged that way through a deliberate action. She scowled at it. Lali would wake not long after the sun rose and would make enough noise to disturb his sleep. Jet lag would likely hit Aaron today, depending upon the quality of his rest.

Though it was unkind, she hoped his night had been as restless as hers.

Guilt nagged at her. A good hostess would shut the door. She rolled her shoulders, stepped onto the landing. And cursed her kind heart. She could not allow Lali to wake him. Their day would be too active. Fatigue from inadequate sleep would drain his mortal strength far faster than it would her own and he would fall behind, slowing their progress at work and in other ways.

A few moments later, she stood with her hand on the doorknob, willing herself to pull the door closed.

Instead, she eased it open and stepped inside, drawn toward his sleeping figure. He rested on his stomach with one knee up and an arm thrown around the spare pillow. His hair lay in disheveled curls on top of the ivory pillowcase. During the night, the bed linens had worked their way down to his waist, baring his upper body to her view.

He wore no night shirt. During their time together, he had often slept in the nude. Did he do so now?

Her fingers itched to find out.

She moved silently, coming to a stop beside his bed. He had often slept thusly, with his face buried in her neck and his arm drawing her tight against his chest. A pang of longing hit her. For the first time in centuries, she had felt safe in a man's embrace, secure in the knowledge that they were building trust together.

The longing turned to bitterness. He had not hesitated to break her trust, precisely when she had learned to count on it.

She gazed down at him, torn between the passion he stirred so easily within her and the need to protect her heart. In sleep, he lay vulnerable. It would be easy to dispose of him now before he had a chance to hurt her again, before he could harm Lali, who had had enough pain in her young life and needed no more.

Hawthorne reached for him, intending she knew not what. Her hand trembled, refusing her bidding, and she drew back. Never before had she hesitated to avenge harm done to her and her family. And yet, here lay a man who had made her feel, then cracked her heart with his refusal to believe in her. Why could she not harm him? Why did vengeance elude her with this man?

The answer came to her in a sudden rush of understanding.

Her heart longed for him still.

This is what had stayed her hand at DragonCon when he had called her insane. This is what had silenced her objections and allowed him to remain in her home, in spite of reason cautioning against it. This is what leashed her temper when he touched her, when any other man who dared such would be dead before his next breath.

Foolish heart. Its weakness shamed her.

She leaned forward and tugged gently at the covers, pulling them over his shoulders, much as she had for Lali. The room's chill would seep through him. She could not allow anyone under her care to fall ill, regardless of his past actions.

He stirred and turned toward her, catching one of her hands. "Hawthorne?"

His hand was warm on hers, its breadth comfortingly familiar. He tugged gently, throwing her off balance, and she fell forward on top of him. He *mmmd* and wrapped his arms around her, sighing into her hair. "Missed you," he murmured. "So much."

Were his words true? Did he miss their time together so much that even in sleep he could admit it? Is this truly why he had come to Tellowee, as he had claimed?

She closed her eyes and lay still atop him, listening to the steady thud of his heart beneath her ear as his breaths evened and his hold relaxed. Her fingers found the bare flesh of his arm. She could not resist touching him there, could not quash the yearning to know him again, foolish though it might have been. A few minutes stolen in the predawn morning would not change anything. She claimed them anyway, reveling in the heavy weight of his arms across her back, in the warmth of his sleeping form and the way their bodies aligned perfectly together through the barrier of clothing and linens.

When light seeped through the blinds and into the room, she slid from his embrace and left his bedroom without looking back, closing his door softly behind her. Lali would wake soon, leaving Hawthorne little time for the run she desperately needed, not to clear her mind, but to search for answers to the questions suddenly crowding her thoughts.

AARON SQUINTED at the digital numbers on his alarm clock and groaned. The night before, he hadn't been able to settle. He'd unpacked, paced around the room, crept quietly downstairs and raided the kitchen, where he'd been appalled to find no bagels.

How could any sane person live without bagels? If he were Catholic, he would've called it a cardinal sin.

He'd scrounged together a plate of fruit and sat at the kitchen table, eating it while he checked e-mails, and put off answering them because he could.

Though he'd taken great delight in deleting all seven of Jeanne's e-mails.

He'd investigated Hawthorne's house in more depth than her cursory tour had allowed and seriously considered using her workout equipment, would've used it if Lali's bedroom hadn't been directly above.

And so the night had gone. When he'd finally fallen into bed at three oh five, his sleep had been filled with dreams of Hawthorne, some of them so real he'd woken, expecting to find her snuggled into the bed beside him.

Her scent lingered in the room, teasing him. How could it be so strong when she'd only spent ten minutes in there the day before? He thumped his head into the pillow and threw an arm over his eyes. Need shot through him, heating his blood as his body reacted to the subtle fragrance.

He could still feel her hands on his skin, stroking him gently, stirring his passion whether she meant to or not.

If she'd been there, which she hadn't. Damn dreams.

He tossed the covers off and slid out of bed, shivering as cool air raked across his bare skin. A run. He needed a run to clear the fog from his head and drive Hawthorne far enough out that he could control his reaction to her. Couldn't run around with a hard-on. She was liable to take offense and chop it off or something.

A few minutes later, he crept down the hallway, iPod and ear buds in one hand, running shoes in the other. Lali's door was open, so he stuck his head in to check on her. She was fast asleep, curled around a floppy ragdoll with the covers down around her feet. His heart softened. Another couple of days and he wouldn't be able to resist this one's charms at all. He pulled the covers up to her shoulders, dropped a soft kiss to the top of her head, and crept quietly out.

Hawthorne's room, he ignored. If he found her sleeping as innocently, he'd crawl into bed with her and wake her the way a beautiful woman should meet the day, with the tender touch of her lover. He had a feeling she wouldn't take kindly to that, and he hadn't quite believed her when she'd insisted Bobby Upton wasn't her new lover.

Aaron sat on the bottom step and pulled on his shoes. A steady thump emanated from one of the workout rooms. He followed it down the hallway and was surprised to find Hawthorne running on the treadmill, her long strides falling on the machine's exercise belt at a sprinter's pace. Sweat soaked through her athletic top in broad patches and glistened on her bare abdomen and limbs, highlighting her toned form. Her breath came in the even puffs of a woman at the top of her fitness level.

As soon as he entered, she jumped lightly off of the belt, straddling it as she cut the machine off.

"Hey," he said. "Didn't mean to interrupt."

"You did not." She slung a hand towel around her neck and sipped from an open bottle of water. "I was nearing the end of my jog."

He huffed out a laugh. "That was a jog? Remind me never to race you."

"Do you not set a challenging pace for your exercise?"

"Challenging, yes. Breakneck, no." He gestured to the curtained window. "Thought I'd take a run toward town and back, learn my way around the streets."

She tilted her head to the side. A slow smile curled her lips into a close approximation of Levi's smirk. "Have fun."

He eyed her warily. "Why are you smiling like that?"

She sipped her water, rubbed the towel across her face. "I shall have breakfast ready upon your return. Bacon and eggs, fruit if you wish."

"I had fruit last night. Much more concerned with that smile. What aren't you telling me?"

"It is turkey bacon, though I am willing to fix another meal, if you prefer." She finished the water and recapped the bottle. "Lali will awaken soon. She will expect you to accompany us to the park again today, so if you wish to run, you should go now. Unless you would rather spend the morning at work in your office."

"Forget it. I'm going to the park." He planted himself in front of her and glared down at her. "While Lali's playing, you and I can discuss your tendency to ignore me when you don't want to talk about something."

"We shall discuss work."

"Nope. Plenty of time for work after we smooth over this communication problem."

"There is nothing to smooth." She stepped to her right. He matched her movement, blocking her exit, and she sighed. "Do not be childish, Aaron. I have much to do today and no patience for a man's foolishness."

"I'm not the one being childish here."

Her eyebrows snapped together. "You dare much."

"Not nearly enough," he retorted. "I had my way, we'd be in bed right now, reenacting the dreams I had last night."

Her expression went blank, her body rigid. She brushed past him without speaking and left the room, her footsteps nearly silent against the hardwood floor.

He rubbed bleary eyes with tired fingers. That went well. At least he hadn't blurted out exactly what those dreams had entailed. No need to tell her the one he really wanted to recreate was of her resting in his arms while they slept, sharing his bed through the long night.

Or hers. He wasn't picky.

Tired, that's what he was. Tired and hungry for her touch and nearly defenseless to the power she had over him. His arms ached to hold her. How desperate was he that a simple embrace was enough to drive him over the edge?

He left the house as quietly as he could, not wanting to wake Lali, and shivered as the cool morning air hit him. Frost covered the ground, turning Hawthorne's lawn into an icy landscape. He tucked his iPod into the holder on his arm, twisted the ear buds into place. He stretched his arms out as he walked down the rock lined path toward the sidewalk, then headed into town. A block later, he broke into a light jog, struggling to lose himself in the rhythm of his feet pounding the concrete and the metal grind of Celtic Frost playing in his ears.

For the most part, he ignored the other joggers taking advantage of the clear mountain morning. Lot of women out, he noted with an absent-minded shrug. Young, fit women who eyed his bare legs and broke into excited chatter that wasn't entirely muted by the thud of music streaming from his iPod.

He reached the gated compound he'd noted the day before and waved at the two women standing guard duty. One of them spoke, her words a soft murmur under the wave of music.

He pulled out the ear buds and slowed to a trot. "I'm sorry?"

The woman that had spoken nodded politely. Unless he was mistaken, she was the same one who'd been on duty the day before. "I said, 'Good morning, Mr. K.'"

"Ah, good morning."

The women nodded, their gazes cautious as he reinserted the ear buds and picked up his pace.

Mr. K, huh. Word spread quickly in the small, Southern town.

How many of them thought he was there as Hawthorne's lover?

He grinned. Oh, yeah. He'd be sure to drop that little tidbit into their conversation, soon as the opportunity allowed.

He jogged through town, noting street and business names, and ignored the catcalls and wolf whistles directed at him. This must've been why Hawthorne had smirked at him. His red-headed witch had sent him through this gauntlet with no warning. He snorted out a laugh. What man with half a brain would mind having a bunch of twenty-something women admiring him?

Especially this group. So far, he hadn't seen one that wasn't attractive and in top physical form. He slowed his pace as the sidewalk rose gently and relished the cool mountain air stinging his lungs. Plenty of men had been out the day before. Maybe they'd already gone to work or had slept in or...

His thoughts trailed off as an attractive forty-something woman with her ash blonde hair pulled into a swinging ponytail jogged past, her mouth moving politely in a greeting he couldn't hear.

Did everyone know his name?

A light bulb went off in his head. Of course. Close-knit town, a lot of women in residence. The phone calls he'd witnessed on his way in had probably been their way of keeping track of a new resident so no one would panic when they saw him.

Though judging by the looks he was getting, no one minded him being there.

Made him glad he kept in shape. Shame to be jiggly in front of this group, even if he wasn't interested. A man had his pride, after all.

He crossed the road at the city limits and jogged toward Hawthorne's house, letting his mind wonder.

His inbox needed a little attention. Scratch that. He didn't want to deal with outside business, not on his first day in town, though Jason deserved a hearty thanks for arranging the job with Hawthorne.

UPS might bring his things today. He needed to research an attachment for a child's seat for his bike. Couldn't walk everywhere with Lali.

They'd gone through most of her library books the day before. Hawthorne seemed to have her on a schedule. Did they have a library day or did they just go as needed?

He'd studied Hawthorne's proposal. They'd work on that today. Maybe he'd soften her up by treating her and Lali to lunch at the café in town.

He smiled, gave friendly nods to the people he passed, and sincerely tried to keep his ego in check at the number of women eyeing his legs. Hawthorne loved his legs, loved running her hands over the firm muscles of his thighs.

And over other parts.

She had, anyway. Maybe she'd love it again someday.

He slowed to a walk a block from her house, pulled the ear buds out, and switched off his iPod. Next time, he'd run without it and enjoy the birds calling through the restful quiet.

Two women jogged past, nodding politely. "Mr. K," they said in near unison.

Well, mostly quiet.

He crossed the street again, bounded up the steps to Hawthorne's porch two at a time, and let himself in. He followed the smell of bacon and the sound of Lali's chatter to the kitchen at the back of the house, and swung the door open in time to hear her describing another dream to Hawthorne, who had showered and changed into yoga tights and a matching top.

Not that he noticed, or admired, or wanted.

Lali greeted him with a wide grin from her perch on the island in the middle of the room. "Airn! You came back."

"Course I did, kiddo." He ruffled her hair on his way to the fridge and grabbed a bottle of water from its cool depths. "Though I nearly didn't make it. I was attacked on the way by a bunch of Amazons who wanted to drag me back to their lair and force me to draw stories *forever*."

Her eyes widened. "Really?" she breathed.

"Naw, but it makes a good story, huh?"

She giggled and rolled from side to side on the counter.

He reached out a steadying hand, catching her an inch from the edge. "Careful now."

She blinked up at him, her gaze full of laughter. "You is a good puppy, Airn."

"I try." He sidled up behind Hawthorne and peered over her shoulder at the eggs she was scrambling, breathing in the warm scent of her freshly scrubbed skin. "You could've warned me," he said softly.

"It is a right of passage." She met his gaze over her shoulder, their faces inches apart. Her eyes drifted to his mouth and lingered there. "No one will bother you unless you wish it."

"The only woman I want to bother me is standing right here." He stepped back before he could give in to the urge to claim her mouth in a kiss that would not be appropriate in front of the avid eyes of a four-year old child. "Shower. Back in a few."

He tugged a lock of Lali's hair as he passed, earning another giggle, and made his way to his bedroom, trying not to think of how close he'd been to finding out if Hawthorne's body fit as well against his own as he remembered.

# NINE

THE MORNING rolled slowly by. Hawthorne helped Lali with her somersaults while Aaron answered e-mails and performed other business related tasks. Once she and Lali finished and dressed, Lali scampered through the house and pulled Aaron into their activities. They all went to the park and Aaron treated them to lunch in town before coming home and settling Lali in for her nap.

And then came the time Hawthorne dreaded, the hour when she had no further excuse to avoid spending time alone with him.

He had settled on the couch in her office with his socked feet propped on her coffee table. She stood in the doorway observing the back of his dark head as he bent over his laptop. He would be eager for this, had likely chosen the couch precisely because he knew it would force them into the kind of intimacy she would rather avoid.

He was right.

Her run that morning had done nothing to clear him from her mind. When he had entered the workroom looking rumpled and warm as if he had come straight from his bed, she had been hard pressed not to relive the few moments before her run when she had lain on top of him, savoring his embrace.

Allowing him to tug her into his bed had been a mistake, one she would avoid in the future. That nearness had thrown her, disoriented her. She, of the icy control, had actually smiled at him, a real smile, an expression she had not formed in years except with her progeny, and then only rarely. All because he had expressed an interest in running into town and back amidst the keen stares and whispers of her distant kin.

Of course, he could not have known exactly what he was subjecting himself to, but thinking on it had sparked a mischief that had broken her control long enough for a smile to curve her mouth.

She eyed him now, remembering his long, muscular legs displayed beneath the short hem of his running shorts and the way his long-sleeved athletic top had molded itself to his toned upper body. Yes, the women of Tellowee would have admired him from both far and near, depending upon whether or not they believed he was under her protection or merely working with her.

Something twisted within her, a confusing, cockeyed mixture of emotion. Surely she could not be jealous of other women showering Aaron with attention. If he wished to consort with another Daughter, then he was free to.

Emotion twisted again. Hawthorne sighed. Perhaps she was, indeed, jealous.

Aaron peered at her over his shoulder. "You gonna come in or stand in the doorway sighing?"

"I did not wish to interrupt your work." She stepped gingerly around the sofa and perched as far from him as she could, which was not far. He had taken the middle cushion, leaving her few options for sitting comfortably without touching him. "It would be easier to discuss the graphic novel at a table."

"Nope." He placed his laptop on the coffee table, exchanging it for a copy of the synopsis and outline she had submitted to her publisher. "You didn't do a detailed script."

"I have never written one before," she admitted. "That is why I wished to collaborate with someone more experienced than I."

"Well, you've got the right guy then. Here. You hold this."

He gave her the synopsis and picked up his sketchpad and pencil. "And I'll draw. Tell me about the main character."

"Una Longshadow. She is a young woman, a handmaiden of the Black Queen."

"I know that part." At her raised eyebrow, he said, "Read the first book."

Her stomach clenched on a flutter of nerves and a storm of questions raced through her mind. When had he found the time? Why had he done so? Had he liked it? What had he thought of her work?

"Relax, Hawthorne."

"I am."

"No, you're not. You look like I'm gonna bite you or something." He tapped one end of his sketchpad against his thigh. "Look, this will go a lot smoother if you'll sit back and pretend you don't hate me."

"I do not hate you."

"Right."

"Truly." She slid backward on the couch, seating herself fully, her arm inches from his, their thighs nearly touching. Warmth radiated from his skin through the flannel shirt he wore untucked from his jeans. From the corner of her eye, she admired his forearms, bare beneath the rolled up sleeves of his shirt, the play of muscle, the crisp, dark hairs lightly covering his skin. "You were the one who did not want me."

"Only for a little while. Sanity hit about thirty seconds after you left." He dropped the sketchpad on his lap and twisted around, facing her. "I looked for you, but you were already gone."

He had come after her? "Ruby took me home," she murmured. Her granddaughter had feared Hawthorne would behead Aaron, as she had every other man who had betrayed her. Only that morning had she learned that this man was safe from her vengeance. Curious that her heart protected him, even as it mourned the loss of his affection. "You should not have sought me out."

"Hard to make amends without seeing you," he said mildly. "Could you at least try to look at me?"

"I am not avoiding your gaze, Aaron. This situation is...uncomfortable."

"Uncomfortable because you don't want to be around me or uncomfortable in the same way that it was unpleasant to be..."

When he hesitated, she faced him. "You may speak plainly."

He shook his head. "I don't want to bring up your past."

"Is it not my past that stands between us, that and your refusal to believe me?"

"I'm willing to listen now if you want to explain."

"I tried to explain," she said in a voice far sharper than she had intended. "For all your talk of building trust, you held yours back."

"No, that's not..." He sighed. "Ok, you're right. I didn't trust you, but when you drop a bomb like that on a guy, what do you expect?"

"Faith," she said flatly. "A moment of consideration for the proof I was willing to offer."

"Proof you're withholding now," he pointed out.

"Because you broke my trust." She inhaled through her nose, stemming the hot ball of anger rising in her gut. "I do not wish to be hurt again."

"Hawthorne," he said gently. He reached toward her with one hand, then pulled back without touching her. "I would give anything to go back and change that."

"Such is impossible, Aaron."

His bark of laughter held a twist of bitter regret. "Maybe. Still want to do it, though." His hand reached for her again and he bit back a mild oath. "Could you at least lift the moratorium on touching while we're working?"

"That is not wise. However, you seem to have difficulty communicating without touching. I am amenable to lifting this moratorium while we work, but only when touching is appropriate."

His grin flashed. "You're something else. Come sit on my left so I won't be so tempted."

"As you wish." And though it was a strange request, she rose and stepped over his legs, still propped on the coffee table, and sat down on his left side. "Is this better?"

"Much." He waggled his eyebrows and a mischievous spark lit his brown eyes. "Now you can lean against me while I draw."

She bit back the smile that threatened. "Do not expect such liberties."

"Just a hope. Now, tell me about Una."

She did, describing the young girl as she envisioned her. She did not reveal that Una had once lived, that the Black Queen quadrilogy was based on an episode in the life of Hawthorne's only sister. That would cause an additional rift between them, a rift she wished to narrow, not widen. Perhaps one day, Aaron would be ready for the truth, though she suspected he was still quite far from it now, and would be until he had earned her trust, if such was possible.

Aaron's pencil stroked long, smooth lines on the blank page of his sketchpad, bringing Una to life once more. Hawthorne leaned forward, fascinated by the image forming rapidly beneath his skilled hands. If her body brushed his arm too frequently, he did not object, and she chose not to notice.

After all, a woman could only hold her control for so long before it broke, even when that woman had had centuries of practice.

LALI'S NAP was a short one. She bounded down the stairs, searching for them only an hour after Hawthorne had put her to bed, and crawled onto the sofa beside Aaron, her eyes intent on the rough concept sketches he made as Hawthorne described characters and settings.

It took her much longer to become bored with their work than he figured. After half an hour of nearly silent observation, she slid off the sofa and heaved a basket of art supplies from under the coffee table. A few minutes later, she settled herself at the table with blank paper and crayons and proceeded to draw picture after picture of the three of them, eyeing each critically for flaws while tapping the end of her crayon against her bow mouth.

He'd never seen anything so adorable in his life.

They broke for a snack in mid-afternoon. Aaron brought his sketchpad to the kitchen and sat down across from Lali while she picked through a plate of fruit and cheese.

"Maria will return next week," Hawthorne said in a quiet aside.

"Maria?"

"Our housekeeper. She watches Lali while I work."

"Oh." Aaron glanced down at his sketchpad, hiding his disappointment. "I kinda like having her around."

"She is a good girl, but her presence is occasionally distracting. If we were not on a schedule, I would allow her more freedom."

"We can always work around her. I don't mind."

Hawthorne's gaze drifted to his. "I see that you do not."

"You sound surprised." He winked at Lali and snagged a piece of cheese from her plate, startling her into a laugh. "I thought we had the whole I'm-not-a-monster thing sorted out."

"You're not a monster," Lali said. "You're my puppy."

"He is a man, Lali, not a canine," Hawthorne corrected gently.

"Silly Nana. I know Airn's a boy." Lali held up a piece of fruit, squinted at it suspiciously, then placed it back on her plate. "Only boys can be puppies."

Hawthorne blinked and Aaron bit back a laugh.

"Finish your snack and we shall play in the leaves for a while before Aaron and I must return to work," Hawthorne said.

"That sounds like fun." Aaron bumped her elbow with his. "Mind if I tag along?"

Hawthorne slid him a bemused glance. "If I said no, it would not stop you from joining us, would it?"

"Not a bit," he said cheerfully. "I'll get our coats."

He grabbed outdoor wear for all three of them while Lali finished her snack and Hawthorne helped the little girl wash her hands. For a blissful hour, the three of them raked leaves shed by the enormous oaks in the backyard into a dormant garden plot on one side of the lawn. As soon as they had a big enough pile, Lali threw down her pint-sized rake and leapt into them, scattering leaves everywhere. Hawthorne unbent enough to smile, softening her expression and, if possible, making her more beautiful.

Aaron wished she would smile more often, and began planning ways to tease happiness out of her. She so seldom showed joy, not because she wasn't happy. He often sensed her amusement and knew she'd found pleasure in his touch. Her control was so rigid, though, that she rarely let anything show. He wanted to change that.

They put in another hour and a half of work, making steady progress on roughing out concept sketches he would later refine. Lali sketched at the coffee table for a while before going to her room to play.

At four thirty, Hawthorne said, "Ruby will be here soon to watch Lali."

Aaron plopped his sketchpad onto the couch. "Why? Are you leaving?"

"I am." She stood and began clearing the coffee table, sorting Lali's art supplies into their proper containers. "I shall not be long."

"And?"

She glanced up from the box of crayons she was methodically straightening. "And what?"

He tamped down on his impatience. Rome wasn't built in a

day, and neither was a woman's trust. "Where are you going?"

Her eyes slid away from his as she resumed cleaning and sorting. "I teach self defense classes at the rape crisis center in Gainesville."

"That's such a great thing to do." And it lifted his hopes that she might actually be dealing with what had happened to her.

"It is my duty to help others protect themselves when I could not." She dropped the box of crayons into the basket and stowed Lali's art supplies under the coffee table. "Knowing how to defend oneself will not always stop an attacker, but fighting back is the number one deterrent for further assault."

He hadn't known. "It is?"

"Yes, preferably with a weapon. I emphasize using whatever is handy." She stood and stared down at him, her expression a blank mask. "Including one's own body and vocal chords. For too long, men and women have been taught to give in, to acquiesce in the face of danger, under the rationale that an assailant will escalate the attack if the victim fights back. Nothing..."

Her voice broke, and with it his heart. He rose and cupped her shoulders, and wished he could wrap himself around her and protect her from the past that had scarred her so deeply. "Nothing?" he said gently.

"They say nothing is worse than death," she said in a hard voice thick with bitter rage. "I disagree."

He pulled her close, couldn't help it. He needed to hold her, needed to ease her pain in whatever way he could, if she would let him. She buried her face in his neck and curled her hands into fists in his shirt, and he thought, *This is it. She'll cry and get some of the anger and hurt out and maybe she'll heal a little more*, but she didn't. Instead, she stepped back, smoothed the wrinkles from his shirt, and left without another word.

He stood in the middle of her office for a long time considering the amount of pain a woman like Hawthorne would have to endure in order to believe death a better alternative.

What he wouldn't give to have been there the day she'd exacted revenge on the men who had hurt her so badly. What he wouldn't give to deliver a measure of pain back on them.

What he wouldn't give to take all of that hurt away from her and never have her feel it, ever again.

RUBY ARRIVED at five on the dot. Aaron sat at the desk in the office Hawthorne had set aside for his use, listening to the rise and fall of the women's voices. A moment after the front door closed, Lali bounded into the room, Ruby in tow.

"Airn, look. It's sitter Ruby," Lali said as she climbed into Aaron's lap.

"She means sister." Ruby propped against the doorframe, her expression granite hard. "What are you doing here?"

"I'm collaborating on a graphic novel with Hawthorne," Aaron said easily. He saved and closed the drawing he was working on and opened a blank document for Lali. "Didn't she tell you?"

"I didn't believe her. So, are you here to break her heart again?"

"Are you here to ask nosey questions?"

She snorted. "You've got a lot of nerve showing your face in this town."

"Well, there you go. I'm nervy." He gently corrected Lali's grip on the stylus, and grinned when she stuck her tongue between her teeth and concentrated on the tablet. "But that's between me and Hawthorne."

She pushed herself away from the doorframe with a pointed glare. "Right. Don't hurt her again."

"Or, what, you'll kick my ass?"

Her mouth curled into a vicious smile. "No, but I won't stand in her way again."

If he hurt Hawthorne again, he figured he deserved a good ass whooping. "Fair enough." When she made no move to leave, he added, "Are you really Lali's sister?"

"Yes," she said, her tone flat. "And it's nearly time for her supper."

"I'll leave the two of you to it, then." He bussed Lali's cheek and lifted her off his lap, unsurprised at her protest. "I'll be back before bedtime."

Lali tilted her head, her gray eyes solemn. "Promise, Airn?"

"I promise. Now scoot, kiddo. Go spend time with big sis."

They left hand in hand, their blonde heads nearly identical in color. Why hadn't Hawthorne told him Ruby and Lali were sisters? What had happened to their parents, and why was Hawthorne raising Lali when Ruby seemed capable of doing it herself?

If Hawthorne ever opened up to him again, he'd be sure to ask her.

He cut off his tablet and stored it out of Lali's reach, shrugged on his jacket, and faced the brisk evening air. His bike hadn't arrived yet, though he didn't mind the walk into town. The Omega had looked promising, and being as it was Tellowee's only bar, he was duty bound to inspect it and sample the local brews.

He let his mind drift as he walked, waved absent-mindedly to the people who called greetings. A few he even recognized. A slender man who brought his son to the park every day. A jogger who'd passed him that morning. The guard on gate duty at what he'd learned was the Institute for Early Cultural Studies.

"Don't you ever go home?" he asked the guard.

"Twelve hour shifts," she said with a grin. "Not all of them on gate duty, though."

"See you tomorrow morning, then, huh."

"Naw. Rotating off tonight. I'll tell the incoming crew not to harass you."

"Appreciate it."

"You're Hawthorne's man." She lifted one black bedecked shoulder in a shrug. "She's liable to skewer anybody who messes with you."

He let the remark go unchallenged. Hawthorne's man he might wish to be, but until she forgave him, they were nothing more than colleagues who'd had a brief affair. As far as her skewering anyone, he highly doubted she could be moved to raise a protest over him, let alone a sword.

The thought depressed him. Not that he wanted her to go hacking away at anybody, but it would be nice if she could show a little emotion every once in a while. Maybe regret that their time together had ended the way it had, far preferable to the blank expressions she'd given him since he'd showed up on her door. They hadn't been apart so long that he'd forgotten how to read her. She seemed to've clamped down on her emotions so hard that precious few bled through.

Damn her control anyway.

He slipped into The Omega behind a laughing couple and ignored a pang of jealousy. The situation with Hawthorne was entirely his fault. Well, almost. Who could've imagined she'd spin such a tall tale about her past? No one in their right mind, that's who, and who could fault him for not taking her story at face value?

He made his way through the early supper crowd to the bar and slid onto a barstool, his stomach rumbling from the scent of fried food wafting from the back.

So, yeah, maybe he should've taken the time to actually look at the proof she claimed to have, and he would've if his first reaction hadn't been, *Not again*. After all of Jeanne's craziness, how could he *not* have reacted that way to Hawthorne?

And now she wanted him to take it on faith, which was asking too much. No one lived to be two centuries old, let alone two millennia. He thought back to his days at day school and silently amended that. No one outside of myth lived more than two centuries. It was physically impossible. Therefore, Hawthorne's tale had to be false, even if it rang true in every other way.

He still hadn't figured out how to reconcile that one falsehood. She seemed incapable of anything other than straight-forward honesty. That's what had changed his opinion, the belief that her mind had simply warped under the damage inflicted on her body. Dammit, she needed to heal, needed to face what had happened head on and see the truth for the horrible reality it was instead of burying it in a story she'd used as an escape. He didn't know how to do anything other than be there for her while she coped with it.

God, he hoped that was enough.

A stunningly attractive young woman with her dark blonde hair pulled into a ponytail stepped up to the other side of the bar. "What'll you have?"

He leaned on the bar and mustered an easy grin for her. "What's good, food-wise?"

A dimple flashed in her tanned cheek. "Whatever cook feels like making."

"As long as it's not pork, I'm game." He eyed the hand-written list of microbrews posted on a blackboard behind the bar. "Which one of those do you recommend?"

"Duck Rabbit," she said promptly. "It's a stout. Smooth. A local favorite."

"Sounds great."

She left and pushed her way through the door into the kitchen. Aaron twisted on the stool and scanned over the crowd of mostly twenty-something women, all physically fit. Most of the men were, too, with a few notable exceptions. He'd never seen so many people obsessed with fitness before, not even in image conscious California.

"Here you are." The bartender handed him his drink as he swiveled around to face her. "Cook'll have your food out in a bit."

"Thanks." He took a testing swig from the bottle she'd given him. As she'd said, it was smooth with a pleasant milky undertone. "This is good."

"We aim to please." She leaned casually against the bar and gave him a friendly smile. "So, are you passing through or are you a new addition?"

"New addition. I'm staying with Hawthorne while we collaborate on a novel."

She recoiled and the color leached from her face. "You're Aaron Kesselman."

"That's me. Are you ok?"

"Please don't tell her I was flirting." She fled, racing past a young man with the same dark blonde hair and friendly features who stepped aside and turned, following her progress through the swinging doors leading into the kitchen.

"What did I say?" Aaron asked.

"With Casey, could've been anything." The young man stuck his hand out. "Will Corbin. My parents own this place."

Aaron took Will's hand and shook it briefly. "Aaron Kesselman. I'm..."

"Hawthorne's man." Will's mouth twisted into a rueful grin. "That'd be why Casey left."

Aaron muttered a choice oath under his breath. "It's not like I bite."

"You might not, but Hawthorne does. Casey's flighty, not stupid."

Aaron rubbed a knuckle over the sudden ache in his forehead. "What's she gonna do? It's not like we're an item." Yet.

"Sorry, man. Word's already out that you're taken. No woman here'll touch you with a ten foot pole."

"Christ." It's not like he wanted to date any of the local women, but still. He'd be here for a while, and it'd be nice to not have women fleeing from him wherever he went. "Any way to head that off?"

"Not a one," Will said cheerfully. "We're a loyal bunch. Until Hawthorne gives the contrary word personally, you're as good as mated."

"Mated," Aaron said flatly. "As in married?"

"That would be it." Will's gaze slid past Aaron to a spot over his right shoulder. "Speaking of."

Aaron glanced over his shoulder. Two women were striding through the entrance, a svelte blonde of Nordic descent and a petite woman with her strawberry blonde hair stuffed under a chunky knit cap. "One of those your wife?"

"I wish," Will muttered. "Pretty sure she doesn't know I exist."

Aaron hunched his shoulders and rolled the beer bottle between his hands along the top of the bar. "Kinda in a similar boat there, pal."

"Yeah?" Sympathy bled into Will's even features. "Wish I could say it'll get better."

Aaron saluted the younger man as he made his way to the two women, who had taken stools at the other end of the bar. The redhead leaned across the bar and pulled Will into a smacking kiss on the mouth. The blonde stared coldly through the younger man.

Yup. Aaron had been on the receiving end of *that* stare a time or two.

Casey stepped tentatively through the doors leading from the kitchen carrying a plastic basket of chicken fingers and fries. She bobbled it as she placed it on the bar in front of Aaron, carefully avoided meeting his gaze with her own, and scurried away, ignoring his attempted thanks.

He scooped up the basket and his ale and wended through the bar to a table. God knew he didn't want to make one more woman *uncomfortable* around him.

To keep his mind busy, he watched the crowd while he ate, checked the score on the soccer game playing on the huge TV mounted to the wall, and generally tried to be as unobtrusive as possible. Casey brought him another beer, only because Will refused to, Aaron figured. A few of the women and all of the men sent curious glances his ways, but she was the only person who came within five feet of his table.

Either Hawthorne's rep was really that bad or the residents of Tellowee didn't take to strangers.

He had a funny feeling it was the former.

When Aaron tried to pay for his meal and the beer, Will refused his money. "I'll put it on Hawthorne's tab and send her a bill at the end of the month."

"What's wrong with paying for it now?"

"That's just the way we do things here." Will held his hands up in a *don't shoot the messenger* gesture. "The women rule. You stick around long enough, you'll see."

Aaron shoved his wallet into his back pocket. "I'm trying to find a way to stick."

"Good luck with that." Will's eyes slid to the Nordic goddess, who was in the middle of a heated argument with her redheaded friend. "Gotta break that up before they bring the bar down. Come back anytime."

"Sure," Aaron said. And he would. The food had been filling, the beer chilled and crisp.

On the other hand, who wanted to go to a place where no one but the owner's son would talk to you for fear of inciting Hawthorne's wrath?

His temper simmered during the walk from The Omega to her home. Hell if he'd put up with that, especially since she barely gave him the time of day. If she didn't want to spend time with him, then she could at least put word out that she didn't have a claim on him. It's not like he wanted to date. Being able to have a simple conversation with a woman without her becoming hysterical about his not-girlfriend seemed like a reasonable wish, though.

By the time he tugged on the front door, a hot fist of anger sat low in his gut. He hung his jacket up on the free-standing coatrack in the foyer and followed Lali's high-pitched screech up the stairs to her bedroom, where he found Ruby wrestling her little sister out of her clothes.

"What's going on?" he said.

"Airn!" Lali wiggled out of Ruby's grasp and launched herself at him. "You came back."

He hefted her into a hug and smoothed her hair back. "Is this gonna be a thing with us?"

"She's been like that all night. Nothing but *Airn, Airn, Airn,* and Goddess help anyone who gainsays her." Ruby sat back on her haunches and eyed him. "If I didn't know better, I'd think you walked on water."

"Ha, funny." He rubbed a thumb across the tear tracks on Lali's cheek. "What's this, kiddo? You been giving your big sis a hard time?"

Lali glared mutinously at Ruby. "She was gonna give me a bath without my puppy."

"Come on, Lali. We've talked about this." Aaron heaved out an exasperated breath and grappled with the anger roiling through him. Lali hadn't caused it, and she sure as hell didn't deserve to have it spill over onto her. "Big guys don't help little girls with their baths. It's just not done."

"But you're my puppy," Lali wailed. Fat tears rolled down her cheeks. She threw herself against his chest and sobbed like her heart had broken in two.

"Wow." Ruby's mouth twisted into a familiar smirk. "You really have a way with women."

"Hush it, you," he said. "Calm down, Lali. Come on now, be a good girl." He shushed and rocked and cuddled her, and gradually, her cries dwindled to sniffles. "There, now. All that fuss and you still have to take a bath."

"Want my puppy," she said, her voice a sleepy murmur against his throat.

"I'm here, sweetheart." He rubbed his cheek against the silky wisps of her hair, and was surprised to find that his earlier anger had evaporated under the onslaught of concern for Lali. "Let Ruby help with your bath and then I'll tell you a story, ok?"

Her arms tightened around his neck. "Ok, but I don't like

it."

Laughter slipped from him before he could hold it back. "I know. Go on now."

He untangled himself from Lali as she slid into Ruby's arms and watched until they disappeared into Lali's bathroom. His head throbbed and his gut ached from the last of the anger, and all he really wanted after helping Lali into bed was a good night's sleep. He doubted he'd get it, not with the state his mind was in. Hawthorne owed him some answers. By God, she was going to give them to him whether she liked it or not.

# TEN

**H**AWTHORNE SPENT the next few days acclimating Aaron to life in Tellowee. He expressed a desire to swim as part of his exercise routine. It was a simple matter to gain a pass for him to the IECS' facilities. When his bicycle and art supplies arrived on Friday, she helped him put the former together so he would have adequate transportation around town.

Apparently, Aaron had not driven a motorized vehicle in years, though he held a current driver's permit. He refused to consider using her Land Rover, preferring instead to walk or bicycle where he needed to go. That someone would deliberately limit his independence baffled her. As much as she endeavored to educate him otherwise, he simply did not understand the reality of life in a rural Southern town, particularly one without public transportation.

The weekend passed easily enough. Lali and Aaron spent much time together, the three of them more so. On Saturday night after a full day of play and work, Aaron insisted on watching a movie on the television in her living room. Hawthorne helped Lali with her bath while he made popcorn and picked out a movie.

The three of them settled onto the couch with Lali between the adults, her eyes wide as she soaked in the rare treat. As Hawthorne suspected, her granddaughter fell asleep before the movie was finished. When she made to move her, Aaron stood and said, "I've got her," and lifted the little girl into his arms with such sweet tenderness, Hawthorne's heart skipped in her chest.

He flipped most of the lights off on his way down the stairs and sat close enough to her for their shoulders to touch. A breathless rush of feeling came over her, building until her blood heated and her skin tingled with anticipation. She waited for him to violate their agreement and touch her, but he never did. Why that disappointed her, she could not say.

When the movie ended, he said, "Want to watch another one?"

Her heart leapt. *Yes*, she thought, and then, *No*. Of course, she could linger in his presence. "It is late."

"It's not even nine thirty." He nudged her shoulder with his. "Come on. Live a little."

"I have lived plenty," she reminded him.

He laughed softly and turned the television to a monster movie marathon. "Just one."

His gaze caught hers, and in his dark chocolate eyes she saw remembrance and a spark of attraction, recognized it because she felt it, too, and longed to recapture the simple joy they had shared at DragonCon.

That he chose to share another monster movie marathon with her told her more plainly than words how remorseful he was over the way they had parted. More, he wanted to build trust with her again, though he did not say so. Even if she could not smell the musky scent of his arousal or sense the increased speed of his heart when she was near, his actions spoke loudly of his desire.

More fool her, she allowed one movie to become two and all but wallowed in the brief contact between their arms as midnight came and went.

She had other concerns to deal with as well. Aaron's presence had distracted her temporarily from her duties to the People and her family. Bobby Upton's accusations regarding Isolde would have to be investigated, an action Hawthorne had neglected in the flurry of emotion storming through her upon Aaron's unexpected arrival. On Sunday, she phoned Yvette, waking the younger Daughter, and asked her to initiate a low-key investigation into Una's daughter. Isolde would learn of it eventually and would make her way to Hawthorne, who would use the opportunity to rattle her niece and gain the upper hand.

At times, it was more advantageous to serve the People away from the spotlight. Those in power always feared losing their authority and were thus protective of it, creating a vulnerability.

Hawthorne had no such weakness.

Maria returned to work on Monday, cheerful after her vacation. The elderly woman fussed over Aaron much as she did her own children, all grown and all, in Maria's opinion, in need of a mother's watchful eye and protective touch.

An opinion with which Hawthorne whole-heartedly agreed.

With Maria home and available to watch Lali, work on the graphic novel went much more quickly. Aaron refined his concept sketches over the weekend and set them aside. By Tuesday, they began a more detailed script, refining the plot and fleshing it out through conversations that were surprisingly agreeable.

Hawthorne created the script on her laptop using their discussions as a guideline while Aaron sketched rough thumbnails of each page. The script would serve as a reminder when he expanded the thumbnails and created over-sized pages from them, pages that would later be reduced to the size preferred by her publisher.

The process fascinated her, as did his skill as an illustrator. Under his hand, the story of Una Longshadow came to life, and with it, the memory of her sister. He had recreated her faithfully from Hawthorne's description, refining his concept sketch until it bore a startling resemblance to Una as a young girl.

He showed it to her, fingers tucked in his pockets, eyes hopeful and wary. Hawthorne held it gently, willing her trembling fingers to still. It had been so long since she had seen her sister, so long since their last embrace. The comfort of Una's presence was a mere memory, lost if not for the curse that kept her image sharp in Hawthorne's mind.

What would Una think of the man who had used his passion to revive her from the dead, if only on paper?

"Hey." Aaron covered her hands with his and chafed them gently. "You ok?"

"I am well."

She stared at the pencil sketch and swallowed around the fist-sized ache gathering in her chest. *Una, my heart. Would that you were here.*

"Ah, if you want, I could do one in full color for you." He cleared his throat and stuffed his hands in the back pockets of his jeans. "I was gonna scan it in and color it digitally anyway, but it would be fun to color a physical copy instead."

Hawthorne lifted her gaze to his. "You would do this for me?"

His expression softened into a smile. "'Course I would."

"Thank you." She pressed the sketch gently into his hands and rose on tiptoe, brushing a kiss over his cheek. His skin was warm under her lips and more tempting than she dared acknowledge. "I shall treasure this portrait."

His eyes lit with an inner glow, as if she had pleased him.

He had pleased her as well. She would not forget the hand he had played in preserving her sister's memory.

The next day, Hawthorne's directions to her young assistant bore fruition. Mid-morning, Isolde knocked imperiously on the front door. Hawthorne heard Lali's scampering feet pause at the front door and just as quickly retreat to the office where she and Aaron worked.

"Nana, Nana," the young girl cried. "It's the mean cushion."

"There's a mean cushion at the door?" Aaron set aside his tablet and stylus and scooped Lali up. "This I have to see."

"No, Airn." Lali flung her arms around Aaron's neck, her eyes round, her face pale. "The mean cushion will get you and then you can't be my puppy no more."

His confused gaze met Hawthorne's over the little girl's head.

"She means cousin." Hawthorne tilted her head toward the low voices at the front of the house. "My niece, Isolde."

"Ah." He jiggled Lali in his arms and patted her back with gentle taps. "I suppose you and me can get a snack while Nana and Isolde visit."

"It is business," Hawthorne said, "and may take some time."

"Then we'll go to the library," Aaron said easily. "Maria can drop us off while she does her shopping. How about that?"

"Yes, puppy," Lali said against his collar. "Don't like the mean cushion."

"Lali is not your responsibility, Aaron."

"What does that have to do with anything?" His arms tightened around the little girl. "Anyway, this is clearly not the place for her to be right now."

"She must learn to face her fears," Hawthorne insisted.

His face set into hard lines. "She's four and has plenty of time to learn how to deal with people she doesn't like."

Hawthorne inhaled sharply. Maria lead Isolde into the office, forestalling Hawthorne's reply.

Aaron stared at her niece, then turned an accusing glare on Hawthorne. "You've got a lot of explaining to do," he said softly.

She returned his glare with an icy stare. If he had not broken her trust at DragonCon, Isolde's uncanny resemblance to the portrait he had created of Una would not have taken him unaware.

Nor would he have been surprised by Hawthorne's much younger appearance compared to her niece's older one. Isolde had lost her mortality nearly two decades before upon falling in love, surprising everyone who knew her, including Hawthorne. Unlike her mother, Isolde had no room for forgiveness in her heart. The lack stretched to the many wrongs forced upon Daughters by men from the time of the Seven Sisters' unjust curse, to Una's treatment at the hands of the Roman army, to the Shadow Enemy's continued assault on the People. That Isolde had submitted her will to a man and become mortal had been seen as wisdom on the Daughter's part, a sign that her unforgiving nature would mend.

Hawthorne suspected it never would, though she had more tact than to say so, in spite of her reputation otherwise.

Isolde's sharp eyes observed the tableau for only a moment before she stepped lightly into the room. She bowed slightly from the waist, then smoothed a hand over the jacket of her tailored business suit. "Aunt. I heard you had taken a lover."

Hawthorne ignored the censure in Isolde's voice. "This is Aaron Kesselman. Aaron, my niece, Isolde."

Aaron nodded politely, his arms protective around Lali. "Hello."

"Don't speak to the cushion, Airn," Lali hissed against his throat. "She'll get you."

Isolde's black eyes glittered, hard and full of disdain. "She's become spoiled and insolent. When will you take her in hand?"

"When she needs it." Hawthorne leveled an even stare at Isolde. "Aaron, have Maria drive you and Lali to the library. I shall see the two of you for lunch."

"Of course," he murmured. He bussed her mouth lightly, nodded goodbye to Isolde, and left, Lali still wrapped around his neck.

As they exited the office, Lali said softly, "Someday, I'm gonna be a great warrior and chop the mean cushion's head off, just like Nana."

Aaron's soft laugh mingled with Isolde's outraged gasp. "Of course, you will, kiddo. Don't think I'd mind seeing that."

His footsteps faded gradually, leaving the office in tense silence. Hawthorne spared a glance for Isolde as she took a seat behind her desk and prepared for a battle of words with her sister's only living daughter.

LALI LED AARON into the local public library, her tiny hand tucked trustingly into his. He pulled the door open for her and snagged her by her backpack as she rushed through it, barely catching her before she plowed into a woman in front of them pushing a baby stroller through the second set of doors.

"Hello, Missy Charlotte," Lali said.

The woman turned around and smiled down at Lali. "Hello, Miss Lali. Becka's already inside waiting for you."

Lali turned huge gray eyes onto Aaron. "Can I go find her?"

"If you walk."

She flashed a smile and ran through the doors, and he heaved an exasperated sigh.

"Don't worry. She'll calm down once she finds Becka." The woman held out a fine-boned hand, her smile friendly. "Charlotte Everheart. I'm Director Upton's daughter."

"Aaron Kesselman." He gripped her hand politely. "Who's Director Upton?"

"Rebecca Upton? Director of the IECS?" She laughed and shook her head, sending her mousy brown ponytail bouncing. "You've not been here long, I take it."

"About a week," he admitted. He held open the door for her. "Here, let me help you. We're causing a logjam."

Charlotte pushed the stroller through the open door and into the library. "Happens every Wednesday. Story time," she said over her shoulder. "It's a lot of fun."

He peered through the glass windows separating the main library from the children's area. Kids were scattered everywhere while adults, many of them men, clustered together in small groups around the perimeter of the room. A buxom woman wearing a plastic nametag too small for him to read took a seat in a small chair at the edge of a brightly colored circular carpet.

"That's our cue," Charlotte said. "Lynette's about to read to the kids."

Aaron followed her inside the children's section and found a spot next to a group of other men. They nodded politely, and if their stares were a little too curious, he ignored it. Lali had already plopped down next to a little girl of a similar age whose hair was the exact same shade as Charlotte's. Becka, he assumed, and was relieved that Lali had, indeed, settled down when she'd found her friend.

The story didn't take long. Lynette read with a clear voice, holding the children's attention, and invited their participation. After, she led the surprisingly well-behaved group through a simple song accompanied by hand movements the children mimicked.

As soon as the song ended, the kids stood and found their parents. Lali bounced up to him with Becka in tow, her bright eyes shining.

"This is my puppy, Airn," she said to Becka. "Isn't he pretty?"

Becka tilted her head back so far, Aaron thought she'd tip over. She blinked at him, her cornflower blue eyes solemn as she took his measure. "He's taller than my puppy."

Lali sighed happily and gazed at him with a soft smile. "He's a good puppy, too. He makes pictures and tells me stories from his head."

Becka screwed her face into a thoughtful frown. "My puppy doesn't do that."

Charlotte came up behind the girls and grinned at him. "You look confused."

"I am," he admitted. He stared down at the little girls, trying to sort out their conversation. Lali gazed back at him with an adoring expression and his heart turned over and fell right into her tiny hands. "Lali keeps calling me her puppy. I thought it was her way of telling me she likes me, but Becka says she has a puppy, so now, yeah, I'm a little confused."

"A puppy?" Charlotte looked from one girl to the other, then smiled as her brow cleared. "Oh. Poppy, not puppy. Becka calls her dad Poppy."

"Oh." He knelt in front of Lali and gathered her into a tight hug. Hawthorne had said Lali missed her father, but she'd never told him what had happened to Lali's parents. He'd meant to ask and never found the right time, and now he cursed the lack. Why hadn't he pushed Hawthorne to explain? "I'm not her father."

Charlotte knelt beside him and pulled Becka into a hug. "You're Hawthorne's man though, right?"

He huffed out a laugh. "Not quite."

"Lali must believe so."

"Puppy," Lali said. She clapped her hands against his cheeks and smiled. "We has to go do the crafts now, Airn."

"Ok, kiddo." He accepted the kiss she pressed to his mouth. Her sweet little girl kiss took on a whole new meaning in light of the puppy nickname. "I'll be right there."

"Okey dokey." She wiggled out of his arms and threaded her fingers through Becka's, and then they were gone, skipping out of the children's section together.

Aaron stood slowly and held out his hand to Charlotte, pulling her into a stand.

"Thanks." She inhaled slowly and blew the breath out on a huff. "This being mortal gig is for the birds."

"Excuse me?"

Her eyebrows inched upward above her round, blue eyes. "Hawthorne hasn't told you yet?"

"Ah, told me what?"

She pinned him with a speculative look. "About the People. Ruby said you were lovers. I thought you were just being discreet when you denied it, but now..."

Heat crept into Aaron's cheeks. "Does everybody think that?"

"Pretty much, and anybody who doesn't will find out soon enough." She placed a gentle hand on his shoulder and squeezed. "It's none of my business, but if you care about Lali at all, consider carefully what happens between you and Hawthorne. Lali doesn't need another heartbreak, not so soon after losing her parents."

Aaron rubbed a knuckle over his forehead. "She didn't tell me."

"Seems like Hawthorne is holding an awful lot back." Charlotte's hand dropped away. "Ever wonder why?"

He stuffed his hands into his pockets and hunched his shoulders. "Pretty sure I know why."

"Fix it before it's too late." Soft whimpers came from the stroller. Charlotte bent down and lifted an infant out, placed him carefully on her shoulder. "My youngest. Thank the Goddess my brother took my middle son to work with him or I'd have my hands full today."

"Wait, is your brother Bobby Upton?"

Charlotte shifted her weight from one leg to the other, patting her son's back. "That's him. You've met?"

"The first day I got here." Aaron tried to keep his expression impassive and failed miserably judging by the smile spreading across Charlotte's face. "He kissed Hawthorne."

"Did he?" Charlotte's smile turned into a grin. "He's a rascal."

"Hunh. That's one word for it."

The baby's whimpers escalated into cries. "Oh, crud. That's my cue. Could you keep an eye on Becka for me while I feed this one?"

"I've got it."

"I really appreciate it." She pulled a diaper bag from behind the stroller and nudged it to the side, out of the way. "Introduce yourself around. And don't forget to mention which Daughter you belong to."

"Lali?

"Hawthorne. Daughter with a capital D, not..." She huffed out a laugh. "Never mind. You'll be fine." She pushed through the doors of the children's section as the baby's cries turned into sobs.

Aaron rubbed his forehead against the confusion gathering there. *Goddesses and Daughters and puppies, oh my.* His life had become a parody of a children's story.

He snagged Lali's backpack from the rug and trailed a group of gossiping fathers into a conference room where Lynette and two other members of the library's staff were guiding the kids through a series of Halloween-themed crafts. He took his place behind Lali and Becka and helped them glue triangular eyes onto an orange Jack-o-lantern made of construction paper, threaded pipe cleaners into egg cartons for spiders, and unwound gauze from around Becka's hands during the making of a mummy from an empty toilet paper roll.

Halfway through the final craft, he bumped into another father, a familiar looking African-American with close-cropped hair and a slim, athletic build who held a wiggling little boy up to the table.

"Sorry," Aaron said. "Too many people, not enough room."

"It's ok. We're used to it." The man's face creased into a smile. "Jim Hornby."

"Aaron Kesselman." He hesitated a moment. "Hawthorne?"

"Right. I heard she'd taken a lover." Jim laughed as dismay flicked across Aaron's face. "Get used to it, man. Tellowee's a really small town. Everybody knows everybody else's business, and they like it that way."

"I'm beginning to get that." Aaron shook his head ruefully. "It's a world apart from San Francisco."

"I hear you. Chicago, born and raised. Small town life's hard to crack."

"Wait, are you Jim Hornby the baseball player?" Aaron laughed around his astonishment. "Holy cow. I thought I recognized you."

"Retired now and happily married. I met my wife while she was in Chicago doing a little scouting for the IECS. We started dating and fell in love, and the next thing I know, she's submitted her will to me." Jim jiggled the little boy. "That's how we got this one."

Aaron glanced between the former baseball player and his

son. "I have no idea what you're talking about."

"Hawthorne hasn't told you." Jim's lips compressed into a thin slash across his ebony face. "I can't believe she'd risk herself that way, or the People."

"Told me what? What People?"

Jim leaned closer and dropped his voice. "Living with a Daughter's hard enough, you feel me? Do yourself a favor and get Hawthorne to explain about the People before you're in too deep."

Aaron's heart dropped into his stomach. Why was everybody so concerned about Hawthorne not telling him things? And what by all that was holy had Jim been talking about? His head spun with Lali's puppy revelation and the conversations with Jim and Charlotte. When Aaron and Lali got home, he and Hawthorne were going to have a really long chat.

And this time, he would follow through and make sure it actually happened.

"I gotta go man." Jim stood and lifted his laughing son onto his shoulders. "See you next time."

"Yeah," Aaron said faintly. "Nice to meet you."

Lali beamed and held up her finished craft. "All done."

"Great."

He scouted the crowd for Charlotte, and breathed a sigh of relief when he spotted her talking to another woman. Hopefully, Maria would be by soon to pick him and Lali up, but until then, he still had a gauntlet to run helping Lali pick out books.

How many of the damn things would he have to face unprepared? Sooner or later, the town had to run out of people and gossip and strange lingo.

Didn't it?

He shouldered Lali's backpack and held out his hands for the little girl and her friend. Hawthorne had to come clean with him, whatever it took.

# ELEVEN

AWTHORNE USED the silence left in the wake of Aaron and Lali's departure to her advantage, allowing it to spool between her and her niece and prick the younger Daughter into making the first move.

Isolde pursed her lips and sank gracefully into one of the two Queen Anne style chairs placed in front of Hawthorne's desk. "Your household is as disordered as ever, Hawthorne."

"Do not fool yourself into believing that I shall tolerate your criticism, Isolde." Hawthorne folded her hands in her lap, regarding the other woman with a calm countenance. "The love I felt for my sister must be earned by her progeny."

Isolde's full, red lips curved into a sly smile. "Have I not won your regard, Aunt, by taking your place on the Council and relieving you of the burden of service to the People?"

"For which I am grateful," Hawthorne acknowledged with a nod.

"Perhaps," Isolde murmured. "Or perhaps, as the eldest of the line of Bagda, you are ready to assume your rightful place on the Council."

"I am quite content to leave such duties to you, niece."

"And yet you sic human dogs on me, delving into my private affairs as if I were an untrustworthy stranger instead of the only surviving daughter of your beloved sister." Isolde leaned forward, her expression politely curious. "Tell me, Hawthorne, to what do I owe this unexpected pleasure?"

"I am merely caring for my house, fulfilling my duties as an elder."

Isolde's light laughter echoed in the room. "Tending house requires a full check into my life? Really, Hawthorne. How gullible do you believe me to be?"

"None whatsoever." Weariness weighed on Hawthorne, driven by the weight of responsibility and the tedious need to guard every word carefully, to time even the most casual inquiry perfectly in order to achieve the maximum benefit. "Perhaps an unsavory rumor has reached my ear."

"Since when does Hawthorne the Beheader heed the trifles of town gossip?"

"Since that gossip involves the only surviving daughter of my beloved sister. It is said you have betrayed the People, though the hows and whys are not yet fully known."

Isolde's smile was crafted as carefully as her words. "Of course, such betrayal could never be. I have and always have had the best interests of the People at my heart."

Hawthorne leveled an even stare upon her niece. "And do those best interests involve an alliance with the Eternal Order?"

"Why, Aunt, you jest. The Order is a figment of the imagination, a morality tale meant to frighten children and nothing more."

"We both know this is not so."

"I know nothing of the sort. First the Blade and now you." Isolde crossed her ankles, the epitome of prim and proper elegance. "The burden of age has twisted your mind to paranoia."

"Has it?" Hawthorne believed nothing of the sort, though a small amount of paranoia was healthy. It had guarded her life through nearly two millennia. "You would have me trust you unquestionably?"

"One does not blindly trust. I believe you were the one to

impart that lesson."

"As was my duty." Hawthorne rose, content that she had gathered as much as she would from Una's daughter. For the moment. "Please give my best wishes to your husband. He has not visited in months and I miss his counsel."

"I shall tell him." Isolde stood and moved around the desk, bussing Hawthorne's cheek. "Well met, Maetyrm."

"Well met, child. Be well."

Isolde bowed slightly and left, her heels clicking against the hardwood floor in sharp taps.

Hawthorne walked to the coffee table where Aaron had left his work and picked up his recreation of Una. The likeness was uncanny and pricked at the well of longing and sorrow buried deep within Hawthorne, carefully hidden from the outside world. Una would never live again. Her seed would die with the intractable Isolde, who had refused to have children. But for Hawthorne's lingering memories and the work of the man who had come into her life in the most unexpected fashion, it would be as if Una had never lived.

She pushed the melancholy away and settled onto the sofa with her laptop, allowing work to absorb her concentration.

AN HOUR LATER, voices sounded from the vicinity of the front door, rousing Hawthorne from her work. The lilt of Maria's accented words, the deep smoothness of Aaron's reply, the bright bubble of Lali's laughter. Tiny feet scampered through the house, their beat along the floor growing louder. A moment later, the little girl burst into the room, her face wreathed with pleasure.

"Look, Nana." Lali climbed onto the sofa pulling a grocery bag full of crafts behind her. "Look what puppy and me made."

Hawthorne set her laptop aside and listened patiently to Lali's chatter, filled with Becka and Aaron and Missy Charlotte and all the happenings from that day's library visit.

Aaron entered the room at a slower pace, his expression

much heavier than Lali's.

As soon as her granddaughter wound down, Aaron sent her out of the room to find Maria and crossed his arms over his chest, glowering down at Hawthorne. "We need to talk."

She patted the sofa, deliberately mimicking his frequent requests to sit.

He ignored her. "What happened to Lali's parents?"

"They died in a car accident not long after her birth." She folded her hands in her lap and girded herself for yet another battle of words. Would that everything could be solved with a strong arm and a sharp blade. "Why do you wish to know?"

He wheezed out a disbelieving laugh. "How can you ask me that? It's Lali."

"Yes, this is so. Yet, you have never asked before."

"Not because I don't care. You're so damn *closed.*"

"I have not always been so with you. There was a time when I was willing to explain and was met by your rejection."

"Don't talk to me about DragonCon," he said in a harsh voice. "You fed me a line of bull..."

"There was no bull between us, Aaron." Hawthorne stood and faced him, biting back the anger and hurt. Why did he continue to accuse her of lying? "You chose not to believe me."

"You chose to..." He compressed his lips into a thin line and gazed at her with eyes gone flat. "Why isn't Ruby raising her?"

"Ruby and I agreed that Lali would receive better care in my household. A Daughter of Ruby's age..."

"What does that mean? All I got at the library was an earful of Goddesses and Daughters and People, and a whole lot of censure because you hadn't told me what any of it meant."

"I offered to show you once."

"You offered me proof of a lie." Aaron shoved his hands through his hair, clenching them into fists around the curly brown strands. "No one lives to be two thousand years old, Hawthorne. It's impossible."

The inevitability of his continued disbelief tugged at her heart, squeezing painfully. "Is it?"

"Yes, of course. Christ. When are you gonna give up this nonsense and come clean with me?"

"When you find a way to trust me, Aaron." She met his confused gaze evenly. "You cannot continue to believe only part of my story. Either it is wholly true or wholly false. It cannot be both."

"I..." He dropped his hands and stared at her with such longing it took her breath. "I want to believe you."

"Wanting and doing are not the same thing," she said gently. "We have much work to do this day. Tomorrow is Halloween and I wish to spend it preparing for the children who will come by begging for treats."

He nodded, a dazed gesture that tugged at her heart. "I can take Lali out, if you want to stay here, or vice versa."

"Whatever you wish."

"I like her." He lifted one shoulder into a shrug. "She thinks I'm her father."

"You would make a fine father." Though Hawthorne had her doubts on whether he would make a good father for an immortal Daughter such as Lali, particularly when he could not find it in his heart to trust her own tale. "Come, Aaron. Our work awaits."

"Yeah." He stared at her, his expression helpless and lost, like a child left to fend for himself in unfamiliar surroundings. "Yeah."

She enfolded his hand in her own and led him to the couch, retrieved his work from the table and placed it in his lap. And reined in the tender emotions the man beside her stirred in the hidden recesses of her heart.

THE NEXT DAY, Aaron took a break from work and alternated his time between Lali and the kitchen, where Hawthorne and Maria cooked up a storm of baked goods. After only a week around the spunky little girl, he'd already lost his heart to her, and suspected she knew it. It was no hardship to love someone who held nothing back.

Unlike some people he could mention.

He'd come away from his discussion with Hawthorne more confused than ever and, after a restless night with little sleep, had finally decided to let it go until he could coax her into trusting him again. If she could do that, maybe she'd open up and tell him the truth instead of clinging to her outrageous tale.

The one thing that really bothered him, the one thing he couldn't let go, was her insistence that he had to either believe everything she said or discount all of it as false. In a single sentence, she'd pinpointed the heart of his conflict.

That evening, Hawthorne helped Lali into her costume while Aaron thumbed through a magazine he'd dug out of the stash under the coffee table in Hawthorne's office. *The World of the People.* He'd never heard of it before and had been curious to see if it covered the mysterious People everybody kept mentioning.

At first glance, it seemed like a combination of a local newspaper and a typical gossip magazine. A familiar looking blonde woman graced the cover, her serious eyes forthright as she stared into the camera and out at the magazine's audience. The caption read, "An Interview with the Blade." Given her upper tier corporate attire, he figured she must be a bigwig of some sort.

He flipped through the pages, stopping to read gossip. Recent college graduates, Daughters who had submitted their wills (*There was that term again*, he thought), promotions. Most of the women had unusual surnames or were listed under nicknames, like Eleanor Shadowfell, who was apparently a member of the Council of Seven. What that might be, he had no clue.

He passed over a plea for help needed in identifying the remains of a Daughter found in a grave in a recent archaeological dig in Sweden, skimmed through an article on advances in small weapons technologies, earmarking it for research, and finally hit the article on the Blade. The lead picture showed the woman from the front cover leaning against an antique desk in a casual pose. *Rebecca Upton discusses her life as the Director of the IECS and the role of the People in modern society.*

Hunh. Interesting.

He turned the page and began reading. *Rebecca the Blade has long been known as one of the People's fiercest warriors...*

His breath caught in his throat. *Rebecca the Blade.* He backed up and began again, read the whole thing through, then focused on the pullout sections. One chronicled the Blade's history from her role in the Battle of Hastings in 1066, during which she earned her famous sword, Silverthorn, to her assumption of the directorate of the Institute for Early Cultural Studies in 1985, a few years after she *submitted her will* to her now-husband, Robert, and gave birth to a Son, Bobby. There was even a picture of her dressed in a leather vest and pants, and holding her sword in a ready stance, her delicate features set in hard, dangerous lines. *Though the Blade now uses words as her weapon, her renowned skill with the sword is as strong as ever,* the caption underneath read.

His heart thumped into overdrive. No. This had to be a joke. Hawthorne had planted the magazine for him to find, her demented way of reminding him of the first time they'd met, when she'd pinned him against a door and demanded to know how he'd learned of the People.

The People. Rebecca the Blade. The Chronicler.

A memory flashed through his mind, of the delicate, middle-aged blonde who had greeted him during his first run through Tellowee. *Dear God in Heaven.* Hawthorne had hired a local to pose as this Blade, knowing he'd used that name in his own work.

*No, wait.* He shook his head as another memory pounced. Charlotte had told him her mother was Rebecca Upton and her brother Bobby, whom Aaron had met. They were real people, but what did it all mean? The sword, the nickname, the completely fake history printed in a seemingly real magazine?

He pinched the bridge of his nose and breathed slowly, searching for calm. He needed to think, needed to sort through everything, put all the pieces he'd been given together into one picture.

Lali bounded into the room, her eyes bright, her mouth stretched into a wide grin. She was dressed in a black turtleneck and thick tights under a plastic, kid-sized breastplate and plated skirt with a wooden sword strapped to her back. "Looky, Airn! I'm an Amazon."

Aaron dropped the magazine on the coffee table and opened his arms. Lali launched herself at him, never losing her grin, and he held her tight, breathing in her little girl smell.

Hawthorne followed at a slower pace and sank gracefully onto the couch beside them. She nodded toward the magazine. "That was not for your eyes."

He snorted. "Like you didn't deliberately plant it there for me to find. Seriously, Hawthorne. You're taking this too far."

"Am I?"

"Yeah, you are." Lali leaned back and cocked her head at him, and he reined in his temper, as much as he could. "I don't appreciate it either."

"Do you not?" Hawthorne's grey eyes were flinty in her impassive expression. "Perhaps I do not appreciate your continued disbelief."

"Maybe if you'd talk about it rationally..."

She slashed her hand through the air, cutting him off. "Rational. As if you were acquainted with the word."

He hissed in a breath, blew it out slowly. "You know, I'm gonna let that pass. Me and Lali are going trick or treating." He stood, shifting Lali to his hip.

Hawthorne rose as well. "Lali will guide you around the neighborhood. Have a care with her."

"I always do," he said around the lump in his throat. As if he'd ever let anything happen to Lali.

He snagged jackets for the two of them while Lali rounded up her Halloween basket, a plastic Jack-o-Lantern with a stiff, black handle. The sun hadn't yet set when they left and the evening air was still balmy, a holdover of the day's warmth. Lali held his hand as she bounced down the sidewalk, chattering about all the people they were going to visit and the treats she might get. He nodded at parents, obediently waited while Lali rang doorbells and received treats, and felt his world tilt into surreal when he realized most of the costumed little girls were dressed similarly to Lali and accompanied by fit women in their early twenties. Gangs of young women roamed the streets dressed in armor and leather, some leading half nude young men by chains or ropes.

The whole town was in on it. Must be. It was like a bad episode of *The Twilight Zone.* Any minute, he expected Rod Serling to pop out from behind a bush and narrate Aaron's journey through the madhouse around him.

Not long after, they ran into Charlotte, Becka, and Becka's younger brother. Aaron sighed, relieved to see a moderately sane person.

"Hey, Aaron," Charlotte said. "Y'all getting a good haul?"

"I think so." He stuffed his hands into his back pockets. "Can I ask you a question?"

She deftly broke up a pending squabble between her children before answering. "Sure."

"How old is your mother?"

"She's..." Her eyes narrowed. "Why do you want to know?"

He shrugged. "I was reading an article about her in this magazine."

"The one in *The World of the People?*" At his nod, she

said, "That was a great piece."

"Was it true?"

Her face closed into a hard mask. "You haven't worked things out with Hawthorne yet, have you?"

"No," he admitted. "I tried, but she keeps coming up with these cockamamie stories."

"Try harder," she said bluntly. "Or leave if you can't accept her."

"I want to," he began.

"That's not enough." She compressed her lips into a thin line. "Look, Aaron, I like you. Really. You're a nice guy and I know Lali loves you, but you have to come to terms with this."

"How? It's crazy, some of the things she says, and that blasted article, which has to be fake..."

"Tell you what. My mother lives two blocks that way." She jerked her chin at a side street. "Go see for yourself how fake she is."

She took her children, one in each hand, and nodded at him.

"Charlotte, wait."

She marched past him, head high, her back ramrod straight. He watched her go, as confused by her reaction as he was by everything else.

So much for asking the sane person.

Lali snagged his hand and pulled him down the sidewalk. As often as not, people stopped to chat with her and introduced themselves to him. By the time they made it to Charlotte's mother's house, his head was dizzy with names and faces and the curious stares of strangers.

Bobby answered the door at the Upton residence and scowled. He lifted Lali into a hug and nodded toward Aaron. "Kesselman. Thought Hawthorne would give you the boot by now."

Lali clapped her tiny hands against Bobby's cheeks. "Silly man. Nana's boots won't fit my puppy."

Bobby's face melted into a fond grin. "Is that so? How about I give you a boot for your treat, huh?"

"That's not a treat," she said, and squealed with laughter when Bobby goosed her ribs.

The woman from the magazine's cover stepped up to the door, her face wreathed in a gracious smile. She held out her hand and shook Aaron's. "Mr. Kesselman. I'm Rebecca Upton. Nice to meet you at last."

"Ah, nice to meet you, too."

Up close, Rebecca appeared as sane and rational as any of the people he'd met in Tellowee, maybe more so. Her gaze was direct, her posture firm. Not exactly the hallmarks of a crazy person or someone who'd allow herself to be dragged into the middle of another person's scheme. But how to tell?

"I just finished reading that piece on you in *The World of the People.*"

"They hounded me for ages to give that interview. I finally gave in and now it's all anyone wants to talk about with me."

"I've had that happen. Crazy how a little publicity stirs people up."

She leaned against the doorframe. "That's right. You're an author."

"I am."

Bobby rolled his eyes. "If y'all are gonna talk, I'm taking little bit here inside to see Dad."

"Sure," Aaron said, and watched carefully as they left, Bobby's boots thumping heavily against the wooden floor as he teased Lali. "My main character is called Rebecca the Blade."

A coy smile flashed across Rebecca's face. "Is that so?"

"Kind of a coincidence that Hawthorne came after me because of a character in a graphic novel whose name is the same as yours."

"Mmm. Do you have a point, Mr. Kesselman?"

He lifted one shoulder in a casual shrug. "Just wondering if she's pulling my leg or if there's something else going on here."

"Did you ask her?" She shook her head slightly, sending wisps of fine blonde hair twirling against her face. "No, I can see that you did, and that you didn't believe her."

"Should I?"

She held his gaze for a long moment, considering him with the canny regard of the field general the article had made her out to be. "What does your heart say?"

"She's telling the truth." He blew out a breath and shook his head. "But that can't be right. Some of the things she claims..."

"Can't possibly be so. Yes, I've heard that before," she said gently. "The war here is not between you and Hawthorne. It's within yourself. Trust her or don't, but at least understand where the true conflict lies."

He glanced away, struck to the quick by her discernment.

"Consider this as well, Mr. Kesselman. I've known Hawthorne for a very long time and have never known her to be anything but honest."

He rubbed a hand across his nape. "Exactly how long have you known her?"

"If I told you, you wouldn't believe me."

"That long, huh?"

She laughed. "Indeed."

"You have to know how crazy that sounds."

She laid her hand on his arm. "Sometimes, the truth is much stranger than fiction. As an author, you must have experience with that."

He stared at her, nonplussed. What a way to put it.

She squeezed his arm, then dropped her hand. "Come inside and retrieve Lali before Bobby makes her a permanent part of our household."

He followed her in, rescued Lali from being completely spoiled by Rebecca's son and husband, and escorted the little girl around town until well after dark, his thoughts in turmoil.

# TWELVE

L ATE THE NEXT AFTERNOON, Aaron dropped his head against the back of the couch in Hawthorne's office and closed his eyes. Since reading that article on Rebecca Upton and talking to her in person, he'd wrestled with the one thing he hadn't considered before.

What if Hawthorne was telling the truth?

Crazy, that's what that was. People didn't live to be that old. They just couldn't. Yet, the number of people he knew who seemed to sincerely believe otherwise was growing by leaps and bounds. Hawthorne, Charlotte and Rebecca, Jim Hornby. Probably their relatives as well, Ruby, Levi, Bobby Upton, Rebecca's husband, and God only knew who else. Maybe the whole damn town of Tellowee. How could people who appeared so sane and rational be anything but? Was it some kind of mass hysteria, or was it simply the truth?

Had he been wrong about Hawthorne all along?

He studied Hawthorne in the soft light thrown from the Tiffany lamp beside the couch. Over the past few days, she'd taken to dressing as he did, wearing comfortable sweaters and jeans when they worked, running around in her socked feet. She slumped into the couch, her fingers flying across the keypad of the laptop propped on her toned thighs.

He remembered what those thighs looked like without the protection of clothes, long and sculpted, pale and strong as she knelt above him and rode them both to release.

Desire stirred and his body hardened. She was the most beautiful woman he'd ever met, stubborn and frustrating when she wanted to be, at times so blunt with her honesty, it bordered on tactless.

He'd begun to fall for her before he'd learned of her past, begun to fall for the way she touched him, for her kind, stoic wisdom, and the flashes of humor he glimpsed when she let down her guard. Making amends had only been part of his reason for pursuing her back to Tellowee. The much deeper need dwelt in his heart. Their time at DragonCon had been almost magical, their friendship so promising, and the closeness more than he'd ever thought to have again. Was that why he was so eager now to believe in her, because he wanted her so much and needed her to be whole? Because with each day that passed, he grew more and more desperate to find a way through her defenses to the woman he'd nearly fallen for, and was falling for still?

She saved her work, closed the lid of the laptop, and placed it on the coffee table. "You are staring."

"I am." He slid the tip of his finger down the smooth curve of her cheek, and was surprised when she turned in to the touch. "You're so beautiful."

Her lashes swept down over soft gray eyes. "So you say."

"Because it's true." He shifted closer, pulled her into a light hug with a casual arm over her shoulders. "Go out with me tonight."

She slid him a sideways look. "That would be unwise."

"Why? Lali's spending the night with Becka. Maria won't be back until Monday."

"I need to remain here should Lali wish to return home."

"So we won't go far. The Omega has decent food, pool tables. Dancing." He brushed his face over her hair, breathing in her scent. "Or we could stay here and do a movie marathon. You and me on the couch, with nobody to interrupt us."

She huffed out a soft breath. "Your wishes are transparent."

"Hey, I'm a man. We're not that complicated." The delicate swirl of her ear beckoned. He dipped his head and nuzzled it, and desire blossomed into something more. "Come on. It'll be fun."

"Perhaps an evening out would not be amiss." She smoothed a crease from her jeans, plucked at a piece of lint. "We have worked hard since your arrival. A short break among others could be beneficial."

"That's my girl." He dropped a kiss to her cheek. She turned her face up for him, and he tried hard not to gloat over the small triumph. "I'll go check on Lali."

He found her in her room packing an overnight bag, and hid his smile at the variety of items she'd stuffed into the small suitcase. The ragdoll she slept with. An assortment of Barbies and action figures, complete with clothes, accessories, and doll-sized weapons. Two of her favorite bedtime stories. Three pairs of shoes, including a pair of hard plastic pink heels with glitter across the toes. A cowboy hat, her Halloween sword, and a deck of Uno cards, but not one item of clothing.

"Need some help?" he asked.

Her face lit up with a happy smile. "Airn! I done gots most of the 'sentials."

"I see."

"It's gonna be so much fun." She flipped the lid over and laid down on it with her tongue between her teeth, and struggled to pull the zipper around. "You should come, too, then you could tell Becka stories and tuck us in."

He lifted her gently off the bag and opened it back up. "Me and Nana are gonna do grown up things tonight."

Her face fell. "Oh."

"You'll have lots of fun without me." He sat down on the edge of her bed and pulled her into his lap. "I bet Miss

Charlotte's already got movies and games for you."

She rested her head on his chest and hefted a heavy sigh. "Yeah, but that's not the same as grown up stuff."

"It's better, almost definitely. You get to stay up late and aggravate Becka's little brother, maybe have a pillow fight and eat too many treats."

"But I will miss you so."

His heart trembled in his chest and flopped right over. He brushed the wisps of hair from her sweet little face and was rewarded with a smile. "I'll see you in the morning bright and early when Miss Charlotte drops you off. Now, how about we rearrange your bag a little?"

He talked her into leaving most of the things she'd packed, all but her ragdoll, the pink heels, and her Halloween sword, and added two nightgowns, clothes for the next day, extra underwear and socks, and her toiletries. She bounced on the bed as she helped zip the suitcase shut, her bright, bubbly chatter surrounding him.

Half an hour later, he and Hawthorne dropped Lali off at Charlotte's. Aaron met the cold gaze of Rebecca Upton's daughter evenly. He'd had a lot of practice at that since Hawthorne had come into his life.

And finally, it was just the two of them, him and Hawthorne, confined together in the spacious interior of her SUV while she drove them into the cozy downtown area of Tellowee. Nerves fluttered in his stomach and his palms dampened. Since his arrival in Tellowee, they hadn't been alone much. Even when they were working, there was a near constant threat of interruption, from Lali or Maria, or from one of the many people who phoned seeking Hawthorne's advice. The occasional quiet evening after Lali's bedtime, that was theirs, but it wasn't the same thing as being completely alone like they'd be after their date.

All alone at night with Hawthorne, just him and her and two lonely beds. He scrubbed his palms across his thighs, and tried desperately not to think that far ahead.

145

The Omega was nearly full by the time they arrived and snagged a table in a corner away from the door. Casey was on floor duty alone. She whizzed through the tables, smiling and laughing with customers, handing out refills and taking new orders.

She reached their table and came to an abrupt halt. "I didn't know he was yours," she blurted. "I swear, if I had, I would've stayed far, far away and never even considered flirting with him."

Hawthorne arched one delicate eyebrow. Casey paled and fled.

"That's a neat trick," Aaron said. "Though it'd be nice if I didn't get that same reaction every time somebody learns we're working together."

She turned her impassive gaze on him. "Those who flee are wise to do so, Aaron Kesselman. I do not share."

"We're not together, by your choice," he reminded her.

She lifted one shoulder in a casual shrug. "During your stay in Tellowee, it would be better for you to remain under my protection."

"Is that why you allowed Isolde to believe we're lovers?"

"She drew her own conclusions on that, though the truth is not so far away her belief could be called a lie. You chose to play along."

He shrugged and leaned against the chair's wooden back. "It seemed like the thing to do at the time. Plus, it gave me an excuse to kiss you."

Will came up to the table, a towel slung over his shoulder, his brows furrowed over glittering eyes. "Hawthorne, please stop terrorizing my staff. Casey won't even come out of the back to work."

"She should not flirt with my man."

Aaron cut an annoyed glare at her. "I'm not your man."

"You are under my protection, which amounts to the same thing." She blinked, a solemn tilt of her eyelids over sparkling gray eyes. "As we just agreed."

He blew out a breath and ignored Will's knowing look. "Are all women in Tellowee this hardheaded?"

"Pretty much," Will said. "I tried to warn you."

"Next time, try harder."

Will laughed and yanked an order pad out of the back pocket of his jeans. "What can I get y'all?"

They ordered and ate, made room at the table for people who dropped by to chat or seek Hawthorne's counsel. Some of it was simple and some not, and some was so personal, Aaron wished he could slip away. Negotiating a mating contract, which he thought might be something like a pre-nup. Advice on whether or not to take a job in Mongolia among, as one acolyte put it, the "hard savagery of orthodox Daughters." A woman who quietly begged for intercession in an abusive marriage.

Aaron did try to leave then, and was stopped by Hawthorne's hand on his. So he stayed and he listened, and the longer he did, the more the woman's situation pissed him off. The People's laws were strict. If he understood them correctly, the woman would be tied to a post and whipped if she abandoned her husband, regardless of what he'd done to her. How could anyone abide such treatment of another human being?

He asked Hawthorne that very question as soon as the woman left.

"It will not come to that," she said evenly. "I shall intercede and resolve the situation if it cannot be resolved satisfactorily."

"Resolve it, huh."

Her face became a hard mask, cold and unfeeling, though her eyes were hot balls of fury, and he realized she intended to *resolve* the woman's problem the same way she'd resolved her own, with a devastating finality.

Violence wasn't the answer. He firmly believed that, or had before he'd met Hawthorne. Now, after hearing her tale and the story of the woman who'd just left, he wasn't so sure. Regardless of whether he believed any of it, the Daughters, the People,

Goddesses and Retribution and centuries-old warriors, the law only went so far and could sometimes be leveraged unjustly. He witnessed evidence of that every time he watched the news. Maybe Hawthorne had the right of it when she took matters into her own hands, especially when answering brutality.

At eight, the lights dimmed, and not long after, someone called up a slow, bluesy song on the state of the art jukebox situated near the bar. Couples came together and drifted onto the dance floor, swaying as one to the beat of the music. Aaron eyed them with the envy of a man who longed to hold the woman who'd captured his interest and couldn't. What would it be like to have Hawthorne like that, to wrap his arms around her and breathe in the woman who stirred him so easily to such great heights?

Her hand cupped his shoulder, startling him with the warm ease of her touch. "Come, Aaron. We shall dance and cement your position within my household."

Relief poured through him, relief and anticipation, and he laughed, couldn't help it. "Cement my position, huh? I guess I can go for that."

They wedged into a narrow, empty spot on the edge of the crowded parquet dance floor. He held her as he wanted to, with her hand over the unsteady thump of his heart and their bodies brushing with each step. Her scent washed over him, the light aroma of tea roses mingling with whatever it was that made Hawthorne unique.

He eased his arm around her back and edged her closer. "I like this cementing thing."

"I thought you might." Her breath fanned across his jaw, sending a shiver through him. "Though, perhaps we should not dance so closely."

"Forget it. I'm not letting you go until it's time to go home, maybe not even then."

"And should I object?"

He tilted her chin up with one finger. "You won't."

Her lips parted and her eyes dropped to his mouth. He cupped her face, mesmerized by the smooth, alabaster skin and her breath catching softly in her throat. The crowd around them faded away until they were the only people on the dance floor, alone with the sensual rhythm of the music filling the air.

"I've missed this," he said. "Holding you, touching you. Why did you ever let me go?"

"I wanted to keep you." Her eyes swept up, meeting his, and the longing there bored into him. Intense, needy, everything he was feeling, reflected in the stormy pull of her gaze. "You would not hear me then."

"I think I'm ready to hear you now."

He stroked his thumb across her face, testing the corner of her mouth, the sensuous curve of her lower lip. Her eyelids fluttered shut and her head tilted back, and her beautiful, luscious mouth was there, inches from his own.

"I'm gonna kiss you now," he murmured, and she *mmmd* and tightened her fingers in his sweater, and then his mouth was on hers and his heart shouted a resounding *yes*. Her lips parted under his, accepting him, taking him in. It was like coming home after an eternity away. The rightness of it flooded through him, urging him to take more, to have more, and he burned with it, fighting the need that rose up, so fierce and urgent it overwhelmed him.

He drew back, exploring her slowly, nibbling her full lips, testing the sharpness of her teeth, tasting the corners of her mouth. She seemed helpless under his onslaught, clinging to him with one hand on his shoulder and the other curled into his sweater over his heart, and he wanted her to be. *God, yes.* He wanted her to be as helpless as he was in the storm of their need, as devastated by the passion that had consumed him since the very first time they'd come together.

The music changed, snapping him back to reality, and the noise and weight of the crowd rushed into his consciousness. He tore his mouth from Hawthorne's and rested his forehead against hers, struggling to still the frantic beat of his heart and the breath that panted in and out of his lungs, mingling with hers. They were in public. *God*, he'd kissed her like a man on fire in a public place, surrounded by her friends and colleagues. What had he been thinking?

The pressure of his erection against the fly of his jeans answered that question, and he nearly laughed.

Hawthorne unclenched her fingers and smoothed the wrinkles in his sweater. "Perhaps we should go home now, Aaron."

He searched her expression, examining the taut need anyone else would miss. Yes, maybe they should go home. He skimmed his hands down her arms, tangled his fingers with hers. She tugged him off the dance floor and wove through the crowd, leading him toward the only place he wanted to be.

THE AIR in the close confines of the SUV was thick with desperate need. Aaron stared calmly into the night, his seatbelt buckled, his hands resting flat upon his thighs. Hawthorne envied him his demeanor. Her own heart pounded so hard in her chest, it would not have surprised her if he heard and reconsidered. As she had told him, the wise fled before her. It had been thus since she had wrested her vengeance from the men who had stolen her honor and her mother's life, and it would be thus eternally.

At her age, she had no expectation of meeting mortality save at the end of another's blade, though the lack of hope would not keep her from trying.

The man beside her was no warrior. He battled the world with his hands, yes, but also his mind, using his creations to explore reality in a way no other could. He was tender, some might even say weak, though only if they discounted the power of his creativity, and of his heart.

Aaron Kesselman had a strong heart.

Their kiss had stoked the desire she had tried so desperately to deny. A woman's control lasted only so long before it collapsed. She had had an eternity to hone and refine hers, had thought it strong enough to survive any salvo, only to have it flee in the face of Aaron's heart.

Perhaps she was the weaker one after all.

She parked her Land Rover in the garage. Switched the ignition off and activated the automatic garage door, waiting for him to speak. He seemed lost in thought, unaware of their arrival. She unfastened her seatbelt and exited the car. Behind her, his car door slammed and his footsteps thumped quietly against the concrete floor. He followed her into the house and through the hallway separating the living room from his office. She could feel his presence behind her, hear the slowness of his breaths and the brush of fabric as he moved. Uneasiness pricked at her. Would he never speak or touch her? Was he waiting for her to set the pace, or had he changed his mind?

Did he regret touching her now, as he had at DragonCon?

Perhaps she had read the situation incorrectly. Perhaps their kiss had meant nothing to him and was simply an extension of his kindness.

The uneasiness shifted into an ugly band that squeezed her chest, closing her lungs and forcing her heart to boom in too small of a space. She crossed to the stairs and climbed them automatically, measuring her steps upward without being aware of them through the thick tears gathering behind her eyes and the bitter heartache clogging her throat. She kept moving, always moving. That was the way a warrior dealt with pain, by forcing it outward, not by bottling it up inside. Is that not how she had always mitigated the cruelty and hardship of the centuries? Had she not held her own through a life well lived, thus thwarting those who sought to harm her?

Her steps faltered at the door to her bedroom. She faced the solid oak with the weariness of a woman who had simply had enough. How long must she survive without a mate to hold her through the long, empty nights, without the love of a companion

151

to break her immortality, without a hope of finally knowing peace after centuries of restless wandering?

Aaron's hands rubbed over her shoulders, a gentle, comforting warmth. He turned her slowly and tilted her chin up, and blanched. "Hawthorne, sweetheart." He pulled her to him, cradling her head on his shoulder, rocking her as if she were a child. "Shh. Don't cry. We don't have to do anything."

She curled her hands into fists against his chest and absorbed the goodness of him. "I am not crying."

His laugh was short and soft, a grunt of sound that pierced the shell of her heartache. "I'm not gonna argue. I've seen the way you handle a stick."

"It is a hanbō."

"Hanbō, stick. I know how deadly you are. Come on."

He opened the door to her bedroom where she had not been able to continue. In her bathroom, he wet a washcloth and scrubbed her face, holding her chin with firm fingers.

Her heart softened. His touch was so gentle, so kind. "You are a good man, Aaron."

"Not so good if I made a woman like you cry twice in one year. Close your eyes."

She obeyed and relaxed while he washed gently around her eyes, cleansing away her sorrow along with the tears.

"There now." He placed the soiled cloth on the sink and cupped her jaws in his hands, kissed her forehead so tenderly she blinked back a bemusing spate of tears. "Better?"

"I was well before."

"You're a terrible liar. What do you sleep in?"

"My skin." She lifted her hands to his, ran trembling fingertips over the warm skin, memorizing the length of his fingers, the alignment of bone and muscle. "You know this from our time together at DragonCon."

"I thought you were doing that because we were..." His voice trailed into a murmur and his eyes dropped to her mouth. "Don't you have a t-shirt or something? I could let you borrow one of mine."

"Why do you wish me clothed thusly?"

"So I can tuck you into bed, take care of you. I'm so sorry. God, am I sorry." He gathered her near again, holding her carefully. "I didn't mean to push. You have to believe me."

"I believe that you did not meant to push me, though I do not recall you doing so. Perhaps you should explain further."

His laugh rang through the bathroom, echoing off the pine and tile walls. "God, I adore you."

If he adored her, why did he insist on pulling away from her, rejecting her twice now? Men were a baffling species, and this man insisted on being among the most baffling. He was not, as he had asserted, an uncomplicated individual. Would that he were, so that she had a hope of understanding what motivated him to kiss her one moment and ignore her the next.

His hands slid down her back, gripping her hands. She followed dutifully behind him as he led her to her bed and prepared it, she presumed, for her entry. He untied the lace-up ropers she wore, pulled them off. Set them neatly by her nightstand, stood and tugged off her sweater, leaving her upper torso clad only in a thin, white camisole.

His breath wheezed out. "Sweet merciful God, you're not wearing a bra."

She glanced down, confused. "Have I need of one?"

He shook his head slowly, squeezed his eyes closed. "Tell me you haven't been wandering around the house braless for the past week."

"It would be an untruth to say otherwise, Aaron."

"Whew, wow. That didn't help." He rubbed a hand over his closed eyes, muttering things like *all week* and *I can do this*. He dropped his hand, leaving his face bare to her gaze. His chocolate eyes were hot and needy and his hand held a fine tremor. "Let me, ah."

He unfastened her jeans and drew them down her legs, his fingers caressing her whether he intended to or not. She balanced with one hand on his shoulder, lifted each foot patiently so he could pull them off, and failed to miss the way his eyes lingered on her. His breath puffed against her skin, fanning it with warmth as he worked, plucking at the desire lingering in her blood.

He rose slowly and all but pushed her into her bed, pulling the covers up to her shoulders before he kissed her forehead. "Goodnight, Hawthorne."

She raised herself onto her elbows and considered the resolve in his expression, and the unmistakable arousal pushing against the fly of his jeans. "You are leaving me?"

"I am. Get some rest." He shoved his hands into his pockets and regarded her solemnly. "We'll talk in the morning."

He truly intended to leave her, though he was aroused and ready and *adored her.* She sniffed delicately, caught the faint aroma of his pheromones, and in that moment, lowered herself to the manipulations of a common human. "Perhaps I need the comfort of a friend this night, after the pushing you did."

He winced and glanced away, and if she had been capable of feeling shame for her own actions, she would have then.

Fortunately, shame had been burned out of her system centuries ago.

"That's a really bad idea," he said. "Really."

She turned down the covers on the opposite side of the bed and patted the mattress. "I insist. You would not wish me to cry again, would you?"

His eyebrows snapped together and he whirled, muttering *God's gonna strike me dead for this* under his breath as he snapped off the overhead light and closed the door to her bedroom. She shimmied out of her camisole and panties and dropped them on the floor while he undressed and climbed into bed. He met her in the middle, and she wrapped herself around his long, fit body.

His hands cupped her bare hip and his breath hissed. "You took off your underclothes."

She buried her face in the crook of his shoulder and slid her hands under his t-shirt, scratching his skin lightly with her nails. It was as she remembered it, warm, firm, beautiful. "Yes."

"And you expect me to hold you all night like that?"

"If that is what you desire." She ignored his constrained laugh and skimmed a hand around his ribs, exploring the muscled plane of his back. "Have you not missed our time together?"

"I have, so much." He slid a muscled thigh between hers and sighed. "I don't want to hurt you anymore."

"Then do not."

"You make it sound so simple."

"It is as simple as you wish it to be. I did not cry from a harm you inflicted, but from a joy you withheld."

"That's...not exactly clear."

"When you kissed me this evening," she explained, "I believed you desired me."

"I did." His arm tightened across her back where he held her. "I do."

"Yet, you refused to speak on the way home, refused to touch me or share your gaze with me. Should I not have taken your distance as rejection?"

"No, Hawthorne. Not just no, but hell no. I want you so much it hurts, inside and out, all day and night. Especially the nights. Dreaming of you, the way you smell and taste, like sunshine and woman and everything I've ever needed, and the way you feel when I'm in you, so tight and hot and good it takes my breath. I've waited so long to have you again, I was afraid my control would snap and I'd take you in the car." His voice dropped to a low murmur against her ear. "So, no, I wasn't rejecting you, sweetheart. I was trying not to jump you."

Her own breath caught in her lungs, refusing to move, choked by the power of his words, the taut need in his voice. "I would not mind this jumping thing so much, if it means having you the way you described. Perhaps you would care to demonstrate."

His laugh was low and male and scraped across her skin, exposing the billowing desire heating her blood. "I thought you'd never ask."

# THIRTEEN

AARON EASED HAWTHORNE onto her back. She went willingly, allowing him to cover her as his mouth found her ear, teasing it with gentle nips of his sharp, white teeth. The tip of his tongue darted out, flicking her earlobe, then trailed hot, open-mouthed kisses down her throat, sucking lightly. Her skin tingled under his attentive touch and her hands clutched the back of his head, tangling in the dark, silky curls.

It was beautiful, the way he built trust, with slow sweeps of his hands along her sides and the brush of his thumbs in the tender creases under her breasts, with his lips sliding over her nipples, then his tongue, until they were tight nubs, aching and tender. She writhed under him, holding nothing back, wishing to please him as he pleased her. Did he know how she yearned for him, that she dreamed of him as he did of her and buried those dreams so they would not haunt her waking hours?

He explored her the way he had that very first night, patiently, tenderly, thoroughly, strumming the need ever higher. Her hips lifted from the bed, seeking his touch, and her heart thrummed in her chest, galloping in time with the rhythm of his hands on her flesh.

His thumb stroked her clitoris, sending ripples of heat through her groin. "So wet," he murmured, and then he tasted her, laving her sex with the flat of his tongue over and over again, pushing her to a fevered pitch with each sweep.

Her hands clenched into fists around his hair and her control shattered completely. "Now, Aaron, please," she begged on a long gasp of air. "I need you."

He *mmmd* against her sex, drawing a cry from her that held, suspended in the air around them. His fingers pushed into her and his mouth latched onto her clitoris, sucking and teasing, and her heart cried for him as he lifted her up and up and up, so high she floated on a hot cloud of need. With another flick of his tongue, she burst like rain on a warm summer day, jolting as lightning raced through her and thunder rolled, and fell until he grounded her and she rediscovered the warm, reassuring presence of her lover.

"Aaron," she whispered.

He rose above her, yanked his shirt off and shoved his underwear down, freeing the hard length of his erection. She saw him clearly in the room's dim light, the glitter of his eyes as he gazed upon her, the slash of his mouth in a face gone rigid with desire, and the long ropes of muscle and sinew curving around the solid frame of his body under the dusky beauty of his smooth skin.

He sat back on his haunches with his knees bent under him and pulled her down the bed, draping her thighs across his. "Tell me if this gets uncomfortable."

She nodded solemnly, content to follow his lead. He braced above her and slid the length of his erection into her waiting body, filling her with his delicious breadth, tightly sheathing himself within her welcoming heat.

She rippled around him, an echo of the pleasure he'd given her. A strangled groan erupted from him and his fingers dug into her hip. "I thought we could do it like this without... God, you feel so right." He panted the words out in shallow breaths. "Maybe you should be on top."

No. *No.* She wanted him above her, wanted to be able to feel him taking his pleasure in this way, wanted to accept him and dig her nails into his back and wrap her legs around his waist, as other women did with their lovers. Two millennia of fear and pain was enough. It was time to begin conquering it.

She opened her arms to him and beckoned him closer. "Come to me, Aaron. Lie upon me and build trust."

He shook his head, a harsh jerk, sending the ends of his hair bouncing along his neck. "Not like that. It's not good for you like that."

"It will be this time," she assured him.

"Promise me you'll stop me as soon as it bothers you." His eyes glittered down at her, the hard need in them a seductive call. "Promise me."

"I promise."

"Don't lie to me," he warned.

"As you said, I am a terrible liar."

He laughed softly and eased down onto her, covering her fully, and her breath choked in her lungs. The memory of that day dredged its way up from the dim recesses of time, the clawing hands and the hard, continual pain between her legs, and the screams of her mother as the lash fell upon her back, no less vivid for that distance. He rolled to the side so that she was not fully beneath him, as if he knew what horrors her mind held, and her breath unclogged and whistled cleanly out.

This was Aaron, her Aaron, who would never knowingly harm her, not like that. Aaron with his gentle touch and sweet kiss and beautiful, clever hands. Aaron, whom Lali trusted so fiercely she had claimed him as her surrogate father. Aaron, who had brought Una back from the dead, and with her, all the good that had been lost upon her death.

This was the man who had built trust with her and introduced her to Godzilla and very nearly captured her heart during their sojourn two months prior. She latched on to his presence and held it in her mind, and it loomed large, crowding out all the evil clamoring through her head.

His fingers trailed over her temple and down the curve of

her cheek. "You ok?"

"I shall be." She nuzzled his hand and brought her own up to explore the strength of his arm, the curve of hard muscle and firm flesh. "Love me, Aaron."

"I will," he murmured. He pressed his mouth to hers as his hips found a quiet rhythm and his hands stoked her desire, and when his breath rushed out of his lungs and his heart pounded so hard she could feel it with her own, he rolled onto his back, taking her with him. She moved over him then, accepting his touch, encouraging the hard thrusts of his body as his hands gripped her hips and their bodies slapped together.

"Hawthorne."

His voice was low and thick and taut. She shivered and her own need rose to meet his.

"So close," he said, and he came, throbbing his release into her on a low, shuddering moan.

She sighed with him, savoring the desire still rippling unreleased in her own body, and lay upon him, enjoying the vestiges of their passion. His arms came around her, holding her in spite of the sweat coating them both.

"You didn't come." He brushed a kiss over the top of her head and tightened his grip. "I'm sorry."

"Why?" She smiled against his chest, secure, content. "You pleasured me earlier, as you will later. It was enough this time to watch you take your own."

"It wasn't right. You shouldn't have let me stay on top."

She ignored the recriminations in his voice, the guilt he held so close to the surface. "Aaron, sweet, if I had not wished you to be there, it would not have been so. You know this."

His chest expanded under her cheek. "I wanted you to be able to find something good there, something to erase all the bad things that happened."

"Those things will never leave me, Aaron. They can only be subsumed." She raised up and caught his gaze with her own, willing him to understand. "I choose to revel in the glory of what we have and not foster regret for that which may never be. Can you not do the same?"

His mouth turned up at the corner, a half smile that warmed her as surely as his touch. "Yeah. I guess I can, if you can, too."

"I shall," she said firmly. "Now, the night is still quite young. How shall we pass the time?"

"I wonder," he murmured, and she laughed and reveled and chose to believe.

THE NEXT FEW DAYS passed in a blur for Aaron. He spent his time working or playing with Lali and his nights sneaking into Hawthorne's bed, loving her for as long as he could before sleep clasped them in its greedy grip.

The puzzle of her past faded from his mind. The more time he spent with her, the more ridiculous his earlier obsession with it seemed. What did the truth matter as long as they were together?

They finished a rough draft of the graphic novel's script at the end of his third full week in Tellowee, not quite two weeks before Thanksgiving. The work went quickly. The closer the script neared to completion, the less input he needed from her. Soon, he'd no longer have an excuse to stay. The artwork could be done anywhere as long as he had her ideas down on paper for how the story should flow.

With the script almost finished, Hawthorne snuck away more and more frequently. Business, she said, though he gathered her absences had something to do with Isolde's visit just before Halloween and, oddly enough, with Bobby Upton's presence the week before that. The people traipsing through Hawthorne's home seemed tougher somehow, closed off and hardened, the way she sometimes was. He puzzled over it in the rare moments when he was alone, and couldn't quite eradicate the knot of worry lodged in his chest.

While Hawthorne was preoccupied with business, Aaron

took care of Lali. Ruby came and went, but seemed more intent on whatever secret project Hawthorne was working on than on spending time with her sister. Lali didn't mind. She was happy to spend time with him, whether he was working or not. He took her to the park and the library, toured Tellowee's primary school with her, and took her swimming in the IECS' indoor pool. The faces in the tiny village soon became familiar enough for him to place parent with child and, often, man with Daughter.

Though he still had no idea what that meant.

He didn't push Hawthorne. Whatever she was doing consumed so much of her energy, he couldn't bring himself to press for answers. They would come eventually. For the first time since she'd told him of her past, he was content to wait.

Maria began to prepare for the upcoming holiday feast a couple of weeks before the big day. One day at lunch not long after, she said, "Will your family come out to visit for the holiday, Aaron?"

"I promised my mother I'd be home for Thanksgiving."

A heavy silence descended around the table. He paused in the middle of scooping a hunk of beef out of his stew. Maria's face had sagged into a worried frown and Hawthorne had gone rigid.

"What?" he asked.

"Now is not the time to leave the protection of my home, Aaron," Hawthorne said. Her eyes were cold and flat, her mouth a thin line. "It is not safe."

"That's ridiculous. What could happen between here and San Francisco? Besides, I promised. If I don't go, Ma will never let me hear the end of it."

"Better to risk your mother's anger." She glanced at Lali, who seemed oblivious to the thick tension gathering between the adults. "We shall discuss this tonight."

"There's nothing to discuss," he said, and refused to wither under the weight of her gaze.

That night, they tucked Lali into bed and read her one story

each, then kissed her goodnight. As soon as Hawthorne pulled
the little girl's door nearly closed for the night, she snagged his
elbow in a hard grip and frog marched him to his room.

She closed the door behind them, and he shook her hand
off. "What is with you today? You've been as mean as a hornet
since lunch."

She rounded on him, pinning him with an hard stare. "You
will remain in Tellowee until it is safe for you to leave."

"No, I won't. Christ, Hawthorne. Ma's expecting me to
come home and I'm not breaking her heart just because you're in
a tizzy."

"Do not be foolish, Aaron. The Eternal Order is on the
move..."

He huffed out an exasperated laugh. "I don't even know
what that is."

"There is insufficient time to explain properly." Her fingers
twitched and clenched together, and her expression softened.
"You must trust me."

"I might if you'd tell me what's going on."

"You would not understand."

"Then make me." He cupped her shoulders, pressing his
fingers into her tense muscles. "Is this about Isolde?"

Hawthorne clutched his waist, digging her fingers into his
flesh. "She may be a key figure in a clandestine group..."

"The Eternal Order?"

She nodded once, a solemn bow of her head. "Members of
the Order seek to undermine the People. It is complicated, the
history too deep for you to learn in such a short time."

"Try me."

"Why should I?" She dropped her hands and shrugged off
his touch. "You have made your position on my past quite clear."

"I told you I was ready to listen."

"It is not enough." Her voice sharpened, slicing through him
in quick twists. "And it is far too late for that."

His heart dipped and thudded. "What do you mean, it's too

late? Are you saying it's over?"

"Foolish man. Would I struggle to convince you to stay if I did not want you here?" She blinked and drew in a ragged breath. "A hundred years ago, I would have felt no compunction in chaining you for your own safety. Now, I must bow to your will."

He stuffed his hands into the back pockets of his corduroys as memory flashed through him, of young women in armor leading their young men through the streets of Tellowee in chains.

"The Order is dangerous," she said. "They will not hesitate to capture you and use your position as my lover to manipulate me. I cannot afford to have you unprotected on the other side of the country."

"It's only for a few days. Surely I'll be ok as long as I stick close to home."

She stepped back, her face as cold and hard as glass. "You are determined to go."

"I have to. My mom..."

"Would rather have her son alive and whole."

"You're being melodramatic."

"And you shame me with your defiance. A Daughter who cannot control her own household..."

Aaron's hands bunched into fists in his pockets. "What the hell is a Daughter?"

"A descendant of the Seven Sisters, warriors cursed to immortality for the sin of avenging their parents' deaths." She touched her fingertips gently to his cheek, though her face remained expressionless. "I am a Daughter, Aaron, a woman tempered in the forge of hardship and enmity."

"You're immortal?" His breath left him and his mind buzzed. *Immortal.* Merciful God. "Is this another one of your delusions?"

Her expression flickered, sagging and reforming so quickly he almost missed the flash of emotion in the alabaster mask of her face. "If you are determined to leave, I shall have young Upton select escorts for your protection."

"I'm a grown man, Hawthorne, not a child."

"It is this or chains." She turned and paused with her hand on the door. "Know that though your leaving shames me in the eyes of the People, I shall welcome you home should you return, and mourn your loss should you choose to remain with your family."

"Hawthorne..." He stared at the rigid set of her back, the droop of her head. "Don't be like that."

"I can only be what I am, Aaron." She shrugged, a restless jerk of her shoulders. "It will never be enough, will it?"

He watched her go, helpless under the onslaught of questions, the riptide of emotions swirling through him. Hawthorne, his sweet, beautiful Hawthorne with her steady strength and frank openness. An echo of Ruby's words drifted through his mind. *Did you never consider that she might be telling the truth?* He'd only just begun to do that when Hawthorne had blindsided him with another revelation.

*Immortal. Cursed.* Sweet God in Heaven. Stupidly enough, he'd thought he was ready, and then she'd dropped another bomb on him. What would she tell him next?

His heart tripped and tumbled in his chest, and fell, taking him with it. No wonder she wouldn't tell him about her past, the way he treated her every time she opened up. Why did he keep doubting her? Why did she keep letting him?

He pushed himself off the bed and jogged after her. She turned with her hand on the knob of her bedroom door and eyed him warily.

"Wait, Hawthorne, please." He slowed his steps when he came to Lali's door and lowered his voice. "I'm an idiot, a complete and total idiot, and you have every right to kick my ass from here to Sunday. You can even use your stick, if you want to."

A shy smile tilted the corners of her mouth. "It is a hanbō."

"I like calling it a stick. Makes it sound less scary." He pulled her into his arms, cradling her the way he should've done all along. "Promise me you'll explain everything to me soon, all at once so I have time to prepare for it, not in dribbles and dabs that take me by surprise and leave me stupid with it."

Her slender fingers curled into his sweater and her scent surrounded him, roses and woman, soft and sharp all at the same time. "I shall."

"I wish I could make you understand why I need to go home."

"As I wish you would heed my words." She buried her face in his shoulder, muffling her words. "You will be safe here with my sword to protect you. I cannot guarantee this should you leave."

"I know." Of course, he did. Hawthorne with a sword had to be close to invincible. He'd never felt anything other than safe around her, even when he'd thought the burden of her past had pushed her over the edge into insanity. "Will it really shame you for me to leave?"

"It weakens my position considerably." Her breath sighed through his sweater, warming his skin. "If Isolde could see my heart in you, others will as well."

Hope was a dangerous thing, he decided when his own soared high. "Are you trying to tell me you love me?"

"I am merely warning you, Aaron. You are my lover. This makes you a target."

"So your heart's not involved at all?"

"My heart is not the issue here."

"Mmm. You give great non-answers."

Her laugh was gentle. "Perhaps."

"Definitely." He tightened his arms around her, aligning their bodies so that they meshed and flowed together. "What if I said others can see my heart in you?"

She stiffened in his grip. "Have you not toyed with me enough for one night?"

"This isn't a game. I was half in love with you before..." He didn't want to bring up his own stupidity at DragonCon, and the repeat he'd made only moments before. "I'm sorry for reacting so badly. You mean so much to me. I don't know why I keep pushing you away."

"You cannot continue to do so, Aaron."

"I know. I know, sweetheart." He brushed his cheek against her temple again, as much to comfort himself as to ease the pain he'd caused her. "Of all the men in the world for you to wind up with, it had to be me, knee-jerk skeptic, all around doubter. I wish I could believe you without that getting in the way."

"As do I."

Her softly spoken words cut him to the quick, though he deserved no less. Any other woman would've skewered him by now. That Hawthorne hadn't spoke volumes about her character, and her heart.

"Let me tuck you in. You haven't gotten enough sleep lately."

"I am fine, though I would not mind your tucking." She drew back and cupped his jaw, meeting his gaze with her own. "You will share my bed."

He grinned, couldn't help it. "Is this how a Daughter coaxes a man?"

"It is how I coax you, Aaron."

He slid his hands down her arms and captured her hands. "Whatever works, right?"

"Indeed."

She led him to her bed and helped him undress. Aaron wrapped himself around her under the thick covers, protecting her the way she wanted to protect him, ashamed that the one thing he couldn't protect her from was his own doubt.

# FOURTEEN

TWO MILLENNIA of dealing with men had not prepared Hawthorne for Aaron's intransigence. In the past, she had handled her men in one of two ways. The ones who pleased her were allowed to live. The ones who did not met the sharp edge of her blade. Until the modern era, there had been no question that a Daughter's word was law and that her man would follow it to the letter.

Life had been so much simpler then.

Hawthorne peeked at her man where he sat on the couch in her office, creating thumbnails of pages for their graphic novel. For such a sensible man, Aaron remained stubbornly blind regarding threats to his safety. Without showing him the evidence in her vault, he would never fully believe her, but doing so would eat away at what precious little time they had left before the situation with Isolde and the Eternal Order came to a head.

The deeper Hawthorne dug into the connections between the two, the more convinced she became that her niece was a member of the Order and was working to undermine the People in some way. Something was coming, though what that something might be eluded Hawthorne. Her focus had shattered, caught on the problems Aaron's presence in her life caused.

He was proving to be a greater distraction than any of her previous lovers had. Those she had discarded at will, dispatched with her sword or abandoned when she had taken her fill of them. Aaron refused to be so easily disposed of. Had she not already discovered her own inability to rid herself of him? And now, yet again, she had forgiven him for his continued disbelief.

Why?

It puzzled her greatly. She had grown fond of him during their time at DragonCon, before he had rejected her so harshly. Since his arrival in Tellowee, that fondness had deepened, a natural extension of their blooming friendship and of their relationship as lovers. But what had it deepened into? Love? Trust? The final submission of her will?

No, that had not yet come about, if it ever would. Until she could fully trust Aaron, her will was her own, a stolid testament to her eternal life and the curse the People endured.

*The sins of the mother.*

She would never trust him until his faith in her was equally as strong, and that would not come about until he believed in her. She would have to lead him to her vault, show him what it held, and allow him to explore it. He would need time to understand it, though, time that they simply no longer had, or not enough of it.

The urgency of her need to have him believe pressed against her, tautening her muscles and bringing with it a sharp stab of pain in her temples. Two millennia of material rested within her vault. Aaron would want to explore it in depth, would need to in order to understand. Would that they could afford such a luxury now. The longer she waited, the more painful his disbelief, and the more fragile her heart. Better to get it over with as soon as possible rather than have it drag out so long.

If she had not clung so fiercely to her pride, he would know by now. Alas, he was not the only obstinate one ensconced under her roof. Pride made a stubborn bedfellow, and a prickly one as well.

Perhaps she loved him. He shifted on the couch, re-crossed his ankles. His pencil moved nimbly over the paper in his lap, bringing Una's story to life in light strokes. A pang of tender yearning washed over her. Beautiful Aaron with his gentle eyes and graceful hands. No ill could befall this man, *her* man.

She lifted her cell phone and punched out the number for BDH Security. Young Upton would have the means to protect her man while he visited his family in San Francisco. And when he returned, she would see to it that he never left again, free will be damned. A Daughter protected those in her care, including stubborn illustrators who refused to see the danger in the world around them.

A WEEK BEFORE THANKSGIVING, Aaron packed a light suitcase and prepared to leave for San Francisco for a short visit with his mother. For the past few days, a security detail had followed him whenever he stepped foot outside Hawthorne's house. When he went on a morning jog, someone trailed behind him. When he took Lali to the library, two men in dark suits with ear pieces escorted them. Next thing, she'd have somebody follow him into the bathroom to make sure he could piss ok.

The whole thing was ridiculous. He was a comic book illustrator, for cripes' sake, a nobody. Who would want to come after him?

It frustrated him no end. It had been a long time since he'd needed somebody else to look out for him, and here Hawthorne was running around like he needed her to hold his hand.

Which he did, but not because he was a kid. He dropped his suitcase by the front door and scowled at it. Needing to hold her hand was proof that he was an adult. He should tell her that. "Hawthorne," he would say in a reasonable tone, the only kind that worked with her, and even that was iffy, "I think I love you and I need to hold you, which proves I'm an adult. So, lay off the bodyguards already, would you?"

Her face popped into his head, the regal tilt of her chin, the impassive gaze. "It is this or chains, Aaron Kesselman," she would say. Hell, he didn't need an imagination to hear that. She'd said it often enough to his face, like she'd really tie him down.

And she might. Hell, it was Hawthorne, the woman who believed herself to be two millennia old and who could damn well wrestle an alligator, a bear, and a mammoth into submission at the same time, if she wanted to. One measly illustrator would be a breeze.

"This or chains," he muttered to his suitcase. "Can you believe it?"

"Who are you talking to Airn?"

Aaron whirled around and found Lali behind him, peering up at him with curious gray eyes. He lifted her up and settled her onto his hip. "Myself. Who are you talking to?"

She patted his face with her tiny hands. "My puppy. Nana said to tell you lunch."

"Just lunch, huh? What if I don't want lunch?" He growled and poked at her belly. "What if I want to snack on a little girl instead?"

She giggled and squirmed and shrieked, and he threw her over his shoulder and carried her into the kitchen, where Hawthorne and Maria were making lunch.

"I found a sack of potatoes in the hallway," he said. "Thought you could make a good snack out of it."

"I'm not taters, Airn. I'm a Lali!"

"Taters, Lali. Good snack food, either way."

He set her right side up in her chair and scooted it in for her. The doorbell rang, and Lali scooted her chair back out, scampering away to answer the door. In the few weeks he'd known her, he had yet to see her sit still unless she was asleep, and sometimes even that didn't slow her down.

He sidled up to the two women and slid a hand across Hawthorne's trim waist. Her skin was warm under her sweater, tempting. The night before, he'd loved her for hours, trying to cram in a week's worth of intimacy in one night in a futile attempt

171

to tide them both over until his return.

It hadn't been enough. No matter how often he had her, the need was still there, strong and alive and ready to feed itself on the low murmur of her moans, the slick heat of her body, the steady beat of her heart next to his.

No, one night wouldn't make up for the week he'd be without her, not by a long shot.

"I don't have time for lunch," he said. "Have to leave for the airport soon."

Maria tutted, her jowly face set in disapproving lines. "A growing boy needs his nourishment."

"I haven't been a growing boy in over a decade, Maria." He bussed her cheek, sending her into a frenzy of titters and blushes. "You can feed me extra when I get back, how's that?"

Hawthorne's gaze was riveted to the yams she was attacking with a thin-bladed paring knife. "Will you be coming back?"

Aaron's earlier annoyance at her overprotectiveness melted away. "Of course, I am. We still have work to do."

"And that is all that holds you here?"

"You know what holds me here," he said softly.

"Do I?" She dropped her knife and wiped her hands on a cloth towel. "You have given me no assurances."

"I didn't think you needed them. If you think I'd let you go again..."

Lali skipped into the room ahead of one of Aaron's bodyguards. "Scootery!"

*Security*, Aaron translated. He gave the suited guard a sour look. "I see the babysitters have arrived."

"They are your bodyguards, Aaron, not your babysitters. You will allow them to protect you during your family holiday, or I shall not allow you to leave."

"I'm not a kid," he said through gritted teeth. "When are you gonna get that through your head?"

"When you trust me to care for you. Your life is in danger, love..."

"No..." His argument ground to a screeching halt. "Wait. Did you just call me love?"

"And I shall not abide threats to those under my protection."

"Let's get back to the 'love' part."

"Mr. Kesselman, your flight leaves in four hours." The bodyguard, a massive, menacing young man named Colin, gazed at Aaron with a flinty stare. "We won't have time to get through airport security if we don't leave now."

Aaron bit back a sigh. Just when it was getting good, the babysitter had to rein him in. "Walk me out?"

Hawthorne dropped the towel onto the granite countertop. She walked hand in hand with him to the door, following Lali.

A whole week without his girls. Seven days without Lali's bright chatter and Hawthorne's sweet smile, and at least that many nights without her in his bed, warming him, loving him. Filling him with heat and need and...

What was he thinking? He'd never make it a whole week without the two of them. He peered down at Lali and nearly crumbled at the solemn gaze on her normally smiling face. She raised her arms, and he lifted her up and held her close, bathing in her little girl scent while a hollow ache settled into his gut.

She wrapped her arms around him and buried her face in his collar. "I don't want you to go."

His throat squeezed tight. "I'll be back soon, kiddo."

"Promise?"

"I promise. You'll hardly know I'm gone."

Hawthorne eased Lali away from Aaron. He wrapped his arms around them both. "When I get back, we'll talk about this whole love thing."

"I love you, Airn." Lali's voice was muffled where she was trapped between him and her nana. "I love you lots and lots, bigger than my whole heart."

His own heart filled with it, overflowing with tenderness for the two females in front of him. They'd had him from day one, and he'd been too stupidly blind to see it. "I love you, too, Lali. And you, Hawthorne. We're gonna sort this out when I get back home."

She curled her fingers in his shirt and lifted her mouth to his, and as his lips moved over hers, he was struck with the certainty that he'd follow her wherever she went, crazy ancient warrior or not.

"Mr. Kesselman," Colin said.

Aaron drew reluctantly away from Hawthorne, kissed Lali one last time, and left before his lead feet weighted him to the floor of her house.

Behind him, Lali's silent tears became sobs. "I want my puppy, Nana."

An agonizing rip sliced down his heart as Hawthorne comforted Lali, shushing the little girl. Colin gripped Aaron's elbow firmly and bustled him out to the waiting SUV with a surprising speed, leaving Aaron no time to look back.

The bodyguard stuffed Aaron into the backseat of the vehicle. Through the door's window, Aaron's gaze met Hawthorne's. *Be safe*, she mouthed. Not *goodbye* or *come back to me*, but *be safe*. The SUV pulled away from the curb, accelerating onto the street. Aaron closed his eyes and dropped his head back onto the seat, shutting out the sight of Hawthorne patting Lali's shaking form, her own shoulders slumped, her expression empty

THE TRIP THROUGH SECURITY at Hartsfield International went much more quickly than it had when he'd arrived, no doubt helped along by his babysitters, who flashed official-looking badges and spoke in low tones to the TSA attendants. Colin picked up their tickets while Brigid, a hard-looking brunette with a tight body and no last name, waited to one side with Aaron, well away from the crowd.

He let them lead him through the ordeal of modern air

travel, ignoring them when he could, following their flat commands when he couldn't. The sound of Lali's sobs echoed in his mind. Why hadn't he brought her with him? A quick trip across the country to visit his mother for a few days, and then he would've had the perfect excuse to come back and spend the holiday with his two girls.

Aaron followed Colin onto the plane, dropped into the seat the bodyguard pointed out, and stared out the plane's window at the tarmac. Lali would love San Francisco, the bustle of the crowds, the rolling hills, the Golden Gate Bridge, and Fran Kesselman would love the precocious four year old. More, she'd love the fact that he was dating someone who could give her grandchildren.

His mother had never liked Jeanne. Cultural differences, he'd always thought, but now that Hawthorne and Lali were part of his life, he understood why. His girls would love him. Jeanne never had.

Fingers snapped in front of his face. "Mr. Kesselman," Brigid said in a sharp voice. "We need you to pay attention."

"I was." Not really, but whatever. Wasn't that what she and Colin were there for? "What's wrong?"

She sat back in her seat and fastened her seatbelt. "Plane's about to take off."

"Right." His gaze wandered while he fidgeted with his seatbelt. Colin had taken the aisle seat, Brigid the window seat across from Aaron. He stretched out his legs, frowned when she didn't have to move hers to make room for his. "What are we doing in first class?"

"Security."

Colin's voice was a low rumble. He sat erect and alert with his hands splayed across huge, muscled thighs. It was the most relaxed Aaron had ever seen the other man. He glanced between the two bodyguards. "I didn't buy a first class ticket."

"Hawthorne told me you were intelligent." Brigid crossed her long legs at the knee and smoothed out a crease in the loose, black slacks she wore. "I'm beginning to have my doubts."

What a hoot.

Outside the window, the tarmac rushed past. The plane took off, accelerating upward, and his gut clenched and fell. The blue autumn sky filled his view. Had Lali stopped crying yet? Did she understand that he'd be back as soon as he could?

Fingers snapped, startling Aaron out of his gloomy reverie. He eyed Brigid speculatively. "You do that again, you might draw back a nub."

"You need to be aware of your surroundings."

"And you need to keep the finger snapping down. I'm not a..."

*Puppy.* Shit. He rubbed tired fingers over his eyes. If Hawthorne hadn't pushed him, he would've put off this trip, nagging mother or not. Then he wouldn't be sitting here missing Lali, afraid to even think about Hawthorne, with a cold-eyed bodyguard to his left and a demanding one sitting across from him. He could be at home, taking Lali to the library, chatting with Charlotte while their two girls made Thanksgiving crafts. They could all walk into town and have lunch at the café on Main Street, and then he and Lali would go home and pretend to rake leaves with Hawthorne and...

Out of the corner of his eye, he noticed Brigid's hand inching forward. "Don't even think about it," he said.

She leaned back in her seat, a satisfied gleam in her eyes. "If you don't want me to do that, all you have to do is pay attention."

"Gimme a break. We're in first class at ten thousand feet. What could happen here?"

"The man behind you could be a plant," she said promptly. "He made it on board with a knife strapped to his ankle."

"Airport security my ass," Colin muttered under his breath.

Aaron lowered his voice and leaned forward. "Wait. How did you know about the knife?"

"The way he walks." She arched an eyebrow at him. "You missed it?"

"I wasn't paying attention." And wouldn't have known what to look for even if he had. "What kind of knife?"

A trim flight attendant in her early twenties stopped beside them, interrupting what Aaron suspected might have been a long-winded description. "Is everyone comfortable?"

"We're fine," Colin said.

"Of course." The attendant's eyes slid down the long, fit length of Colin's body in a quick assessment that even Aaron caught. "Ring if you need me."

When she moved away, Aaron said, "Do you get that a lot?"

"Sometimes."

"Ever take advantage?"

"Never."

The flatly spoken word surprised Aaron. "Seriously? Hot women throw themselves at you and you, what? Ignore them?"

"Women are a distraction."

"Really? Hmm. Hadn't noticed."

Which was an out-and-out lie. Hawthorne drove him to distraction from the time he woke in the morning to the time he fell into bed with her at night, and pretty much every moment in between. She was driving him to distraction now and they weren't even in the same state together.

Aaron settled back into his seat and observed his babysitters. They both held themselves like warriors, with tense gazes that saw everything without their eyes seeming to move. Both were fit and obviously active, quick reflexes, no-nonsense attitudes.

And neither had a last name.

He caught Brigid's gaze. "Are you a Daughter?"

"Yes."

"Immortal?"

Her head turned toward him, reminding him eerily of the way Hawthorne focused whenever she encountered a problem. "I am."

*Hmm.* "How old are you?"

"Six hundred and forty eight. Would you like my résumé?"

What would it say? He turned the possibilities over in his mind. Have sword, will travel, plus first-hand knowledge of history? Like he could believe that, his promise to Hawthorne to be more open notwithstanding. Was everyone in Tellowee crazy, or did they just bring it out for him? "Just curious. What about you, Colin? Are you immortal?"

"No."

"Why not?"

Colin shot him an impatient glare. "Hawthorne should've already explained why."

Aaaaand, yet another person who believed that. If he had a nickel... "Humor me."

"Sons are only born to mortal Daughters, which you should know."

*So why are you bothering me with it?* Aaron filled in, and ignored Colin's dig. "How old are you?"

"Twenty-two."

"Ah." Well, Aaron hadn't been expecting that. Colin carried himself well, not with the lanky confidence of a kid, but with the sureness of a man who knew how to handle himself. A memory flashed into Aaron's mind of another young man who carried himself the same way. "Do you know Levi?"

"We went to school together." Colin stood abruptly and buttoned the jacket of his black suit. "Time for a sweep."

He strode away without glancing back, his long strides eating up the distance down the center aisle.

Aaron turned to Brigid. "What did I say?"

"Colin's not a talker."

He waited for her to elaborate, and blew out an exasperated breath when she remained stubbornly silent. "He's not the only one," he muttered.

"We're not here to entertain you."

"Never thought you were."

*God, no.* They were there because Hawthorne didn't trust him to look out for himself. His mood went from gloomy to sour in a heartbeat. If that's the way she felt, why had she asked him to stay? Why not get rid of him in one fell swoop, send him on his merry way back to San Francisco, and be done with him once and for all? *Oh, no.* Not Hawthorne. Stubborn woman. She wanted him in her bed, so she sent bodyguards to protect him from an imagined threat.

Only, she hadn't treated it as imaginary. He fumbled for his carry on and pulled out his sketchpad, flipping to an empty page. A few minutes later, Hawthorne's sprite-like face stared back at him. Dark shadows under her eyes. She'd been slipping out of bed before he woke in the mornings. Tense lines around her mouth, her lips pressed together firmly. The changes were so minute, no one else would notice them. He should have, though, her lover, the man who might actually hold her heart.

He flipped the page and began another sketch, this one of Isolde, based on the snapshot held in his mind from their one meeting. Cold, empty. Colin resumed his seat, and Aaron ignored him, concentrating on the portrait coming to life under his pencil. He shaded in glossy black hair, a touch of silver. Faint lines around her eyes, the hard slash of her mouth. Not a mean woman, as Lali insisted, or not that Aaron had gathered, but a determined one. A woman with a purpose, ambition, fortitude. That was the impression he'd gotten of Hawthorne's niece.

If that's what the two women were to one another. He rubbed a knuckle across the furrow between his eyebrows. *If, if.* Hadn't he promised himself he wouldn't obsess over Hawthorne's past anymore? Hadn't he promised her that he'd be open to it and wouldn't jump to any more conclusions until she'd had a chance to explain? That left him with only one option: To take everything she said at face value until evidence arose to the contrary.

That had always been his first instinct with her, and he'd ignored it and fallen back on skepticism, hurting her not once but twice with his inability to believe her.

If he loved her, he had to trust her, just like she had to trust him.

Did he love her?

The tight pressure around his heart said so, as did the need in his gut, the empty ache of his arms from her absence. She'd asked him to trust her.

He wanted to, so badly.

They would sort it out when he got home. He flipped to a clean page and began a sketch of Lali in her Halloween costume with wooden sword raised high and a fierce look on her cherubic face.

The plane touched down at the San Francisco International Airport while Aaron was in the middle of a study of his bodyguards. He glanced over the quick sketches of various poses and body parts, the alert postures, the flat intensity of their eyes. They would be good reference material for the next time he needed to portray a character that held his cards close to his chest.

As soon as Aaron tucked his sketchbook and pencil into his carry on, Colin hustled him off the plane at a fast clip.

"Bodyguards in movies always go at the client's pace," Aaron grumbled.

"One, movies aren't real, and two, Hawthorne is our client. If anything happens to you, we'll lose more than our jobs."

Aaron tightened the grip on his bag and threw a grumpy glare at his youngest babysitter. "She wouldn't really cut your head off, would she?"

Brigid slid up to Aaron's other side and grabbed his arm. "We've got a problem. Bobby's been kidnapped."

"Bobby who?" Aaron said.

Colin muttered a curse under his breath and tightened his grip on Aaron's elbow. "Signal ahead. Three minutes to a go."

Colin and Brigid picked up the pace, walking Aaron at a near jog through the remainder of the airport while Brigid pressed a hand to her ear and spoke quietly. The terminal was crowded, jammed with people heading out early for next week's holiday or hopping a short commuter flight to a nearby city. Colin and Brigid strong-armed their way through the crowd, barking at anyone who got in the way as they pulled Aaron along between them.

Three minutes later, they were outside, racing toward a black SUV nearly identical to the one that had dropped them off at the airport in Atlanta. Colin opened the back door, shoved Aaron in, and slid in behind him. The driver cut in front of a taxi, away from the airport, leaving Brigid on the sidewalk. Within minutes, they were on the freeway, bracketed by rush hour traffic.

Aaron sat up and was promptly pushed back down into the soft leather seat. "Cut it out!"

"Stay low," Colin barked. He turned and glanced out the rear window, and kept one hand on Aaron's shoulder, pinning him in place. "Until we know what's going on, we have to assume you're a target, too."

"I thought that's why you were tagging along."

"Didn't Hawthorne explain anything to you?"

Aaron winced at the exasperation in Colin's voice. She'd tried a couple of times. He hadn't been a very receptive listener. "She said something about Isolde and the Eternal Order. That's all I really know."

Colin whistled out a breath. "Isolde holds a seat on the Council of Seven, a seat Hawthorne should by rights have filled when it came empty. She passed it on to Isolde instead."

"What's the Council of Seven?"

"The People's ruling body. Sort of. It's complicated."

"I gathered. What does all that have to do with me?"

"Short version, Hawthorne's really old, really wealthy, and really powerful. It makes anyone connected to her a target." Colin shifted in the seat, easing his grip on Aaron's shoulder. "You're sharing her bed."

"We're supposed to be working together. How could anybody possibly know we're lovers?"

"The way you treat Lali. Your smell..."

"My smell?"

"Pheromones. And you kissed her at The Omega."

Aaron thumped his forehead against the seat. *That kiss.* "You heard about that?"

Colin gave a grunting laugh. "Everybody heard about that. Levi was relieved as hell, let me tell you. Thinks his nana might actually be mellowing, to let a man touch her like that in public."

Right. A man touching Hawthorne in public. In the past, that had probably been sword worthy. "Who was kidnapped?"

"Bobby Upton."

"What?" Of all the people to be kidnapped, thuggish Bobby Upton would've been his last guess. "How many people did he take out on the way down?"

"No idea. We don't know any details yet, only that he's been taken."

Shit. If someone could get to a man like Upton...

"Relax. We'll take you to your mother's house, lock you down there until we know more. We already have a team there securing it, had one in place per Hawthorne's orders already, but now, we'll double the guard."

Well, that would go over well with his mother.

Aaron tuned out Colin's rapid fire lecture on exactly what methods the security team would take to protect him while he was in San Francisco. The details weren't important as long as Ma was safe. His mind kept looping back to Hawthorne's plea. *Be safe*, she'd said, after a week of not quite subtle attempts to persuade him to stay.

He slumped in the seat and closed his eyes as Colin droned on and the road thundered away beneath the wheels of the SUV.

# FIFTEEN

IT TOOK HOURS to calm Lali down, hours of Hawthorne promising that Aaron would come back, though she was uncertain whether he would or not. Promises came easily to the mouths of mortal men, that and notions of love.

She touched trembling fingers to her chest where an awful ache throbbed. *Love.* The word had slipped off her tongue through the barriers of her natural reserve. How long had it been since the emotion had overwhelmed her good sense?

The long road of her memory stretched before her, as clear and sharp as the days when each segment had been created. Love for a man had never tempted her, not to the point of unreason, as it did with Aaron. What was it about him that scattered her reason to the four winds? The gentle touch of his clever hands? The way he consumed her when they copulated, as if he would never have enough of her?

And still, his disbelief continued, settling into an uneasy acceptance while he waited for her to find the courage to confront him again.

One more rejection of the truth on his part and she would have no choice. Aaron could not be allowed to hold knowledge of the People, regardless of his belief or lack thereof. Such a man was a liability. She would be forced to dispose of him.

The trembling in her hand spread to her knees and she sank

weakly down onto the edge of his bed. Only once had she failed in her duty to the People, by passing representation of the line of Bagda on the Council of Seven to Isolde, a duty Una's daughter had fulfilled with the seriousness such a position demanded.

Unless she was a member of the Eternal Order.

Even knowing the possibility, Hawthorne could barely credit the notion. Isolde was many things. Ruthless, blind to the changing world, arrogant to the point of cruelty, but faithless? Never. Her loyalty to the People was an enduring strength. She would, and had, done anything to forward their common goals, and tolerated the political aspects of her seat on the Council far better than Hawthorne could have. If Isolde was a member of the Eternal Order, she had a reason, one that intertwined with her own notions of the People's correct path toward the future.

What ideal could possibly align with the People's ultimate goal of breaking the unjust curse laid upon them and not clash with the Order's touted purpose, to stop the Prophecy of Light from being fulfilled?

A beep drew Hawthorne's attention to her cell phone. She flipped it open and read the text message on the display, a blast alert from the IECS.

*Bobby Upton kidnapped. Eternal Order suspected. Guard your families.*

Hawthorne sagged against the bed. *Aaron.* Sweet Goddess, her man was in San Francisco protected only by two bodyguards, neither of whom had Hawthorne's skill or ruthless determination to protect him. Her heart boomed in her chest and her fingers fumbled. The phone slipped from her grasp and dropped to the floor with a quiet thud. She had to warn him.

*No.* She had to protect Lali first. Hawthorne scooped her phone up and dialed Ruby, left a sternly worded message requesting the girl's immediate assistance, then phoned Yvette to begin planning. Hawthorne's other family members would have received the same message she had and would, even now, be working toward protecting their families. They were not vulnerable the way Aaron and Lali were, her lover through his disbelief and Lali through her youth.

Precious Lali, who had always despised Isolde, had loved Aaron from the moment of their first meeting. *I love you bigger than my whole heart,* she had said, showing more courage and wisdom than most Daughters could summon after centuries of living upon being confronted by their heart's vulnerability.

As Aaron had forced Hawthorne to confront hers. A Daughter who could love so unreservedly was wise indeed, a lesson she vowed to learn from her tiny granddaughter.

She slipped quietly down the hall and peeked in on Lali, tucked the sleeping child under a layer of covers to ward off the late autumn chill, and made a thorough tour of the house, checking locks and bolts, resetting the security system. When at last she had finished, Hawthorne climbed the steps back to the second story on quiet feet and settled herself on the floor in front of the portrait of herself, her mother, and her sister, where she had a good view of the front door and Lali's room.

Her fingers were steadier, her heartbeat contained. She inhaled slowly, exhaled through her nose, then dialed Aaron's cell phone, counting the rings as they sounded through the line.

He picked up on the third. "Hawthorne?"

"Aaron." She clutched the phone to her ear. "You are safe?"

"As safe as I can be in an SUV in the middle of rush hour traffic. Are you ok? How's Lali?"

"We are well and safe, love. You must not worry."

"Can't help that." Static filled the line for long moments before his voice came softly through. "I miss you."

Hawthorne closed her eyes and leaned her head against the wall. "I wish you to return home as soon as it can be arranged."

"I can't." A scuffle sounded in the background, then Aaron's muffled voice said, "Dammit, Colin, cut that out."

Hawthorne's heart dropped into her stomach. "Aaron?"

"Yeah, sorry. That gorilla you hired keeps shoving me into

the seat."

"It is for your own protection," she said, and heard an echo of her words as Colin's voice drifted into her ear. "Listen to Colin. He and Brigid will keep you from harm."

"That's what they keep saying. Look, they're taking me to Ma's house until we know what's going on. Have you..." He cleared his throat, a muted sound that barely filtered through his phone. "Have you heard anything about Upton yet?"

"Colin and Brigid would know before I could."

"Right. Because they work for him. Sorry. Everything's a little crazy here."

"Come home to me, Aaron. *Please.*"

He groaned and sighed. "Hawthorne. *God.* Don't beg. I can't stand it. It's worse than when you cry. Cuts me right in half."

In the background, Colin said, "Hawthorne *cries?* What the hell, man."

"Look, as soon as I've had a good visit with Ma and can pick up some more supplies from my flat, I'll come back. I swear it, sweetheart."

"I shall expect you, then." Hawthorne thumped her head against the wall. "Do not tarry long, Aaron. Lali needs you."

His voice went soft and warm. "And what about you, Hawthorne? Do you need me?"

"A woman who does not need her lover..."

"Hawthorne."

The quiet warning in his voice prodded her into stark honesty. "Yes, Aaron. I need you. Do not prolong my need."

"I... Dammit, Colin. Just give me a minute."

"Aaron?"

"Yeah, sorry. Again. Colin's trying to take the phone away. Something about talking too long and security. I don't understand half of what he says."

"He is trying to explain what I have told you for days now. You are a high priority target and at great risk. Visit your mother,

Aaron, and be prepared for my close attention when you return."

"That sounds very promising. Take care of yourself, Hawthorne. Give Lali my love and tell her I'll be home soon."

"I shall. Be safe, love."

"Hawthorne?"

"Yes?"

"We're gonna talk about the love thing when I get back."

A delicious warmth filled the emptiness left in Aaron's absence. "So you have said."

"I mean it, too. When I get back, we're gonna talk about a lot of things, and I swear, this time I'll listen."

"I shall hold you to that."

"Do. You can even bring out that stick of yours, if you need to."

"It is a hanbō. Will you never learn its name?"

"Then I wouldn't need you to remind me." His voice lowered again, taking on the intimacy she craved. "I don't want the first time I tell you how I feel to be over the phone."

"You do not need to say it, Aaron."

"Yes, I do. I think you need to hear it, too."

Yes, she did. She needed to hear it from his own mouth, but not until he was in front of her, where she could see it in his face, feel it in the gentle strokes of his fingers on her skin. "Colin is growing impatient. We shall talk again prior to your leave taking."

"Yes, we will. Don't think I can go a whole day without hearing your voice."

Nor could she go long without him by her side. The desperate need he aroused in her would not be tucked quietly into its corner, there only when it was convenient. It raged and stormed and demanded, as she had always believed love should do.

After Aaron hung up, Hawthorne sat in the alcove, replaying the sound of his voice in her head while she waited for Ruby's arrival.

WORD CAME IN two days later, early in the afternoon. Bobby Upton had been recovered, bruised and beaten, but otherwise fine. When Aaron heard the news, relief flooded through him. He was no fan of Upton, still hadn't forgiven or forgotten that kiss, but he wouldn't wish a kidnapping on anybody.

As soon as Colin and Brigid could get Aaron from the airport to his ma's house, they locked him down and commandeered a small army of men and women in black suits and ear buds to stand watch. He and his mother existed in an uneasy peace under the watchful gaze of so many stoic eyes. She fretted and fussed and wailed the whole time, pacing through the house with not a strand of her graying hair out of place. Aaron buried himself in work and tolerated it. A man respected his mother, even when she went a little crazy.

It was a feeling he understood well. His babysitters wouldn't let him touch a toe outside the front door, not for a long run to get away from his ma's grumping, not for groceries or a lunch with friends, not even to do yard work. The curtains stayed drawn, Colin or Brigid monitored all phone calls, and they turned every visitor away who wasn't on a pre-approved list.

Approval through Hawthorne, of course. Aaron had no say in it, though it tickled him no end when Colin slammed the door on Jeanne's screeching maw.

Ma twisted her hands together around an embroidered handkerchief. "That's no way to treat your wife, Aaron."

"She's not my wife, Ma," Aaron said mildly, his focus on the panel he was sketching. "Hasn't been for a long time."

"Marriage is a sacred..."

"Don't." Aaron dropped his stylus and speared her with a hard stare. "Jeanne chose to leave. It wasn't up to me. Besides, I'm involved with someone else now. You should be happy for me."

Ma perched delicately on the edge of Pop's recliner. A decade that chair had been sitting there, empty and untouched, waiting for Ma to move on or Pop's resurrection.

"Is she Jewish?"

Aaron saved his work and set his tablet aside. "Pretty sure not."

"Christian?"

"Don't think so." He leaned forward and grasped her hand in his, careful not to squeeze her slightly arthritic fingers too hard. "Does it matter, as long as she loves me?"

Ma touched the handkerchief to her lips, a not quite disapproving gesture that hid the slight wrinkles around her mouth. "What about this Lali girl?"

"She's adorable. Precocious, sweet. You'll love her." Her bright laughter sounded in his mind and the crack in his heart widened. God, he missed her, as much as he missed Hawthorne. "Why don't you come out to Tellowee with me, stay a while and get to know her? Don't say you don't have time."

"Well, I don't. Your sister's coming in soon with the babies."

"So you can come after that." He patted her chilled hand gently, warming it between his own. When had his mother become so frail? "I'll probably be moving out there soon to be with Hawthorne. Her home is beautiful, the people kind. Say you'll visit so I won't have to worry about you."

She turned her hand into his and squeezed his fingers. "A mother's job is to worry, Aaron. A son's job is to live."

He pressed a kiss to her powdered forehead. "I think it should go the other way, too, Ma."

"Always with the smart remarks, just like your father." She patted his cheek none too gently and rose from Pop's recliner. "I hear the big one coming. What's his name? Colin, yes. Tromping down the hallway. How one man can make so much noise, I don't know..."

Her voice trailed off as she left the room, twisting her handkerchief in her fingers.

Colin came in a moment later, his feet silent against the carpet, his expression thunderous. "Your mother just told me to quiet down. I don't know how anybody can be quieter."

"Ignore her. She likes to fuss."

"Yeah?" Colin eyebrows veed down over hot blue eyes. "Maybe she should fuss about something else."

"Don't hold your breath." Aaron picked up his tablet and stylus and flipped to another page. "You need me for something?"

"Hawthorne wants you to come home. She's sending a private jet out."

"Is she, now? I guess you've arranged it already." Since his input wasn't even needed, apparently. Yet another thing he and Hawthorne would straighten out when he got back. The high-handed treat-Aaron-like-a-child crap had to stop. "Can I at least go by my flat and pick up some more clothes?"

"On the way to the airstrip."

"And not a minute before," Aaron muttered. "My sister's coming in tomorrow with her kids."

Colin's expression went blank and flat and cold. "You'll have a day with her. That's the most I could give you."

Well, at least there was that. "Thanks."

Colin turned on his heel and marched out of the room as silently as he had come.

"Colin, wait."

The bodyguard paused, half turned toward Aaron.

"Will my family be safe after I'm gone?"

"We'll leave someone to watch until this blows over, but yeah. Should be."

Aaron sighed out his relief. "Ok, then."

Colin nodded and slipped into the hallway, leaving Aaron alone with his work. A day more, two at the most, and a nice visit with his family under tighter security than the President enjoyed. Some holiday this one had turned out to be, and Thanksgiving was still days away.

RUBY PACED around Hawthorne's office, making a continuous round between the fire burning brightly in the wood heater, the room's entrance, and Lali, who sat on the floor in front of the coffee table, coloring quietly. Hawthorne observed her granddaughter walking the loop from one point to the other, her tread silent on the antique rug protecting the wooden floor. Occasionally, Ruby would pull out her phone and check it with a frown, other times with the small, secretive smile of a woman contemplating her lover.

It was a feeling Hawthorne knew well. Since Aaron's departure days before, she had mooned over him like a young girl in the throes of her first love. As reports came in from among the People about young Upton's capture by the Daughter India Furia, of his rescue by his fiancée, Indigo, and of the turmoil the kidnapping had caused, Hawthorne found her mind drifting at inconvenient moments to Aaron. Was he safe? Were Colin and Brigid protecting him adequately?

Did he miss her, long for her, dream of her?

Ruby marked off another loop around the room.

"You will wear a path in the floor if you continue," Hawthorne said. "Have a care for it, if not for your own footwear."

Ruby shoved her cell phone into the front pocket of her jeans and dropped onto the sofa. "Happy?"

Hawthorne regarded her evenly. "It is unlike you to demonstrate such restlessness."

"Got a lot on my mind." A muted beep came from Ruby's phone. She dug it out and flipped it open.

"A young man, perhaps?"

Ruby's fingers flew over the tiny keyboard of her cell. "Butt out, Nana."

"Since your own mother is no longer here to monitor your actions..."

"Forget it." Ruby slid her phone shut and speared Hawthorne with a flat gaze. "I can handle my own love life, thank you very much."

"I neither stated nor implied that you could not. However, as your elder, it is my duty to arrange the best match possible, for your happiness and well-being, and for the connections such a match might bring to our line."

Ruby rolled her eyes and muttered, "And you wonder why Levi doesn't come around."

"Pardon?"

"Never mind. Don't you have another granddaughter to bug?"

"I do not bug," Hawthorne said stiffly. "I monitor."

Ruby laughed. "Monitor. Right."

Hawthorne's cell rang. She sent Ruby a stern look, a reminder that their conversation would not be forgotten, and answered the call. "Hello, Yvette."

"We have a problem. A couple, actually. The PI you hired to dig into Isolde's past was found not long ago, knocked unconscious a few blocks from his home."

Hawthorne's fingers dug into the arm of her chair. "How seriously was he harmed?"

"His wife has him at the hospital now. Says he'll be fine."

"Do you have knowledge of who might have injured him?"

"Not yet, but probably Isolde, if not someone allied with her. She's been making noises..." A car roared by on the other end of the phone, throwing the line into a hiss of static. "Sorry. I'm outside the hospital now, waiting to see him."

"As soon as you have, please phone me with a report."

"Yes, Maetyrm."

"You said there were a couple of problems."

A deep breath sounded over the line. "Right. The other problem. Olivia the Good was found badly beaten near the house where Bobby Upton was rescued."

Hawthorne's gaze shot to Ruby. She and Olivia had attended school together some four decades earlier. After graduating, Ruby had gone on to work for Hawthorne whereas

Olivia had taken a position with the Daughter Miriam, the representative of the line of Marnan on the Council of Seven. "Has any connection between Olivia and the Eternal Order been established?"

"She's not talking, not about anything, including the name of the person who apparently tried to take her out."

Not an unsurprising development. "Please apprise me of any developments."

"I will." A soft whoosh sounded, and then relative quiet. "What about the other? Would you like for me to have someone take up surveillance on Isolde?"

"No, I shall see to that myself." Who better than family to track down an errant niece? "Have a care, Yvette."

"I will, Maetyrm. I'll call as soon as I can."

Hawthorne disconnected the call and stood. "Gather a bag for Lali. I have errands and do not wish to leave the two of you alone."

"I know where we can go." Ruby slid off the couch and ruffled Lali's hair. "Come on, little bit. Time to go play with the cousins."

Not long after, Hawthorne followed Ruby to the home of another of Hawthorne's granddaughters and saw Ruby and Lali safely inside. On her way out of town, she dropped by the hospital near Tellowee, staying only long enough to inquire of Rebecca Upton into her son's well-being.

Nearly two hours after leaving her own home, Hawthorne parked her SUV at the curb near Isolde's residence, an imposing Greek Revival situated more than half an hour away from Tellowee in the Betty's Creek area. The building and its meticulously maintained landscape were dark save for a lamp glowing dimly through the curtained living room windows. She stepped out of her vehicle and closed the door quietly. Nothing stirred that shouldn't, nor was the neighborhood unnaturally quiet.

She made her way to the door and knocked gently, alert for

any sign that someone was at home. Light footsteps arose from the interior, and she backed away from the door, allowing plenty of room for Isolde to appear on the other side.

Isolde's husband, Mathias Zellinger, opened the door and grinned at Hawthorne. The years had been kind to him, casting only a few wrinkles around the sharp intelligence of his nearly black eyes, leaving his erect posture untouched. "Hey. Long time no see."

She lifted her cheek for his perfunctory kiss. "You appear well, nephew."

"And you are simply stunning." He stepped back and waved her in. "I hear you have a new man. A good one, I hope."

"He is, indeed."

"But you're not here about that, I'm sure. Isolde's not home, but you're welcome to come in and wait for her."

Hawthorne followed him into the living room and sat on the hand-embroidered seat of a delicately fashioned wooden chair. "I have come to discuss Isolde with you, Mathias."

"Oh?" He smiled easily and dropped onto the loveseat across from the fire dancing noisily in the fireplace. "Who has she offended this time?"

"I wish it were only a matter of someone finding offence with Isolde's blunt tactics." She eyed him steadily, gauging his manner, the relaxed slope of his shoulders, the openness of his expression. "Has she mentioned the Eternal Order?"

"She never has, though I've heard it from a couple of others over the years. I thought the Order was a myth."

"It is a closely guarded secret, one known only to the eldest of the People and a handful of others. Has Isolde had many visitors lately, strangers in particular?"

"No, but you know her. She rarely brings work home." Mathias leaned forward and braced his forearms atop his thighs. "What's this about, Hawthorne?"

"Isolde may be working at cross-purposes to the People."

"No." He shook his head, an emphatic gesture that was both

immediate and precise. "She's always been devoted in her duty. You know that."

Hawthorne nodded once. "Indeed. It has come to my attention that her devotion may not be as wholesome as it appears. Are you aware of the Eternal Order's purpose?"

"To stop the Prophecy of Light from being fulfilled." His wide mouth tilted up at one corner into a rueful grin. "Even young children know that."

"That is part of it, yes, but the overall goal is and always has been for the People to retain their immortality. If the Prophecy is fulfilled, all Daughters become mortal..."

"And not just the ones who submit." Mathias sat back with a frown. "You know, Isolde never said so, but I always got the impression she resented the loss of her immortality, resented me for tempting her."

"She is a hard woman, Mathias," Hawthorne murmured.

"She is, but a good one. I know what people say about us. No," he said when Hawthorne made to speak. "I've overheard enough to know. In spite of what anyone thinks, we have a good life together."

"As anyone would wish."

His gaze drifted to the flicker of the fire's flames. "You think she's up to something."

"I have reason to believe so, yes."

"Does it have anything to do with this young man who was kidnapped?"

"Perhaps."

His soft laugh held a touch of melancholy. "Until I met Isolde, I never knew women could play their cards so tight to their chests."

"It is the price of being a Daughter." Hawthorne rose and gazed down upon the man who had given his heart to her niece, the cold-hearted progeny of Hawthorne's only sibling. "Isolde may not return home, Mathias. Prepare yourself for such an eventuality."

His features seemed somehow older than the ones that had greeted Hawthorne upon her arrival. "Whatever you think she's done, I hope you remember how much I love her, how much I still need her. Be kind to her, Hawthorne."

"If I can. For your sake, if not for hers." She touched her lips to his and then to his forehead. "Farewell, my kindred. I shall speak with you soon."

Mathias slumped onto the loveseat, alone in the shadows cast by the cheery fire. Hawthorne saw herself out, sparing all of her sympathy for her niece's husband, and none for Isolde.

# SIXTEEN

ARON COUNTED DOWN the days until his return to Hawthorne. His sister came in with her children, and Colin, a man of his word, gave Aaron a full day to enjoy his family. As much as he loved them, he was anxious to get back to his own family, the woman and child he'd left in Georgia who had wormed their way so stealthily and quickly into his heart.

After saying goodbye to Ma and his sister and her kids, Aaron was hustled out to a waiting SUV for a quick stop by his flat, his patience thinning at the forced rush by his bodyguards. He unlocked the door and stepped into an echoing foreign land, sterile and emotionless compared to Hawthorne's home, filled as it was with the warmth she carefully hid and with Lali's bright laughter.

He'd never thought to grow old in this space. As he looked around, that thought echoed inside his mind. Someday, he would remarry. It had always been his dream to meet a woman who captured his heart, a woman who would willingly give him the children he'd always wanted, who would let him love her with everything he had. Someday, he'd planned on outgrowing his bachelor life and moving on to another home, a bigger one with a yard and a garden and a family to love.

Someday had been building since the moment he'd seen Hawthorne pick up her stick in that ring.

His heart expanded in his chest, filling him with the endless possibilities of a life with her. If she would have him, if he could understand her past and accept it, or what she believed of it, would she want to make a home with him? Would she welcome him there, share her family and the life she'd made? Would she open her heart to him?

He packed quickly as he contemplated the future. A couple more sweaters, another set of cords. His favorite pair of hiking boots and a ragged denim jacket that needed either a good mending or to be thrown into the rag pile.

The last item to go into his overstuffed suitcase was the drawing he'd made of Hawthorne at DragonCon. Beautiful Hawthorne bathed in the light of a lamp, her sensual curves hidden beneath the sheet. He rubbed the dust off the frame with his thumb, traced the line of her cheek, then slipped it carefully into the folds of a sweater.

It was a relatively quick trip by air between San Francisco and Atlanta, then a long drive north to Tellowee. Aaron obeyed Colin and Brigid, allowing them to move him around like the puppet he was, subject to the whims and whimsies of Hawthorne's heart.

And at last, the SUV pulled into the driveway of her home, headlights flashing in the dusky twilight against the wood and rock siding. The front door banged open, and Lali flew through it and down the stairs. Aaron pushed out of the car and dropped to the ground in front of her as she went skidding down the sidewalk, caught her up and buried his face in the wispy sunshine of her hair.

"Puppy! You came back."

"Course I did, kiddo. Told you I would, didn't I?" Damned if he'd leave her again, though. "You're stuck with me."

She leaned back and patted her hands against his cheeks. "We misseded you."

"I misseded you, too."

Hawthorne and Ruby waited on the porch outside the open

door. Aaron's gaze met Hawthorne's and he forgot the chill of the November air, forgot the rushed almost-holiday with his family in California, forgot everything but her and the promises they'd made to talk about her past, and about love.

He rose, taking Lali with him, and strode up the walkway, up the stairs and across the porch, rushing toward the woman who'd become such a huge part of his life in such a short time. He shifted Lali onto his hip and held out his other arm, and Hawthorne walked into it, curling herself into him and around him and through him, her scent, the smile shining in her stormy eyes, her warmth and grace. She lifted her mouth to his, a sunflower blooming into the sun, and he kissed her, taking everything she was and would be, and giving her everything in return.

Footsteps thudded gently on the porch behind him. Colin cleared his throat and said, "Hawthorne laughs?"

"I know," Ruby said. "Freaky, right?"

Aaron huffed out a laugh. "What is it with these guys? Have they never seen you get emotional before?"

"Only rarely." Hawthorne's hand slipped to his waist and squeezed. "Come. We have much to discuss and little time."

He followed her inside and set a squirming Lali down. Hawthorne grasped his hand in her slender one and led him to her office, shutting the door behind them. As soon as she did, he pulled her into his arms. "I missed you."

She leaned into him and toyed with the button resting over his heart. "If you had not left, you would have had no reason to miss me."

He clamped down on his patience. God above, she was persistent. "Ma needed me. The holidays are always hard on her, have been since Pop died."

"Your safety..."

He cut her off the best way he knew how, by hauling her as close as he could get her and capturing her luscious mouth in a hard kiss. Her nails scraped into his chest through his flannel shirt and she opened, blossoming as she had on the porch. His sunflower. He gentled the kiss, savored the quick darts of her tongue on his, the breathy catches in her throat as passion rose. It filled him, bringing a solid heat to his blood that punched through his reason and *demanded*.

He drew back, touched his lips to the sensitive skin behind her ear. "Is there a lock on that door?"

"Ah." She tilted her head and skimmed her hand up, cupping his nape. "No one would dare enter this room without my permission."

"So, you wouldn't have any objections to getting naked right now, would you?"

She threaded her fingers into his hair, and it was all he could do to rein in the need that spiked through him. "That would be unwise."

"You said nobody would come in."

"We must be circumspect..."

He licked his way down her throat, and her voice hitched and softened.

"Aaron, please."

"Please what? Please take you? Please make you come?"

He shoved her sweater up, yanked her camisole out of her jeans, and found the smooth silk of her skin.

She hissed in a breath and shivered. "Your hands are chilled."

"Sorry." He pulled his hands away and dropped her sweater with a sigh. "Nothing a hot shower won't fix. Join me?"

"I cannot, much as I would enjoy having you there. Isolde has disappeared. I must find her, as quickly as I can."

He drew back and met her gaze, still heated from the kiss. "What happened?"

"It is nothing with which you should concern yourself."

"Yeah?" He backed away from her and shoved his hands into the pockets of his jeans. A hard knot of anger wormed its way through the heat they'd shared. "Here's the thing,

Hawthorne. I want to be with you, all the way with you. I thought you wanted that, too."

"I do."

"Then you need to quit treating me like I'm not capable of understanding what's going on. I'm not a kid."

"I never thought you were."

"Really?" He speared her with a heated glare. "Well, here's a way to prove it. Tell me what happened."

She blinked, a singular drop and lift of eyelids over her stormy eyes. "You are not ready for the truth, Aaron."

"Am I not?"

"Until you accept me..."

"Haven't I tried?"

Her voice went flat. "Not hard enough."

He sighed and jabbed stiff fingers through his hair. "Ok, you're right. We were supposed to clear this up when I got back."

"Time works against us, as it has for days now." She slid her arms around his waist, rested her head against the beat of his heart. "You must trust me a while longer."

Her scent tickled his nose and raised a fresh rush of heat. "I'll try."

"Do not try, Aaron. Accomplish. My niece is a dangerous woman. We must all guard ourselves now."

"Ok." He tightened his arms around her. She was right. Love and trust went hand in hand. If he loved her as truly and deeply as he suspected, it only followed that he had to trust her to know what was best, at least when it came to her family. Lali was one thing. For her, he'd fight and argue, but for Isolde? No. Hawthorne had to take the lead there. "Ok. What do you want me to do?"

Her shoulders relaxed under his embrace. "Stay with Lali. Mind Colin and Brigid a while longer and allow them and Ruby to protect the two of you while I track Isolde."

"I can do that." And he would, by God, even if it killed him.

"When are you leaving?"

"Tonight, as soon as I can." Her breath sighed against his skin through his shirt. "I should have left two days ago, would have if you had been here."

"I'm sorry. Ma..."

"No, Aaron. Do not apologize for loving your mother. A son who eschews his family is a sorry man indeed. I would not have you act thusly."

"Then why did you try to keep me here?"

"Because it was not safe." She eased back and cupped his jaws in her hands. "Kiss me once more before I leave. I have missed you terribly."

"Terribly, huh? You sure about the naked thing?"

"Quite positive, love." Her lips tilted into a gentle smile and her eyes went soft and dreamy. "Though perhaps a little petting would be permissible."

"Happy to oblige," he said, and did for long moments as their soft murmurs competed with the crackle of the fire to fill the room.

An hour later, Aaron slumped on the edge of Hawthorne's bed, quietly watching her gear up in a turtleneck, cargo pants, and a leather jacket over sturdy work boots, all flat black in color. She tucked a black knit hat into a jacket pocket, dropped a compass and other gadgets into the leg pockets of her pants, and armed herself with enough weapons to take down a small army. Once her jacket was zipped up, she shrugged on the holster for her sword and slid it into place across her back.

"Is all that really necessary?" he asked.

"You have not been around the People long enough to know the capabilities of an immortal Daughter."

"I've been around you." And he knew enough to know who would come out the winner if he went at her with a weapon. "How bad can Isolde be?"

Hawthorne loaded a clip into a heavy, lethal-looking handgun and slid the top part back with a loud snick. "As a warrior, her skills nearly match mine."

He huffed out a disbelieving laugh. Another woman who could fight the way Hawthorne did, with liquid grace and lightning fast reflexes? He'd pay to see that.

"Scoff all you wish, love. She is not one to ignore."

"I didn't think she was."

Hawthorne leveled a stern gaze at him. "Remember that caution should you ever face her."

"That's what the babysitters are for."

"They are not babysitters." She stepped into the space between his open thighs and rested her hands lightly on his shoulders. "And you will mind them whilst I am away."

He dug his fingers into her waist and rocked her forward, bumping her hips against his, right where he wanted her to be. "See? Babysitters."

"When I return, we shall talk and build trust, and you will learn to defend yourself. Your *bodyguards* will not then be as necessary as they are now."

He laughed, couldn't help it, and would've pulled her onto the bed with him if he didn't know exactly how many weapons she'd tucked into the nooks and crannies of her outfit. "Come back to me soon."

"As soon as I can," she promised. "Care for Lali, will you? She has so few who love her."

"You're wrong there, sweetheart. Everyone loves that sweet little girl."

"All save Isolde." Hawthorne touched her forehead to his. "Care for yourself as well. I have no wish to begin building trust with another man."

A hot shaft of green envy shot through him. Hawthorne with another man? Why would she even bring that up? "I don't particularly want that either."

"Good, then. It is settled. Stay within the boundaries of the house and follow Colin and Brigid's instructions. I shall return as quickly as I can."

He accepted her kiss, took his time exploring her, ended it gently. She slipped away, disappearing through the entrance to her room, and he rubbed a finger over the vee of his furrowed brows. How worried did he have to be? Hawthorne could handle Isolde, no doubts there. No, what worried him was what would happen between now and then, and after, when she tried to explain her past and his knee-jerk skepticism reared its ugly head.

Lali bounced into the room, smiling as she skipped, and scrambled into his lap. "Why is you sad, puppy?"

"Because sometimes, even adults can't control their hearts."

"Aw." She laid her head on his shoulder and toyed with the button over his heart. "You can'ts be sad, Airn. You just can'ts be."

"I'll try." For her, of course he would. He brushed the silky strands of her hair out of her eyes. "Why aren't you sad? I figured you'd cry up a storm as soon as Hawthorne left."

"Silly puppy. Nana always comes back."

The simple faith in her words touched him. *Nana always comes back.* Just like she always kept her promises and always spoke the truth.

Except about her past. Or did she?

He shoved it out of his mind. He'd made a promise, too, to open his mind as wide as the love in his heart, to listen and believe. This time, he'd keep it.

THE HOURS DRAGGED once Hawthorne left. Lali refused to let Ruby care for her and pitched such a fit at bath time that Aaron compromised and stood outside her bathroom while Lali bathed, reading a story to her. It took both Aaron and Ruby to get Lali into bed. At last, they crept through her door, drawing it nearly shut, and heaved twin sighs of relief.

Aaron scrubbed his hands wearily over his face. "I've never seen her like that."

"I think she knows something's wrong." Ruby snuck a

furtive glance at Lali's door and lowered her voice to a tense whisper. "Lali might be young, but she's got great instincts."

The first day he'd met Lali popped into his mind, how she'd wrapped her arms around Bobby Upton's neck and asked him to be her other husband. "Sometimes."

"Always," Ruby shot back. "Trust me. Lali's not a fool."

"She's four."

"And? Sometimes age doesn't have anything to do with wisdom." Ruby's mouth tilted into a tired smirk. "Take you, for instance. You're, what? Thirty-three?"

"Thirty-four."

"And you've not exactly made rational choices where Nana's concerned, have you?"

A rueful grin tugged at the corners of his mouth. "Does anybody when their heart's involved?"

She laughed softly and threaded her arm through his. "You've got a point. Hot chocolate?"

"Sure."

They ambled downstairs arm in arm, sat around the kitchen table drinking Ruby's homemade hot chocolate, laced with shavings of milk chocolate, and talked quietly about whatever came to mind.

When their mugs were nearly empty, Ruby's cell phone beeped. She fished it out of her pocket and read the message, her smile soft and secretive.

"Boyfriend?" Aaron pointed with his mug to her phone. "You've got that look a woman gets when she's thinking about someone special."

"He might be." She set her phone aside and sipped hot chocolate. "Someday."

"Who is he?"

"No one you know." At his steady gaze, she huffed out a sigh. "A guy I know. Jordan. He's a Son..."

"Son?"

"Born of a Daughter who's become mortal. I guess you and

Nana haven't sorted this out yet, huh?"

"We're getting there, though not as quickly as either one of us would like." He sipped hot chocolate and eyed her carefully closed expression. "So what's the problem with Jordan?"

"Nothing. He's a great guy. Sweet, hard-working. Funny, when he wants to be. Maybe a bit too reserved sometimes." She cupped her mug between her hands and rolled it back and forth. "Maybe a little too young, too."

"Yeah? How old is he?"

"Twenty-two, almost twenty-three."

"Yes, I can see how that would worry you, what with your advanced age of, oh, twenty-two-ish?"

She laughed softly. "You're so adorably naïve, Aaron. I wouldn't worry about his youth if I were the same age."

"How old are you then?"

"You sure you want to know?"

He met her gaze steadily. In for a penny. "Yeah, I do."

"Fifty-one."

His breath whooshed out in a rush. "Fifty...?"

"Yup. Hit the big five oh last year. You see why I'm worried about the age difference?"

"Ok, let's say you're really fifty-one and Hawthorne's really nearly two millennia old, and all the other women around here are the same, ancient but youthful looking."

She speared him with an icy glare. "Yeah, let's assume that's true, since it is."

He waved her comment away. "So you're all in the same boat. It's not like there are a lot of men out there who are the same age, are there?"

"Lots of fifty-year old men around, Aaron."

"Don't be obtuse."

"I'm not..."

"You are," he said firmly. "How many men your age have you dated in the last few years?"

Her gray eyes, so like Hawthorne's, dropped to her mug.

"None."

"Uh-huh. That's what I thought. And how long have you and Jordan been dating?"

She slumped into her chair and her voice dropped to a near whisper. "Since he turned eighteen."

"To paraphrase, age doesn't have anything to do with it, sweetheart." He leaned forward and cupped her hands in his. "Love is what it is. There's no rhyme or reason to it. The sooner we accept that, the easier we'll have it."

"Is that how you think about Nana?"

"Sometimes. When she's really ornery."

Ruby laughed. "That's pretty much all the time."

"Yeah, it is." He stood and pulled her up out of her seat. "Come on. It's past your bedtime."

She shot him a haughty glare. "I'm not a kid."

"So we can watch a movie and then you can go to bed."

Her brows shot down over stormy eyes. "I told you, I'm not..."

"A kid, I know, but right now, you feel like my kid, so humor me."

Her expression turned thoughtful. "I never knew my father."

"God, Ruby." He stuffed his hands into his pockets. Did all the women in this family have tragic pasts? "I'm sorry."

"Don't be. It was a long time ago." She threaded her arm through his elbow and tugged gently. "Come on. I've got just the movie for you."

A couple of hours later, after a light-hearted comedy and a bowl of popcorn, they trudged up the stairs to the second floor, Ruby yawning as she stumbled to her room across the hall from Lali's, and Aaron thoughtful. He'd never considered that by loving Hawthorne, he'd be taking on all of her family as well. Lali, sure, and maybe even Ruby and Levi, but she had to have other progeny, possibly numbering in the dozens or, God help him, hundreds. Would he have to learn to love all of those people, too?

He tucked it away and got ready for bed, slipping under the sheets, his mind in turmoil.

He drifted into a restless slumber full of dreams. Hawthorne hacking her way through an army of angry, sweaty men, her eyes cold as her arm lifted and fell, delivering justice with each stroke. Ruby running from a faceless, nameless enemy draped in shadows, her eyes wide and frightened as she ran ever faster from the monster chasing her. And Lali, lying in a broken heap on the living room rug, her beautiful gray eyes staring sightlessly up at him.

He sat up and gasped, trembling and sweaty, his heart a solid roar in his ears. The sound of scuffed footsteps and harsh whispers came from the hallway a moment before his door snicked shut and tiny feet pattered toward him.

"What is it, Lali?"

"Sh." Though she stood at his elbow, her whisper barely reached him. "Ruby's fighting the mean cushion. We has to go, Airn."

"What?"

"Sh." Her hand grasped his and tugged. "You has to come now."

Ruby's earlier words flitted through his mind. *Lali might be young, but she's got great instincts.* He slid from the bed and shrugged on a t-shirt. "Tell me what to do."

"Come with me, Airn."

She took his hand in her ice cold one and led him to his closet. Inside, a narrow door in the back wall stood open. He'd never noticed it before, and probably wouldn't have anyway. Most of his clothes were stored in the chest of drawers in his bedroom, not in the closet.

Lali disappeared into the blackness on the other side of the door. He slipped in behind her and fumbled with the interior knob, pulling the door as tightly closed as he could. A light flashed on with a loud click, illuminating an inter-wall passageway barely wide enough for a small woman to walk through. He turned sideways and shuffled after Lali through twists and turns, down a flight of stairs, then another.

After ten long minutes of brushing cobwebs out of the way and cursing the tight confines of the narrow passage, he stumbled to a stop behind her. She pressed her ear to the wall and listened for a long while before pushing against it. This door opened into an anteroom, one he wasn't familiar with. Lali touched a finger to her lips, then crept toward a thick, metal door embedded into the wall to their right, opposite a staircase. The floor was solid concrete and the space held the musty smell of a basement.

She held her hands up to him. When he lifted her, she pointed to the red-lighted keypad mounted on the wall next to the metal door. "P-u-p-p-y," she said under her breath as she keyed in five numbers, then pressed her right thumb firmly to the blank screen above the keypad. The light flashed green. Lali squirmed out of his arms and opened the door, revealing a black void.

He patted the interior wall, flipped on the lights, and gaped at the view illuminated beneath the harsh fluorescent lighting. The room was a massive space of row after row of bookcases, each one filled to the brim. Weapons of all shapes, sizes, and kinds hung from the sides of the shelving and on the walls, what he could see of them. Down the center of the room, directly in front of him, a series of glass cases held a variety of antiques and artifacts.

Lali pushed against the back of his thighs. Aaron obliged, moving farther into the room, his gaze caught by the assortment of books and objects collected within it.

Lali shut the door and sighed. "Now we is safe from the mean cushion, Airn."

"What is this place?"

"Nana's vault. She's got lots of stuff in here." She skipped down the center aisle, still carrying the flashlight. "I gots a bed back here. Nana said if I ever had to come in here and hide that I had to go straight to bed *or else.*"

A laugh pushed its way out around the sheer awe lingering over the museum Hawthorne had hidden away somewhere in her house. His bare feet chilled on the cold concrete, reminding him that Lali was shoeless, too. "Come here, kiddo. Guess I need to tuck you in, huh?"

He swooped her up, fed her giggles with gentle pokes to her tummy, and tucked her into the twin bed located along the back wall in a corner where the light didn't quite reach. "Want me to cut the lights off?"

"Not until Nana comes," she said around a yawn, and snuggled into the small bed with her eyes closed and a smile on her face.

He kissed her cheek lightly. "I'll be close by if you need me."

He walked back to the entrance of the vault. Hadn't he heard Hawthorne refer to it, or maybe Ruby?

If Lali was right, her sister was at that moment battling Isolde somewhere above them. Short of throwing weapons to Ruby as she needed them, there was nothing he could do about it. Hopefully, she could handle the older woman on her own, though how Isolde had made it into the house in the first place was a mystery, considering all the guards Hawthorne had left behind.

His curiosity over the room's contents gradually edged out his concern for Ruby and the guards. He examined each case, tapped lightly against the glass of one holding the remnants of an ancient book written in an unknown language. Climate controlled or just protected? He moved on to the next case and the next, lingering over each one and their respective contents. A wooden shield with cracked leather peeling away from its surface. A short sword pitted with rust and age. A silver armband in the shape of a coiled serpent, mounted in the same case as an intricately made heavy gold necklace and a lock of curly red hair, dulled by time.

A row of leather-bound volumes caught his eye. He pulled

one carefully from the shelf and flipped it open. It felt familiar, the slant of the handwriting, the density of the pages. It took him a moment, but his mind finally hit on the reason why. He'd held two volumes similar to the one in his hand back in California, the ones written by the Chronicler containing the tales of Rebecca the Blade.

He slid the book into its spot on the shelf, selected another, and nearly laughed. This one he could almost read. The language was... He struggled to put his finger on it. An older English, but not so old he didn't recognize some of the words. *There.* He squinted and finally made out *Una* and reared back. Una Longshadow. Had Hawthorne, like him, borrowed tales from the ancient volumes she collected and turned them into stories?

He pulled down two newer looking volumes, found a chair, and hauled his booty to the corner where Lali slept peacefully, safely protected, much like the artifacts Hawthorne had sealed behind glass. His eyes grew gritty as he studied the texts, deciphering them slowly, engrossed in the simply told stories.

A distant hiss sounded behind him. He looked around, glanced up at the vents spaced evenly along the tops of the walls. Probably just the heat coming on. He shrugged and went back to the texts. A moment later, a whoosh startled him into dropping the book and a heavy object connected with the back of his skull, knocking him off the chair. His head erupted in pain and his vision blurred and wavered. Lali. He had to get to Lali. She was crouched on the bed waiting for him, her gray eyes wide and innocent and full of tears. Lali, his angel.

He shook his head and pushed himself off the floor on wobbly limbs. Another blow thudded heavily on his back and he grunted. A third blow bounced off his skull and Lali's screams echoed in his ears as his vision narrowed and dimmed, and he floated endlessly down into darkness.

# SEVENTEEN

AWTHORNE TRACKED ISOLDE using the notes gathered by the private investigator Yvette had hired. A handful of foreclosed properties, one of which had been Bobby Upton's prison after his kidnapping. Isolde's personal business interests located throughout northeast Georgia. An upscale bar in Lawrenceville she habitually visited, occasionally with Mathias, more frequently alone.

As Hawthorne entered the bar, she assessed the metal and glass décor, the plastic nature of the patrons, their laughter empty, their expressions brittle, and the annoyingly bright music playing through the overhead speakers. It was not what she would have expected from her niece. Isolde had always preferred enduring quality over ephemeral fashion.

A hard-eyed, lean-cheeked young man with his tawny hair cut military short manned the bar, polishing glasses with a clean towel. Hawthorne slid onto a barstool and met his even gaze. "I am searching for a woman who frequents this establishment. Black hair, haughty. Appears to be in her early forties or perhaps younger."

"Yeah?" The barkeep shelved the glass and slung the towel over his shoulder. "Lot of women like that come in here."

"Isolde is unlike other women." Hawthorne pinned him with a glacial stare. "She would be accorded deference. Those who refused to kowtow would pay a heavy price, through the application of her fist or the lash of her tongue."

A smile twitched around the man's thin lips, though his gaze remained steady, watchful. "The table in the back corner."

Hawthorne nodded and slid a twenty across the bar to him. She turned casually and surveyed the corner the barkeep had indicated. A lone woman sat there, hunched over a mug half full of an amber alcoholic brew, staring morosely into the liquid. Her copper hair fell in loose waves across her shoulders and down her back, partially hiding a smattering of multi-colored bruises along her jaw.

Olivia the Good.

Hawthorne waited patiently, surveying the crowd, searching for other members of the People or Isolde's possible allies. When none appeared, she slid easily through the mindless mass of humanity, pausing beside the woman who had been beaten badly shortly after young Upton's kidnapping and left to rot.

Olivia's gaze remained on her beverage. "What do you want?"

"Information."

"I don't have anything to say." Olivia raised her glass and sipped. "You know that."

"For the sake of the People..."

Olivia laughed, a morose noise that hung in the air between them. "Do you think I've ever acted for anything else?"

"You were a member of the Order, were you not?"

"I was. Not anymore." A tear slid down Olivia's cheek, glinting over bruised flesh. "I gave my life for the cause, gave everything to save the People from the certain misery of forced mortality, and what did it get me?"

An unfamiliar emotion tugged at Hawthorne, something close to pity, though not quite.

"I tried to save him, you know. The Blade's Son. India wailed on him for a solid hour before her anger broke." Olivia's hand trembled as she raised her glass and drained it in one long swallow, ending with a grimace. "And then she wailed on me when she figured out what I'd done."

A waitress came by and exchanged the empty glass for a full one.

"Never could abide drinking out of a bottle," Olivia said. "Dear old mom. Old habits stick, huh?"

"Why are you here, Olivia? Why have you not sought refuge?"

The glass hit the table with a thud. Golden liquid splashed over its sides. "There's no refuge for a traitor, Hawthorne. Even if I wanted to run, I wouldn't. No Daughter is that much of a coward."

"Some are," Hawthorne murmured. "What do you know of Isolde?"

Olivia's voice went as flat as her gaze. "Nothing. She never shared her plans with any of the minions. Even if I knew something, I wouldn't tell. I'm not a damn snitch either."

"Yet you readily worked to save young Upton."

"He's a Son," Olivia snapped. "I couldn't stand by and let India kill him."

Hawthorne stifled the contempt that rose. "You twist your loyalty and honor to suit your own needs."

"Honor, loyalty. *Duty.*" Olivia bit the words out between clenched teeth. "The by-words of sheep."

"The by-words of a People on the brink of extinction," Hawthorne corrected grimly. "Do you truly believe prolonging our immortality will solve that problem?"

"It doesn't matter what I think." Olivia hunched over her glass again, cupping it between her hands. "If you don't mind, I'd like to be alone now."

Hawthorne bit back a sigh. Obstinate. Olivia had always been too stubborn for her own good.

She turned on her heel, leaving the young woman who had once been Ruby's friend to her solitude, halting when Olivia spoke, too low for Hawthorne to understand.

"What?" Hawthorne asked.

"Leverage. Isolde once said that she had enough leverage to always find her way out of a tight spot."

*Leverage.*

Hawthorne nodded once, a silent thank you, and wound her way through the crowds and out the bar's doors into the chill November night.

What sort of leverage would Isolde seek, now that she had been loosely linked to the Eternal Order?

Hawthorne jogged to her Land Rover and slipped inside, started the car and waited for the engine to warm. Leverage depended entirely on those involved in the gambit. Isolde's leverage would be personal, directed at removing the current threat she faced.

An oily knot of fear slid into Hawthorne's gut. Isolde valued the power she wielded above all else, including the love of her husband and the remnants of her extended family. If that power were threatened, she would search out the threat and eliminate it, beginning with those who held knowledge that might endanger her position.

Or those who *potentially* held such knowledge.

Hawthorne shifted into gear and eased into the street, steering with one hand as dialed her cell phone with the other. Mathias' phone rang four times before switching to voice mail. She left a message, then texted him with one eye on the road as she sped through the heavy late-night traffic toward the home he shared with Isolde.

It was a long way from Lawrenceville to Isolde's home just south of the North Carolina state line. Hawthorne whipped quickly through the clogged streets, merging onto I-985 not long after leaving the bar. She edged the Land Rover up to eighty, focusing her will on negotiating the ever thinning traffic and not on worry over her nephew by marriage, slowing when the speed limits changed.

Less than an hour later, she crossed into Dillard and turned left onto Betty's Creek Road, following it to the private drive leading to Isolde's home. The SUV's tires squealed against asphalt as Hawthorne bore down on the brakes and skidded to a stop outside her niece's house. She left the vehicle running and darted out its door, racing up the sidewalk to test the front door's handle. Relief jolted through her on finding it unlocked. She slid her Glock 19 silently from its holster and entered quietly. The low notes of Beethoven flowed from the direction of the sitting area Mathias preferred, drawing her attention as she stepped stealthily through the house.

He was sitting on the sofa facing the fire with his back to the door, so quiet and still her heart leapt in her chest. *Goddess, please spare his life.* Surely even Isolde would not stoop to killing her husband, regardless of the threat he presented.

He lifted a blue hand-thrown mug from the end table, and Hawthorne exhaled her relief in a nearly silent sigh.

He turned and glanced at her. "Hawthorne. What are you doing here?"

She holstered the Glock. "Searching for Isolde."

"She's not been home in days, not since the last time we spoke." He stood and faced her, his brows knit together. "To be honest, if she hadn't come home by morning, I was going to contact you to begin a search."

"Has anyone else been by? Friends, distant family, other Daughters?"

He shook his head. "Not a soul. In fact, it's been unusually quiet around here."

Hawthorne nodded. Such was to be expected, given the nature of Isolde's role within the People, and perhaps her role in the Order. "It is not safe for you to remain here, Mathias. You must pack quickly and leave as soon as you can."

"Sure, if you think I should." He eyed her carefully, seemed to hesitate over his next words. "Any reason I shouldn't wait for Isolde to come home first?"

"She may be the one seeking you harm." When he tensed,

she added, "I would spare you such knowledge if I could."

"I know." He rubbed a hand over his eyes, pinched the bridge of his nose. "I know you would, Hawthorne. Can you hang around for a while until I'm ready to leave?"

"I had planned on it, nephew," she said with a gentle smile.

She followed him to his room and stood guard while he packed, her thoughts a whirling dervish in her mind. Perhaps Isolde's heart had not hardened so much that she would eliminate her husband and perhaps it had; yet the fact remained that Mathias remained unfettered. Isolde's more immediate threat must be something else, or someone else.

Such as the one who sought to connect her definitively to the Eternal Order.

Hawthorne cursed under her breath and yanked out her phone, dialing her house's landline. When no one answered, she went through individual cell numbers, letting each one ring until voice mail picked up. Colin and Brigid, Ruby and Aaron. No one answered. She shoved her phone into her pants pocket with trembling hands as a well of panic bubbled up in her gut, engulfing her in a tide of nerves and fear.

Mathias packed quickly and secured the house. Hawthorne saw him safely to his vehicle, then jumped into the still-running Land Rover and pointed it toward Tellowee.

Isolde's leverage wasn't information. It was people, and the threat she aimed to eliminate was none other than her mother's only sister.

AARON SWAM into consciousness through the steady throb of pain pounding like an industrial asphalt drill into the back of his skull. He touched unsteady fingers to the root of the pain and came away with blood. His vision wavered and nausea roiled upward. Concussion probably, no doubt thanks to Isolde, unless Ruby or Colin or Brigid had taken a sudden notion to off him.

Which was possible.

He touched the wound again, prodding the tender flesh, and hissed out a curse when his fingers aggravated the cut. Nothing broken, but damn, it hurt.

He pushed to a stand on legs that wobbled and threatened to fold. Lali's bed was empty, the chair he'd used for reading overturned, Hawthorne's books scattered along the concrete floor. The dim echo of a scream reached him. Lali had screamed. No, he thought as a second scream rang through the house, Lali was screaming *now*. He had to get to her, had to help her.

He turned sharply on his heel. A wave of blackness swam over him, sending pinpricks of light through his vision. He steadied himself against his knees, stood upright slowly when his vision returned, and made his way on shaky limbs toward the vault's entrance.

Damn bookcases jumped out in front of him more often than not.

He fell against them, knocking books and weapons loose, and almost tripped over a rack of various sized sticks that slithered out of their rungs and found their way under his feet. Hawthorne was gonna kill him for hurting her precious sticks. She carried one with her wherever she went, seemed like. Always pointing one of the damn things at him. A man couldn't even create a graphic novel without her sticking one in his stomach.

He shook his head and blackness rose, lapping at his mind like a tidal wave with a heavy undertow. Lali. He had to get to Lali. Hawthorne's sticks could wait.

His brain stuck on those words. Hawthorne's sticks. They were a jumbled mess on the floor right in front of him. He chose one about a yard in length and stabbed an end into the floor, using it as a cane, and stumbled out of the vault toward Lali's diminishing screams.

HAWTHORNE PARKED her vehicle two blocks from her home and walked the rest of the way in, her weapons holstered. Moving fast was a higher priority. If weapons were needed, they were readily at hand, though her own body often proved weapon enough.

She circled around her nearest neighbor's yard, avoiding the open sidewalk as she eased around landscaping and fixtures. She hunkered down behind the stairs leading to her neighbor's front porch and observed for long moments. From the exterior, the house appeared empty. No lights shone from within or without, no trace of movement stirred in the windows, and an unnatural hush hung over the area.

She crept toward the front of her house and found Colin lying facedown in the hedge near the walkway, out of sight though not hidden well. Her probing fingers found a hard lump at the base of his skull and a thready pulse. He stirred silently under her hand, making not the slightest moan as he rose to consciousness.

Such was the training of a Son.

Pride rose within her for the man Colin had become. He and Levi had been friends since her great-grandson's arrival in the States at the age of six. They had grown up together and spent hours romping through her home and the surrounding countryside. It had been a pleasure to watch them become men, to instill the values of her ancestors in them even as they became individuals, strong and determined and more than worthy of their stature as beloved Sons.

When Aaron had needed protection, Colin had been her first pick. She trusted him as well as she trusted her daughters and their progeny, down to Levi and Ruby and Lali. He was a good man and nearly as much a member of her family as they. How any mother could abandon one such as him was beyond her.

She leaned down and placed her lips next to his ear. "Allow three minutes to pass before locating your team."

His nod was so slight as to be imperceptible. She squeezed his shoulder and rose, picked her way silently through the frost-coated grass and up the steps to the porch, clinging to the railing, testing each wooden slat carefully before placing her full weight upon it.

The front door stood slightly ajar, its lock scratched so minutely only she would notice the scars. Hawthorne drew her sword from its sheath and placed a hand upon the door, pushing lightly. It swung open easily, baring the empty, shadowed foyer to her gaze. She peeked inside, listened attentively for the slightest noise.

Lali's piercing scream sounded from the entrance to the basement halfway across the house's width. The noise cut off abruptly. Hawthorne pushed the tension from her muscles, relaxing in spite of the leaden beat of her heart and the oppressive silence of her home.

Ahead of her, the floor squeaked.

She slipped through the entrance into the foyer quiet as a church mouse and stationed herself in the doorway leading to the living room. A sallow light filtered through the open front door into the hallway, piercing the deep shadow. She trained her eyes on the area from which the squeak had come, not far from the entrance to the basement, and waited.

And was rewarded for her patience when Isolde moved silently into the thin light, Lali clasped firmly to her chest.

Hawthorne stepped into her niece's path, her sword held point down. "It is late for a visit."

Isolde halted, her face an impassive mask. "I would have knocked had you been home."

"Perhaps," Hawthorne acknowledged with a nod. "Or perhaps you would have snuck into my bedroom and slain me as I lay sleeping."

"Death is not my objective tonight, Hawthorne."

"Then you will not mind allowing my granddaughter to go free."

A thin smile touched Isolde's cold lips. "She goes with me. After all this time, can you begrudge me the gift of this child, a daughter to carry on my line and memory?"

Lali's eyes went wide above the hand Isolde held firmly over her mouth.

"She is not your daughter," Hawthorne said, "nor have I the right to gift her to another."

"Ah, yes. Ruby the Unready." Isolde's smile grew into true amusement. "She is a tad indisposed at the moment, certainly not in any shape to negotiate Lali's future."

The groan of a wooden tread drifted from the basement. Isolde shifted slightly, angling her back to the wall. Hawthorne hefted her sword in both hands and rested it upon her left shoulder.

"Lali's future is with her family, with me and Aaron and Ruby, when she is able."

Isolde scoffed as she faced Hawthorne again. "Aaron," she spat. "A mortal man raising an immortal Daughter? What were you thinking, Hawthorne?"

"That a mortal man can love as well and true as a Son."

Isolde laughed. "Is that so?"

"It is so." Behind Isolde, Aaron eased into view, bracing a hand against the corner of the wall and his weight on a hanbō. Hawthorne monitored his progress as he teetered down the hallway, careful to keep her gaze on Isolde and Isolde's attention on herself. "Is your irrational distrust of men the reason you aligned yourself with the Eternal Order?"

"I aligned myself with the Order, as you put it, in order to prevent a travesty." Isolde jerked Lali upward, tightening her grip. "This child you profess to love will have her immortality broken should the Prophecy come to pass, and with that comes frailty and death. The path of her life will no longer be hers to decide."

"Have our lives ever been our own, Isolde? Truly?" Aaron lifted the hanbō slowly over his head. Hawthorne shook her head slightly. Goddess help her, he was going to use it as a stick, a

221

strategy that would be useful in any situation other than this one, with Lali held so tightly in Isolde's grasp, inches away from losing her life to the twist of hard hands. Had the dear man learned nothing from her? "The People were forever altered when the Sisters were cursed. A vengeful god set us on this path against the wills of our mothers, against all reason and sense and hope. The Prophecy rights that wrong for all of us."

"The Prophecy takes what is rightfully ours and delivers us into the hands of our enemies." Isolde loosened her grip on Lali and her expression melted into one of pleading. "Why do you not understand?"

"I do, beloved niece. I understand that your fear of dying pushes you into a place even your thirst for power does not reach." Hawthorne swung her sword off of her shoulder, falling into an attack position with her left foot to the rear and her arms raised, pointing the tip of the sword toward Isolde's heart. Aaron swayed unsteadily as he mirrored her position, with the hanbō pointed a foot away from the space between Isolde's shoulder blades. "This, I can remedy."

Isolde drew Lali ever closer, tightening her grip. Lali closed her eyes and panted sharp breaths through her nose, her face pale and tense in the moonlight washing through the open door.

"You would not dare," Isolde said, "not with your precious progeny in the way."

"Think you that I could not strike without harming her?" Hawthorne allowed humor to bleed into her expression. "Yet again, you underestimate the abilities of another to protect a loved one."

Aaron leapt, shoving the hanbō into Isolde's back with all of his strength. Isolde jolted forward, her grip on Lali slipping enough for the young girl to break free and drop to the floor in a writhing heap. She scrambled around Isolde's legs, kicking and slapping as Isolde reached for her. Hawthorne surged forward, lashing out with the butt of her sword. It connected with the crown of Isolde's head with a solid thud and she crumpled to the floor, nearly taking a skidding Lali with her.

Lali flung herself at Aaron, sobbing his name. He dropped to his knees and caught her. Over her head, his eyes met Hawthorne's. In them, she saw the love they shared for Lali and a steady determination to protect the child at all costs.

Colin burst through the front door and skidded to a stop just as Ruby stumbled down the stairs from the second floor, clutching her head in one hand and the stair's railing with the other.

"The cavalry's here." Aaron dropped onto his ass and teetered to the side. "Thank God."

Hawthorne breathed out a laugh. "You did well, Aaron Kesselman."

"Yeah. Gotta lay down now."

Aaron collapsed onto the floor, taking Lali with him. Hawthorne's heart leapt into her throat. She raced through the hallway and knelt by his side, running unsteady hands over the cuts on the back of his head. Her hand came away bloody. Nausea roiled through her stomach, lockstep with the first tendrils of anger. How many times had Isolde hit him?

Colin squatted down on the other side of Aaron's prone form. "I called an ambulance, told them to come in silent. We'll get everybody sorted out."

Hawthorne nodded and curled her fingers into a fist around Aaron's blood. He lay silently on the floor, his breaths uneven, Lali cradled at his side.

Ruby slumped onto the bare floor beside Hawthorne. "Looks like Isolde gave us all goose eggs."

"And received one of her own." Hawthorne tugged Ruby into a one-armed hug and touched Lali's disheveled locks with the other. The little girl clung to Aaron's shirt, her thin shoulders heaving, her sobs muffled. "We shall be safe now, all of us."

"Thanks to Aaron," Ruby said.

"Thanks to each of you," Hawthorne corrected. "Though Aaron played his part well, for a mere mortal."

Ruby snorted.

Aaron lifted one eyelid and peered solemnly at her. "I heard that."

Hawthorne laughed and pressed a tender kiss to his beautiful mouth. This man had saved Lali. Though he had barely been able to stand steadily, he had collected his wits and acted wisely.

Isolde stirred, her clothes rustling, disturbing the stillness surrounding them.

Colin pushed himself into a stand. "I got this."

Hawthorne observed the casual way the young man clocked Isolde on the head with his massive fist and dragged the errant Daughter's limp body out the front door. Yes, she had trusted the right man with the protection of her loved ones.

Her gaze strayed to Aaron, pale under his natural tan, his arm curled around Lali, protecting her even as he lay upon the floor unable to protect himself. Hawthorne had trusted him to follow her lead and he had, in turn, trusted her to provide the correct guidance. Perhaps hope yet remained between them.

# EIGHTEEN

AARON REMEMBERED very little of the next few hours. Most of it was one endless blur of people and light and noise. The paramedics who checked him over, the short ride to the hospital, the frazzled nurse who assessed the damage Isolde had done to all of them and clucked her tongue. "Been a madhouse around here tonight," she told Hawthorne. "Had an attack on the Oracle. India Furia. The Blade's dealing with it now."

He had no idea what they were talking about. Thankfully, no one expected him to. His head throbbed and his vision wavered and his shoulders were stiff where Isolde had bludgeoned him. Lali clung to him, refusing to let go, and finally, everybody stopped trying to separate them.

Hours later, after x-rays and another check by a yawning doctor, Hawthorne took him and Ruby and Lali home in her SUV, leaving Colin, Brigid, and the rest of the security team behind for further care. Isolde had stabbed one of the women and broken one man's arm. Brigid had a concussion. Colin had skated through with a knot on his head and a couple of bruises.

Aaron tried to find compassion around the ache in his head. Those men and women had been injured guarding him and Lali. He slumped against the rear seat of Hawthorne's SUV, shifting into a comfortable position. Maybe when his own concussion healed, he'd find some gratitude for their help. For now, he was simply grateful they'd all made it through Isolde's attack alive.

Lali rested her head on his arm, fast asleep, her tiny fingers clutching the flannel shirt Hawthorne had helped him into. Tears stained the little girl's cheeks and her face was pale in the predawn light. When he'd woken to find her gone, all he'd thought of was finding her again. Determination had propelled him in staggering zigzags through the vault and up the stairs. Thank God he'd taken a stick with him, though he'd intended it more for balance than anything.

When he'd rounded the corner into the hallway and realized that Isolde held Lali, his heart had frozen in his chest. It was a miracle the woman hadn't heard him clamoring around. At the time, the tiniest noise had seemed to rebound through the air, as loud as a shrill siren over the thunder of his heartbeat.

And Hawthorne had stood there, casually blocking Isolde's path, showing him what to do as if they'd worked together hundreds of times before. She'd trusted him to help her, trusted *him*, the man who had rejected her truth over and over again.

*That vault.*

What little energy he had left seeped from him in a mad rush. His head lolled on the back of the seat and he closed his eyes against the blur of the passing scenery. Sleep first and then they'd talk, concussion be damned. It was past time for them to sort out their problems, long past time for him to repay Hawthorne's trust and patience with a little of his own.

They ended up bunking down in the same room together. Aaron tucked a sleeping Lali into the little girl's bed while Ruby dragged out an electrically inflatable mattress and Hawthorne made the rounds in the house, securing it. She entered Lali's room carrying extra pillows and bedding, and refused to let him help make up the air mattress or move it close to Lali's side of the bed. Finally, they all slipped into bed, Ruby with Lali, and Hawthorne and Aaron on the floor next to them, cushioned from its unforgiving hardness by the portable bed.

He held her close, ignoring the pain stabbing through his temples. She skimmed gentle hands over him and the tension lingering after a raw, hectic night slid away.

"I'm ok," he murmured. "Doctor said so."

"A concussion is not ok, Aaron. Had I anticipated Isolde's actions..."

He pressed a finger to her soft lips. "None of that, now. Nobody could've known she'd come here."

"I should have."

"No, Hawthorne. Even you couldn't have known that."

Her breath feathered across his face. "You did well tonight."

He huffed out a laugh. Pain rocketed through his sinuses and he winced. "I had no idea what I was doing. Thank God Lali had the presence of mind to come get me."

"She led you to the vault?"

"Yeah, through the walls." He stifled a yawn. "Had no idea those passages were there."

She brushed his hair back from his forehead. "We shall discuss the house's layout on the morrow, love."

"Among other things."

"Shush, now, and find your rest. Lali will rise early."

He ran his hands down Hawthorne's slender back, tucking her tightly against him. It felt so good to hold her again, just hold her and share her warmth. "Promise me one thing."

"Yes?"

"Promise you'll never leave us again."

She tucked a hand under his t-shirt, curved it over the bare skin of his waist. "I shan't, not unless it is unavoidable."

Behind them, Ruby shifted restlessly. The rustle of covers reminded Aaron that he and Hawthorne weren't alone. He closed his eyes as Morpheus' steady hand tugged him under. Tomorrow, he promised himself. Tomorrow, he would choose to believe, not because of any proof Hawthorne offered him, but because of the strength of her word and the love he held for her. He yawned, mumbled an indistinct *I love you* into her hair, and fell asleep, secure in the promise of her love.

MARIA CAME IN early the next day and fixed a huge breakfast. Hawthorne heaped food onto plates for Aaron and Lali and Ruby, so thankful was she to have them safely at home.

The night before, Colin had dropped a bound and gagged Isolde off at the IECS guard station at the main entrance. She'd been taken to a secure room deep within the mountain housing the Archives, there to await the judgment of the Council of Seven.

Hawthorne placed her own plate of food on the kitchen table and took the chair next to Aaron. If the Blade's beloved son had not been in the hospital, Hawthorne had no doubt Rebecca Upton would, at that moment, be knocking on the front door, demanding an explanation. Soon, Hawthorne would be forced to make a decision regarding the position on the Council once filled by Isolde.

As one of the eldest Daughters in the line of Bagda, if not *the* eldest, Hawthorne's duty paved a clear path through her future. She had eschewed it once in favor of Isolde, and could now no longer indulge in the luxury of passing duty's mantle to another.

She cast a wary glance at Aaron from the corner of her eye and stifled a sigh. Duty assumed many forms, but it could not be forced. She had not submitted her will to her lover when she had trusted him to help her defeat Isolde and rescue Lali. The love growing within her would wither without that trust, yet how could she extend it knowing he did not trust her in return?

His arm brushed hers as he reached for Lali's napkin. The fabric of his shirt clung to the sweater Hawthorne wore, tugging at it much as he tugged at her. They could not go on as they had been, with the truth an unscalable, impenetrable wall between them.

She seized her chance to knock a small portion of that wall

down during Lali's nap. When the little one had fallen into a deep sleep, Hawthorne coaxed Aaron away from the guard he kept. She entwined her fingers with his and led him quietly down the stairs. "You will spoil her with your attention."

His shoulders lifted in a casual shrug. "She deserves a little spoiling. Besides, it's not putting me out to care for her."

"What you do goes well beyond care. She will cling to you as long as you allow it."

"Then let her cling," he said in a flat voice. "I'm not pushing her away, not after everything she's been through."

Hawthorne paused outside the door to the basement. "Pushing her away and encouraging her to stand on her own are two different things, Aaron."

"She's four, hardly old enough to stand on her own, as you put it."

"She's a Daughter."

"And? It's not like she has to go out and fight the world right now, is it?"

"Did she not just do so?"

"That was different."

"Not as much as you believe." Hawthorne opened the door and flipped on the stairwell light. "Come. We have much to discuss."

She led him down the narrow stairs, past the now-hidden entrance to the passages snaking through the walls, and into the basement. "I bought this house upon Ruby's birth more than half a century ago. The owners, a mortal Daughter and her mate, had refitted the basement as a fallout shelter. I expanded on their work, reinforcing the walls, adding this door and a tougher security system and, eventually, a series of climate control units. Place your right-hand thumb here."

Aaron scrubbed his thumb on his thigh and pressed it to the screen of the security system. "Why am I doing this?"

"So that you may access the vault at will." She flipped quickly through the steps for setting a new entrance code. "For now, your password is 'puppy.' You may change it, if you like."

One corner of his mouth lifted into a crooked smile. "Puppy's fine. I didn't get a chance to really explore this last night."

"You will." She swung the door open, felt for the light switches, and sighed as the light illuminated the weapons scattered across the floor. "I see Isolde had her fun."

"I'm afraid that was all me. She whacked me pretty hard and I sort of staggered through here." He rubbed the back of his head in an absent-minded gesture. "You're lucky I didn't bring the shelving down. Think I left the books I was reading near Lali's bed."

Hawthorne paused in the middle of gathering staffs of various sizes from the floor and sorting them into their proper holders. "Oh? Which ones caught your attention?"

"The leather-bound volumes near the entrance. Like this one." He tapped the glass case holding the earliest book in her collection. "Fascinating stuff."

"Hmm."

His gaze met hers, truly open for the first time. "Did you write them?"

"I did."

"All of them?"

She turned away from him, unwilling to witness the disbelief she was sure would bleed into his expression, and gave her attention to the weapons she had collected over the years. "Yes."

He tapped the case again. "Even this one here?"

"Yes." Her hand tightened on her first hanbō, the wood worn smooth from hours of practice under the tutelage of an ancient sensei who had once lived in a remote village on a tiny island near what was now Japan. "I began that one a few years after my mother's death, once justice had been served."

"So it's a diary." His voice was as careful as the words he chose. "How old were you when you started it?"

"Perhaps sixteen, before I learned to keep a careful record

of the date on which events occurred." Curiosity pressed at her, outweighing the uncertainty. She pivoted on her heel and faced him, released a breath she had not known she held at the acceptance in his expression. "So much time has passed since then."

"Too much. You mind if we sit down? I'm getting a little dizzy, surrounded by all this history."

More likely, his head hurt and he was too stubbornly proud to admit it.

They wound up in the corner of the vault where Lali's emergency sleeping quarters were set up. Aaron picked up the rag doll Lali slept with and dropped onto the bed, sitting with his back against the wall and the doll in his lap.

Hawthorne righted the chair he had used the evening before, retrieved the two volumes lying scattered on the floor. A few pages were bent, though none were torn and the binding held firm. She smoothed out the pages and placed the books on the chair.

He patted the space next to him. "Plenty of room here."

"We must talk."

"Yeah, I guess. Might as well be comfortable while we do it, though." He patted the bed again. "Let me hold you."

A plea she could never resist, not when it came from him. She crawled onto the small bed and curled into him with her head on his chest, snuggling within his comforting embrace.

"I have a feeling there's more to your story than what you've told me, a lot more." He murmured the words into her hair, brushed his cheek across the top of her head. "I don't get how it's all connected yet, but a lot of people have handed me different pieces of it, like the prophecy Isolde was talking about last night and the goddess everybody refers to and how a lot of women around here claim to be really old."

"It is an ancient tale, Aaron, and a complicated one. Are you certain you wish to hear it?"

"If it helps me understand you, yeah, I am." He rubbed his

cheek over her hair again, savoring the silky slide of it against his skin. "Tell me."

She sighed into his chest, breathing in his warm scent. "A hundred hundred years ago, seven sisters lived with their parents. They were part of a band of nomadic hunter-gatherers living, we believe, in what is now Anatolia. They called themselves the People."

She condensed the Legend of Beginnings into its most basic parts. The deaths of Mother and Father at the hands of the men of the People. The enslavement of the men's wives in the name of safety or property or some other ideal not yet discovered. The Sanctuary the Seven Sisters sought where they tamed wild horses and honed their skills with the bow and spear. The dream the eldest sister had that led the young women back to the People, where they avenged their parents' deaths and freed the women of the People. The curse laid upon them by the god An, who heard the cries of the men as they died, but ignored the injustices those men had perpetrated. And finally, the nature of the curse, that the Sisters and their daughters would live on, forever without the comfort of love or the ability to bear sons.

"Wait, you mean after all the sisters went through, he cursed them anyway?" Aaron shook his head. "That's just wrong."

"Do not fret, love. Ki, the Lady Goddess, was unable to ignore the plight of the Sisters. She tweaked the curse, allowing each one to break it if she could submit her will to the man who held her heart. Thereafter, that woman would be mortal and could bear the sons denied her by an angry, ignorant god."

He was silent for a long time, so long Hawthorne's nerves grew short and frayed. "Later, it is said, Ki bestowed a prophecy upon the People. In it, she detailed a way that the curse might be broken once and for all."

"That was what Isolde was talking about, wasn't it?"

"Yes. The Prophecy of Light. Its existence passed from reality into memory and then to rumor. Until recently, the People had no concrete knowledge of it. Not even the eldest of us could ascertain the truth of its existence, as it was so closely guarded before it was lost."

"Back up a little bit and explain this submission thing to me." His hand found hers where it rested on his stomach, pressing her closely to him. "So, a Daughter has to love someone before the curse can be broken and then what? I mean, what happens to her? Is she still immortal?"

"Once the curse is broken, she becomes mortal, free to love and live as she wishes."

"But it can only happen when she falls in love."

"There must also be trust."

His head made a gentle thud as he rested it upon the wall. "Well, damn."

She twisted around, peered at his expression with concern. "What is it, love? Is your wound aching?"

"No, I'm fine. My head is anyway." He breathed out a quiet, sad laugh. "Don't think my heart's gonna make it, though."

"What do you mean?" She sat up and patted his chest as alarm shot through her. Had Isolde harmed him in some other way, some way that could not be detected by modern science? "Should I call the doctor?"

"No. Hey, cut that out." He grabbed her hands, holding them to his chest, stopping her from running them over him in the hopes of discovering what ailed him. "There's nothing wrong with my physical heart, Hawthorne. I was talking about my feelings, the way you've wormed your way inside and taken over until I can barely go a minute without thinking about you and needing you. God, I love you so much."

"You love me?" She sat back on her heels. "Truly?"

"Yeah, truly. I'm so, so sorry I didn't believe you before."

She inhaled deeply, searching for the correct words. "Many men do not, regardless of what is in their not-physical heart."

"Could you... Do you think you could ever love me enough to trust me like that, to become mortal and live with me and make a family together?"

233

She glanced away. "The love is there."

"But not the trust. Damn me for not believing you the first time, for not giving you a chance to explain." He scrubbed his hands over his face in short, sharp motions. "So what happens now? You go on being young Hawthorne and I grow old, wishing I could have a do over and make things right between us?"

"It would not be the first time such a relationship has existed among the People."

"Yeah? Well, those people weren't us." He dropped his hands and stared at her with such bleakness in his chocolate eyes, it twisted into her heart like a thin-bladed knife. "I'm not a fool, Hawthorne. I know what'll happen. Eventually, I'll be nothing but a burden to you and you'll wonder what you ever saw in the foolish old man I'll become. I don't think I can handle watching you learn to hate me."

She said nothing. There was nothing she *could* say. When a Daughter could not bring herself to trust the man who had captured her heart, it seldom ended well. Every school child heard the tales whispered from ear to ear, a warning to the unwise. *Give your heart carefully,* mothers schooled their immortal daughters, *else your love will wither before trust is earned and the curse shall never be broken.*

Had she not cautioned her own daughters thusly?

Yet every Daughter, or mostly so, wished to find the man who could earn her trust, a man who would love her fiercely and give her the sons denied her by a vengeful god.

"You will not leave," she told him.

His smile was gentle, tender. "Is that a command or a request?"

"It is what it is. If you leave, we shall never know if I can learn to trust you."

"True." He reached out, drew her in until she rested against him, heart to heart. "How long will you let me cling to hope?"

"As long as you can stand doing so." She curled her fingers into his shirt, willing her heart to trust where, she was very afraid, trust would never again grow. "Come. Lali will wake soon. If you are not there when she does, she will become frightened."

"What happened to making her learn to stand on her own?"

"She is four. Such will come in time."

He tilted her chin up, cupped her face in his graceful hand. "I love you."

"I know." She pressed a testing kiss to his lips, and another, simply because she could. "I know, my love."

They made their way to Lali's room hand in hand, uncertainty stretching between them. As they passed the painting displayed in the alcove on the second floor, Hawthorne sent a weary prayer to the Lady Goddess.

*Please help my heart learn to trust.*

It was the first time she had ever uttered that plea in her long, lonely life. She suspected it would not be the last.

# NINETEEN

AARON'S HEART teetered between the love he felt for Hawthorne and disbelief over her story. Even after her explanation, he had a hard time buying it. That she believed it, lived it, really, there could be no doubt. He'd known her long enough to understand her basic nature. Hell, it hadn't taken him three days to know that whatever else Hawthorne might be, a liar she was not.

As he alternated his time between helping with Thanksgiving preparations and caring for Lali, his mind lingered more and more on the one reason he had for not giving in.

It had nothing to do with the incredulity of her story or the thinness of the evidence she'd laid before him. He had a sneaky feeling that the more time he spent in her vault, the less those would be a problem. No, what bothered him the most was the fact that if everything she said was true, they could never be together. Forever for a mortal man was only a few decades. For an immortal Daughter who'd already lived nearly two thousand years, eternity took on a whole new meaning.

Believing that she was immortal meant coming to terms with having to give her up, not in a few decades when death claimed them, but in a few years when he began to age and she remained forever trapped in her youth.

He rubbed absent-mindedly over the ache gathering in the region around his heart and, for the umpteenth time, cursed his own lack of faith. The memory of Pop's voice drifted through his mind, and with it came the antiseptic stench of the hospital and a hopeless sense of impending loss. Pop had been weeks from death, his strength siphoned off trying to fight the cancer eating him alive from the inside out. His faith had never flagged, not once, and it had pissed Aaron off. His own faith was being tested under the twin pressures of his father's illness and the growing knowledge that his marriage would fail, and there'd been nothing he could do about either one.

One day, sitting there reading a dog-eared copy of *The Old Man and the Sea* to his father, his mind had wandered from the story and Aaron had snapped. How could a merciful god allow a good man to wither and die?

"Death comes to everything, Aaron," Pop had said.

"Not like this, Pop. You don't deserve this."

Pop's hand had twitched against the sterile white of the sheet he lay on. "No man deserves the death he receives. God has nothing to do with it. It just is, like the sun setting over the ocean or the moon hanging in the sky."

Aaron's laugh had been bitter and hard.

"Laugh if you want, my son, but remember this. Without death, there can be no life, no rebirth, no beginning, and without beginnings, we have no reason to hope or believe. Faith is what carries us through. Every morning when you get up, do you worry that the sun might not rise? No. That simple faith tells you to worry about something else."

"That's not faith, Pop, that's science."

"Science, faith." Pop's hand had twitched again. "There's not such a big difference between the two. Use your brain a little less and your heart a little more. And pray. You young people never pray enough."

A few days later, Pop drifted into a coma, and not long after, he was gone. Aaron had never found his faith, not the way Pop had wanted him to. Praying had gotten easier, yes, but faith? It wasn't such an easy thing to come by with the world falling apart around him.

And now, that lack of faith had come back to haunt him.

He reclined on Lali's bed, brushing a hand over her fine hair as she slept deeply, sprawled across his lap. She clung fiercely to him, had since she'd scrambled away from Isolde two days before. Since then, she'd been subdued, quiet, her eyes wide and watchful. Lali's faith had been broken, too, and it hurt, knowing he'd had a hand in it.

Was this what Pop had felt when he'd lectured Aaron about faith, this quiet pain of knowing you'd destroyed your child's ability to believe?

If he'd been stronger, Lali would never have been taken. If he'd trusted Hawthorne the first time she'd told him of her past, when everything between them was still new and good, he would've had time to learn how to protect the little girl, or at least to be more cautious. But no, he'd fallen back on his natural skepticism and refused to entertain the possibility of what had seemed like an impossibility. Worse, he'd allowed his relationship with Jeanne to color his view of Hawthorne, as if the women were in any way similar.

He was pretty sure the only things they had in common were their sex and him. They didn't even live in the same reality.

Jeanne's delusions had been an excuse, a way for him to protect his still-fragile heart, and like an idiot, he'd been blind to his own reasoning, ignorant of his own lack of faith.

It had destroyed the one hope Hawthorne had of living a normal life. How could a man profess to love a woman, believe it with all his will, and still be the root of her deepest misery?

Though she wouldn't say it directly, he knew she loved him. After everything he'd done to her, all the doubts and hurt he'd caused, how could she let him into her bed otherwise? How could she make love to him night after night without loving him, knowing their time ticked steadily toward its end because he hadn't been able to believe in her?

Because of his lack of faith.

He smoothed his hand over Lali once more, gently eased himself out from under her, and dropped a kiss to her forehead. There were no easy answers here, no paths he could take to redeem himself and erase the past. He would work harder at believing Hawthorne and find a way to regain her trust. That was all he could do now.

Building trust. Hadn't they been doing that all along?

He snagged a baby monitor and crept quietly out of the room. Somewhere buried deep in Hawthorne's past, there had to be a way to repair his faith, and with it her trust. Two thousand years of accumulated knowledge lay beneath his feet. It had to be good for something.


THE HECTIC RUSH of Thanksgiving absorbed Hawthorne's attention, drawing it from the quagmire of her relationship with Aaron. What was left of her far-flung family assembled in her home, accepting his role in her life with a surprising equanimity as gossip passed from mouth to ear and the meal was presented and eaten. No one looked askance when Lali clung to him, no one dared question his place at the opposite end of the table, in the seat of honor usually reserved for a Daughter's husband.

No one asked if she had laid claim to her mortality through his love.

*Would that it were so.*

The thought whispered through her heart. How she ached to be with him, sharing a life, loving him, carrying the son denied her by that wretched curse. Her gaze fell on the sons borne by her daughters or their daughters, through generations of her female progeny, seated at irregular intervals around the massive table in her formal dining room. She adored them all, down to the last child, but it wasn't enough, would never be enough until she was blessed with a son of her own.

Her needing time drew near.

In a few short weeks, she would ovulate and enter into a short frenzy of need so strong she would be unable to deny it should Aaron remain. They would copulate again and again, drawn by the heat of lust that overtook a Daughter this one time each year, a side effect of the immortality laid unwillingly upon them all, and she would in all likelihood become pregnant with his child.

Would he wish for such a circumstance or would he spurn her, leaving her to raise their offspring alone?

Her gaze met his down the long table, across the plates of food and the centerpieces of flowers, and through the curious stares of her kin. His face softened, lighting with the love he claimed to carry for her, a love not quite deep enough to extend into trust.

Why did his disbelief linger?

She lowered her gaze, hiding the hurt clawing its way through her. She was a fool to continue their charade, in spite of his attempts to understand, to know. The day before, he had snuck into the vault and retrieved the volumes he had been reading when Isolde had bludgeoned him, along with a stack of back issues of *The World of the People*, and then the questions had begun. Why is the Sandby borg site significant? What is the Eye of Marnan? Which Sister are you descended from? Why are Sons so protected? How do you worship the Lady Goddess? And on and on in the bits and pieces of time they had snatched since she had led him to her vault.

He was trying. It should have been enough. Much as her grandsons were no substitute for the son she desired, though, Aaron's attempts to believe were not as good as belief itself.

And still, she could not bring herself to push him away.

Was she so desperate for love that she lowered herself to this? Was she not worthy of a man who loved her enough to accept her past and earned her trust because of it?

Or had her heart discovered a truth her mind refused to

acknowledge, that Aaron was the one man she had met to whom she could actually submit her will, if only she were patient enough?

A slight breath stuttered from her chest. After two millennia, her patience had at last petered out.

She peeked at him again and her heart melted. He and Lali were bent toward one another, their heads nearly touching as they talked softly. The two had been inseparable since Isolde's ill-begotten attempt to kidnap Lali and thus gain leverage over Hawthorne. It had not been a bad plan, all in all, and might have worked if Isolde had not discounted Aaron's fierce love for the little girl, a love that was returned equally and openly.

Aaron had proven himself worthy of the little girl's faith and continued to do so each time he placed Lali's well-being above his own. Another man might have hesitated in that hallway. A weaker one would never have dragged himself after another man's child the way Aaron had.

Hawthorne stilled. Here, she trusted him implicitly. Her fingers clutched around the napkin in her lap, wrinkling it into an untidy wad as she prodded the emotion. Yes, she trusted him with Lali, enough to concede to his reason and logic where her granddaughter was concerned.

She *trusted* him.

Her lips lifted into a smile and laughter bubbled up in her chest, spilling out. The table fell abruptly silent and the shocked gazes of her kin turned toward her.

The trust was small and would never be enough to break the curse on its own, would never be enough for her to subsume her will to his, but it was a start.

Aaron grinned and raised his half-full glass of water. "A toast. To Hawthorne, the matriarch of our family, and to the love and laughter she shares with us all."

Chairs scraped back, scuffing against the carpet as her family stood, raised their glasses, and drank to the woman who had finally learned to trust.

THE DAY WENT much as any other family gathering. Hawthorne played the gracious host as her family came and went. She cuddled children and discussed finances with their parents, listened attentively and doled out advice whether her family wanted it or not.

Through it all, Aaron never strayed far from her sight, as if he knew she drew comfort from his presence.

Near the fall of evening, Levi stopped by with an unwelcome surprise in tow, a familiar looking young woman and her son. The woman was nearly a foot shorter than Levi with dark waves of hair floating down her back and gently rounded curves. The boy had his mother's silver eyes, a like intelligence shining from them, and was slender as a whip. His hand was tucked in Levi's, though when he saw Hawthorne, he dropped it and threw his thin shoulders back, meeting her gaze steadily.

Envy tugged at Hawthorne's heart. Did this mortal woman know how lucky she was to have such a son?

Hawthorne rose from her seat on the living room couch, her gaze as cold as the frost gathering on the grass each morning. Beside her, Aaron rose as well, and with him Lali, who gasped.

Levi met Hawthorne's gaze with a level stare of his own. "Nana, this is Sera Noland and her son, Peter."

"Petey!" Lali ran to the surprised little boy and threw her arms around his waist, nearly knocking him over with her exuberance. "I been waiting and waiting for you."

Petey sent a helpless look to his mother, who looked at Levi, who winked at the little boy and said, "Peter, this is Lali, my cousin."

"Ah. Um. Hi?" Peter laid a tentative hand on her shoulder and patted gently. "Um, maybe you could not squeeze so hard."

Lali unwound her arms and slipped her hand into his, beaming up at him. "I gots so much to tells you. My puppy came to live with me and I gots to carry a sword and the mean cushion came, just like the pretty lady said she would. Do you want to play dolls with me?"

"Ah." He glanced up at Levi again, then at Hawthorne, and shrugged. "Sure."

Hawthorne halted the little girl's headlong rush. "Lali, wait. Who is the pretty lady?"

"You know." Lali's huge gray eyes widened. "The pretty lady. She comes to visit me sometimes through the window when my tummy aches here." She patted her heart. "She sings to me and tells me stories about stuff I'm supposed to do, like finding my puppy and my Petey. She tolded me I had to hide when the mean cushion came and hurted my sitter and my puppy."

A tight fist of fear encircled Hawthorne's heart, squeezing until her breath faltered. "A woman has been sneaking into this house?"

Lali laughed, a light tinkle that jarred Hawthorne's nerves. "Silly Nana. I lets her in."

"Lali." Hawthorne inhaled sharply through her nose. "What have I told you about allowing strangers into the house?"

"But she's not a stranger, Nana. She's the pretty lady and she watches over me. She told me so."

Aaron knelt beside Lali and smoothed a stray wisp of hair from her forehead. "Can you tell me what the pretty lady looks like, sweetheart?"

Lali's eyes lit up. "I gots a picture. Hold on."

She tugged on Petey's hand and dragged the dazed little boy behind her toward the stairs.

"Aaron, would you bring Lali's picture of the pretty lady to me in my office when she retrieves it? Levi, come with me."

Hawthorne pivoted on her heel, ignoring Levi's soft murmurs as he introduced his mortal woman to Aaron and the few other family members who had lingered through the afternoon. A moment later, a small hailstorm of feet pattered after Lali, no doubt belonging to everyone who had witnessed the odd exchange between the little girl and the boy she had claimed on sight.

Hawthorne stalked into her office and sat behind her desk,

tamping down the worry over Lali, the suspicion gnawing at her as to the pretty lady's identity, and icy fury at Levi's temerity in bringing a mortal suitor here. One of his floozies, no doubt, a gold digger who had not the strength or presence of mind to grasp the worth of the man who had so foolishly intermingled his life with hers.

Damn him. Levi was her best and favorite, intended to strengthen the family's position among the People or, at the very least, to secure ties with a powerful mortal family through his intermarriage with a suitable candidate. The soft woman with her silver eyes and timid manner was no match for a Son of Levi's quality and status.

The door snicked shut behind Levi. A moment later, he planted himself in front of her desk, gaze firm as he stared down at her.

"Have a seat."

His beautiful mouth curled into a sneer. "Think I'll stand."

Hawthorne blinked at him. Her great-grandson had always been an individual, pursuing his own path as often as not, but he had never been openly defiant. Until now. "Why did you not tell me you had formed a relationship with a mortal woman?"

He laughed. "Seriously? You have to ask that question? Every time you even think I'm considering a woman, you interfere. Who I date is my business, not yours."

A shaft of hurt pierced her. How could he say that, when she had only his best interests at heart, that and the interests of their family? "That woman is unacceptable."

"*That woman* is my future wife."

"I forbid it."

Levi snorted. "Like you have any say."

Hawthorne clamped her jaw shut. "She is mortal and not of the People."

"Hypocrite." He uttered the word calmly, his voice mild and even, though his whiskey-colored eyes burned fiercely down upon her. "How dare you throw her mortality at me when you're living with a mortal man?"

She placed her palms flat on the desk in front of her, willing the cool surface to bleed the heat from her temper. "Our situation is different."

"Not a bit. Do you think you're the only person in this world entitled to love?"

"No, of course not." Of course, she didn't. How could he think that? Did every Daughter not struggle each day toward that elusive emotion, and laud any who found it? "You could at least have found a Daughter, mortal or not."

"I looked, hard," he said flatly. "And you know what I found? Not a single one I wanted."

"You're young still, barely a man."

He laughed, hard and bitter. "I've been a man since I was sixteen, and treated like one for a lot longer, and you question the direction my heart takes?"

"It is not a question of the direction so much as your state of mind, your vulnerability." Not to mention the potential alliances lost, though she knew he would not want to hear such, not with his emotions clouded by lust. "How do you know this mortal has not latched on to you in order to siphon your wealth into her own coffers?"

"Because Sera's not like that." He dropped his arms and stared down at her. "I should've known better than to bring her here, should've known you couldn't just be glad I'd found somebody. As long as you've searched for your heart, I thought you'd be happy I found mine."

"Levi..."

The door opened on Aaron, Sera, Lali, and Peter, the younger pair walking hand in hand behind their elders.

"Lookit." Aaron waved a sheaf of papers held tight in his fingers. "Lali's got a stack of drawings she's been hoarding up in her room."

He moved around to stand behind Hawthorne, placing his hand on her shoulder as he dropped the drawings onto her desk, pulling her gently against the firm strength of his body. She fanned the pages out even as she noted from the corner of her eye the way Levi drew Sera to him in much the same manner, with his hand on the indent of her waist and his eyes focused so intently on her, there was no doubt in Hawthorne's mind as to their true relationship.

Levi had taken the mortal as his lover and allowed his heart to soften far past love into devotion and need.

Hawthorne stifled a sigh. There would be no dealing with him, then. He had made his choice. Whether wisely or not remained to be seen. On the morrow, she would discuss the matter with his mother. If this mortal, Sera Noland, refused to treat Levi with the proper respect due a Son of his stature, Hawthorne would intervene and do what she must to protect her great-grandson.

She turned her attention to the papers spread before her. Her gaze caught on a crude drawing of what she took to be a woman with coal black dots for eyes, but no nose or mouth. "Lali, sweet, did the pretty lady tell you her name?"

"Nope," Lali said cheerfully. "She just told me I has to be good, and I is. Ain't that right, Petey?"

Peter glanced hopefully toward Levi, then back to Lali. "Um, yes?"

Hawthorne met Levi's gaze. Here, he had done well. The woman might be suspect, but her son was certainly a treasure in the rough. Perhaps the one might be tolerated in order to bring the other into the fold of the People's protection. A mortal male was always of value, even if he was of no blood relation to the People.

"Forget it, Nana. He's eight." Levi's gaze hardened under Hawthorne's watchful stare. "You're not gonna get your hooks into him the way you did with me."

Sera placed her hand flat on Levi's abdomen with entirely too much familiarity for Hawthorne's peace of mind. "What are you talking about?"

"Nothing of consequence." Though Hawthorne would do what she must regardless, as Levi well knew. "Why does the pretty lady have no mouth in this drawing, Lali?"

"'Cause she wore a piece of wood over her face." Lali scrunched her face into a thoughtful frown. "Like at Halloween, 'cept it wasn't Halloween."

Aaron touched a finger to another picture of an amorphous blob surrounded by straight, black lines that could have been a woman's face. "But she took it off for you?"

"Yup. And she told me to tell you, the prosephy..."

"The Prophecy?" Hawthorne guessed.

"Yeah, the prosephy. It needs you to finish, that you're s'posed to do your duty, but you don't has to behead the mean cushion." Lali's expression turned mutinous. "I didn't like that part."

Aaron coughed into his fist. "If anyone deserves a beheading," he muttered.

Sera's fingers curled into Levi's shirt. "Would someone please tell me what's going on here?"

Levi caught her hand with his, pressing hers close to his stomach. "Later. Trust me, ok?"

Sera's mouth slid into a sly grin. "I'll think about it."

Hawthorne eyed that grin with dismay. Yes, it was too late to stop Levi's slide into love, far too late if the woman loved him in return.

Peter nudged Lali with his elbow. "Show her the triangle."

"Oh, yeah." She dropped her new friend's hand long enough to dig into the pocket of her jeans and pull out a small piece of paper. "The pretty lady gave me this."

Peter took it from her and laid it on Hawthorne's desk on top of Lali's drawings. Hawthorne lifted the rough paper gingerly and stared impassively at the triangle set on point with a half circle dropping down from its top line, even as her breath froze in her lungs. The Woman with No Face. Surely there could be no other who would dare use such a symbol.

Three words were written in even lettering around the triangle, one to each side. Duty, love, honor. At the bottom was the simple phrase, *Submit to your heart.* Hawthorne's heart leapt and raced in her chest. The words seemed personal, a message from a feared and mysterious woman.

"Can we go play dolls now?" Lali shifted from foot to foot as Peter stepped back and took her hand in his slightly larger one. "We been good."

"You want me to come with you?" Aaron said.

"Naw. We'll be ok. Won't we, Petey?"

Peter threw his shoulders back and gave them all level stares. "I'll take care of her."

"Petey," Sera said.

Hawthorne interrupted. "They will be fine as long as they stay within the confines of the house. Lali, do not go outside without telling me or Aaron first."

Lali nodded, and then the children ran hand in hand out of the room, Lali leading the way. Sera stared after her son, her forehead furrowed over worried eyes. "I've never seen him like that."

Levi ran a hand up and down her back and dropped a kiss onto the top of her head. "He's learning what it means to be a man, to protect the people who need him. Don't take that away from him."

"But he's so young." Sera sighed the words out. "And she seems so certain."

"It is our way." Hawthorne stood and pinned the other woman with a dispassionate stare. "You will learn soon enough."

Levi's gaze met hers over his lover's head. Hawthorne leaned into her own lover's embrace. Was her great-grandson correct in his assessment of her, that she was a hypocrite for taking love when it came her way and dissuading him from doing the same? Was she perhaps a tad too zealous in her familial duties by pressuring him to marry within the People, when he had found his heart in a woman who seemed to love him in return?

Her eyes dropped to the drawings scattered across her desk and to the tiny fragment carrying the mark of the Woman, the ancient assassin who had haunted the People for longer than their collective minds remembered, a dangerous woman who would as soon kill as appease. She had passed a message through a young girl, reminding Hawthorne of her responsibility.

Duty.

The word fell like dust in her mouth, dry and unpleasant, yet upon her shoulders, certain duties fell. Protecting her family, ensuring the survival of the People, and her duty to herself, to find a way to break the curse holding her in its thrall.

Aaron shifted behind her, tightening his hold on her waist. "It'll wait until tomorrow."

"Yes, my love. It will." Hawthorne met Levi's gaze again, refusing to soften, though she would welcome Sera Noland readily enough, as a good hostess would. "Come. It is near supper time and the children's stomachs will soon rumble with hunger."

She gathered the drawings together with the Woman's symbol and stashed them on one side of her desk, ignoring the way Levi drew his woman under his protective arm. Aaron's place in Hawthorne's life *was* different than Levi's relationship with his mortal.

Wasn't it?

# TWENTY

HE WEEK after Thanksgiving delivered mixed blessings into Aaron's life. After turkey day, Hawthorne seemed more relaxed, open even. Smiles tilted her beautiful mouth more frequently and she even unbent enough to laugh once or twice a day, when humor moved her.

The revelation that a woman had been visiting Lali had worried Hawthorne deeply, though she refused to discuss it. He hadn't pushed, hadn't been in any shape to between the intermittent headaches caused by the concussion, Lali's care, and work.

On the Monday after the holiday, Dr. Phillips cleared Aaron for normal exercise, which Aaron decided extended to sex as well. Since the morning after Isolde's foray, Hawthorne had refused to share a bed with him. He missed holding her, missed waking in the dark with her curled around him, her head on his chest and her arm draped over his waist. Missed the silky heat of her body and the way her gray eyes softened as she moved them both to release.

That would change tonight.

He'd taken every opportunity he could to study the texts in her vault, to hound after her with questions, to learn about her world. The more he knew, the farther away a real life with her seemed. He could feel her slipping through his fingers, dripping away like water through a pinprick in the bottom of a bucket. Every moment he had left was a treasure, another memory waiting to be stored as a precaution against the time when he would grow old and she would not.

That day loomed over him, a thin line of black clouds along the horizon, gathering momentum for the coming storm.

Maria picked him up at Dr. Phillips' office with Lali in tow. "Hawthorne is in a meeting," she said, and that's all Aaron could get out of her. Probably, she had no idea who Hawthorne met with. People came and went through the house so frequently, it was hard to keep up with everybody. Aaron shrugged it off, shelving his worry. He managed to keep it there right up to the moment when they pulled up to Hawthorne's house and he glimpsed Rebecca Upton stepping gracefully down the front stairs, dressed in a tailored business suit and heels with her light blonde hair swept up into a chignon.

Aaron lifted a hand in a casual wave as Maria drove past and pulled into Hawthorne's driveway, around the house, and into the garage. He unbuckled Lali's car seat and swung her out of Hawthorne's SUV. She promptly broke into a run straight into the house, the soles of her tennis shoes pattering on the concrete floor.

He snagged grocery bags from the back of the SUV and followed Maria inside at a slower pace, mulling over Rebecca's presence at Hawthorne's house in the middle of a work day. Couldn't be a social call. Was she there about Isolde or had something happened that she needed Hawthorne's help with?

He dropped the bags in the kitchen for Maria to unpack and followed Lali's laughter through the house to Hawthorne's office. The two were snuggled together on the couch, Hawthorne listening attentively as Lali recited the smallest detail of her outing.

He leaned against the door's frame, content to watch. They were a pair, his two girls, with the same warm gray eyes and hearts as big as the sky, though only someone who knew Hawthorne well would understand exactly how big her heart was. Too many people relied upon her cold demeanor and hard-won reputation to judge her, and never looked below the surface to the woman she was.

He had tried. God knows, he'd tried hard. A twist of regret corkscrewed through him. Maybe he hadn't tried hard enough. Without trust, she would never truly love him, and without love, they had no future.

Every bit of that was his fault.

Each day, he scoured the knowledge stored in her vault, searching for a way to earn her trust, and each day, a little voice told him he was wasting his time. The only way Hawthorne would trust him was for him to believe in her, and he did. The past didn't matter. It just wasn't that important to him, to them. Still, he was beginning to believe that everything she'd told him was true, absolutely and without exception. All he had to do was convince her of his belief and earn her trust.

He sighed and rubbed his nape. That was a lot easier than it sounded. How could he earn the trust of a woman who relied on no one for anything, a woman who refused to discuss the important parts of her life with him, like why Rebecca Upton had visited in the middle of the work day?

That one, at least, he could remedy.

He pushed himself away from the doorframe and walked toward the couch. "Sounds like the two of you are up to no good."

Hawthorne turned toward him, a slight smile lighting her face. "Lali tells me Dr. Phillips has approved your return to exercise."

"Among other things." Aaron dropped onto the couch beside her, slung an arm around her shoulders. He buried his face in her hair and sniffed. Roses. Would he ever smell that flower again without thinking of her? "Do you have a minute?"

"For you, of course." She pressed a kiss to Lali's forehead

and scooted the little girl off her lap. "Lali, darling, if you will give us a few minutes, then later, we shall all walk to the park."

"Okey dokey." Lali skipped out of the room, saying in her sing-songy voice, "We're going to the pa-ark, we're going to the pa-ark."

Aaron closed the door behind her, then resumed his seat next to Hawthorne.

She turned toward him on the couch, her expression soft. "You have the appearance of a determined man."

Oh, he was determined, all right, determined to push those boundaries Hawthorne refused to budge on. "What did Rebecca Upton want?"

Hawthorne's gaze slid from his. "Council business. Trivialities, really."

"Trivialities like Isolde?"

"In part."

"And your place on the Council?"

She peered at him from beneath lowered lashes, part seductress, part warrior.

"I've been doing a lot of reading this past week." He took her narrow hand in his own, threading their fingers together. "She wants you to take Isolde's place."

"I am considering it."

"Do I get a say?"

"Why should you?"

He breathed past the hurt etching its way into his heart. "Because I'm your lover."

"And?" She lifted her shoulder in a casual shrug. "This is my decision."

"It affects me. Lali, too."

"Aaron, love..."

"Love," he gritted out. "If you love me, why won't you talk this over with me?"

"Why are you so insistent?" She shook her head, her expression caught between confusion and wariness. "You have never questioned my decisions before."

"I have. Yes, I have," he said when she shook her head again. "You bottle this part of your life up, keep it a secret from me. Every time I ask, you push me away. How can I earn your trust if you refuse to share something so basic?"

"Aaron. Sweet." She brushed her fingertips over his cheek and captured his mouth in a brief kiss. "Is that what this is about?"

"Some. Maybe I think it's time we both started including each other in these decisions." He thumbed the bridge of his nose and took a deep, fortifying breath. "I've finished the thumbnail sketches for the graphic novel. The rest of it, I'll do on my own."

Her expression went carefully blank as she lowered her eyes, hiding herself from him. "I am aware."

He squeezed her fingers. "I can go back to San Francisco any time now."

"Will you?"

"Do you want me to?"

"I would have you remain, though I know I cannot keep you." She slid off of the couch and stood, studying him dispassionately. "This I have learned well."

"Don't hold that against me, Hawthorne. I had to see Ma."

"You know I speak of something other than filial devotion."

He scrubbed a hand over his face. "Are you ever gonna forgive me for DragonCon?"

"Perhaps I cannot."

His heart sank like a stone. That's what he was afraid of. "If you can't, you'll never learn to trust me."

The corners of her mouth lifted into a secretive smile, bringing a soft glow to her gray eyes. "The two are not mutually exclusive."

"Eh?" He sat up, the weight of her distrust lifting from him. "How so?"

"I shan't tell, Aaron Kesselman."

"Yeah?"

He tugged on her hand, reeling her in. Her legs bumped the edge of the couch between his.

"I bet I can make you," he said.

Her smile widened as she tilted her head. "Do you, then?"

"Oh, yeah."

He pushed her sweater up, taking her camisole with it, baring her stomach, and pressed his lips to her smooth skin. Her fingers tangled in his hair on a sigh. He wrapped an arm around her waist, holding her in place as he explored.

"Aaron, love," she said. "The doctor…"

"Said I was fine. Shush, now. I'm busy."

He hitched her sweater higher, made sure his hold around her waist was firm, and blew a raspberry on her stomach. She shrieked out a laugh and wiggled, pushing against his shoulders when he blew another one.

"What are you doing, Aaron?" she asked, her voice mingled with laughter.

He wrestled her down onto the couch and covered her, bracing himself above her. "Getting you to tell me how you're starting to trust me."

Her fingers found the collar of his shirt as a smile tugged at her mouth. "I told you. I shan't tell."

"Look, I'm not afraid to do that again."

Her eyes widened. "You would not dare."

"Sweetheart, you oughta know me better than that." He buried his face in her neck, couldn't resist tasting the skin under her jaw. Silky, sweet. "Mmm. If only you hadn't promised Lali a trip to the park, we could be upstairs right now, building trust."

"Later," she promised. "As often as you want."

He scraped his teeth along her jaw, flicked his tongue against the edge of her earlobe, and felt her low, appreciative hum all the way to his toes. "Yeah? That sounds promising."

Lali burst through the door. Aaron rolled quickly off of Hawthorne and yanked her sweater down a moment before the little girl rounded the corner, her eyes wide in a frightened face, her wooden sword held high in both hands.

"Is the mean cushion back?" Lali panted. "I gots my sword this time. She can't take you, Nana, not you or my puppy neither one."

"Oh, Lali. We are safe from Isolde." Hawthorne sat up and held out her arms. Lali scrambled into her grandmother's lap, and Hawthorne's eyes met Aaron's over the little girl's head. "Aaron and I were playing. We did not mean to frighten you."

"I wasn't scared, Nana." Lali's voice was muffled where her face rested in the crook of Hawthorne's neck. "I was gonna get her this time."

Aaron scooted closer and rested a comforting hand on Lali's back. "Atta girl, Lali."

She peeked at him, her eyes so like Hawthorne's, it took his breath. "I was brave, wasn't I?"

"The bravest," he agreed.

Later, after Lali calmed down and they'd come back from a trip to the park and settled in to work, Aaron replayed his conversation with Hawthorne over in his mind, smiling at the memory of their play. She'd taken his teasing well, for a centuries old warrior. If they'd been somewhere else, he would've taken her then, eased her pants down and pressed into her, building trust in the only way she left open for him.

His eyes widened on a sudden realization. He'd yanked Hawthorne onto the couch and pinned her down, and not once had she looked upset or frightened. No, not upset a whit. She'd been loose and relaxed the entire time, right up until Lali had burst in on them.

His heart thumped and flopped and turned over so hard, it staggered him. His gaze met hers across the expanse of her office where she sat behind her desk, engrossed in paperwork. Maybe she was beginning to trust him, at least enough to believe that he would never intentionally hurt her, not ever again.

THAT NIGHT, Aaron made love to Hawthorne with a fierce tenderness that stole her breath, wiggling its way beneath what was left of the armor she had erected around her heart. Afterward, he held her tightly, his hands caressing her softly as he whispered sweet words of love to her. How he would never leave her, never hurt her again, never, ever let another day go by without showing her how much he loved her.

It was then, in the still of the night with her lover wrapped around her, that Hawthorne made a decision she had never before considered. Aaron wished for her trust, pleaded for it with an earnestness she was beginning to believe was genuine. The Council would meet two days hence to decide Isolde's fate. Aaron would be there. His presence would count among the People, as both a victim of Isolde's hand and as Hawthorne's lover. No man had ever accompanied her into the heart of her People in that manner. If he held up under the harsh scrutiny of the Seven, now six, thanks to Isolde's betrayal, then he would have proven himself worthy of the trust he wished to engender.

Whether she could submit to that trust was another matter, but here, as with Lali, was as good a place to begin as any.

That she even entertained the notion surprised her. She slid her hand along his sweat-soaked flank, cupped the firm muscles of his ass. "What was this about loving me forever?"

He nuzzled her hair as a soft laugh escaped him. "You know I will."

"Perhaps." She scraped her nails along his lower back, pleased at the low moan he gave. "Perhaps I wish another demonstration."

He captured her hands and held them above her head, out of the way. "Anything you want, sweetheart. Anything at all."

He dropped his weight onto her and captured her mouth, demanding her submission as her heart wavered on the edge of surrender.

Two days later, Hawthorne dressed in a tailored black pants suit and matching sling backs, affixed sedate pearl clip-on earrings to her earlobes, and brushed on enough make-up to appear presentable. She stared at the woman reflected in her bathroom mirror, with her professional demeanor and coldly neutral expression, so unlike the woman she wished to be. She far preferred the short strands of her hair tousled by Aaron's fingers and her dress as casual as his or, when they were alone, reduced to nothing but skin.

Duty called, pulling Hawthorne from her heart's desire, that and a need to mete retribution upon her niece at the end of a sword.

Duty, love, honor. Were those not the words the Woman had given her through Lali? All three seemed applicable here. This one final duty to Una, whom she had loved even unto death, and the honor lost to them both so long ago, reclaimed only through the judicious slash of her sword and the spill of men's blood across the better part of an island.

Hawthorne made her way down the stairs to Aaron's office, and was unsurprised to find Lali sitting in his lap, doodling on his computer. "Lali, darling, Maria has a snack waiting for you in the kitchen."

"Okey dokey." Lali put away the stylus and slid off of Aaron's lap, though not before bussing his cheek. "I'll be back, Airn. Don't eraseticated my stuff."

"I won't." He watched Lali bounce out of the room, then did a double take. "Wow. That outfit is hot. What's the occasion?"

She compressed her lips together, hiding her humor. "I have a business meeting. Would you like to attend?"

"Eh." His brow furrowed as he swiped his palms over his toned thighs. "What kind of business?"

"The kind you wished me to share. Come along, now. Time is short and you will need to change into something more appropriate."

He manipulated the switches on his computer before standing. "Are you gonna tell me what this is about?"

"You will see." She raked a gaze over his lean form, oddly put out that he should have to change out of the flannel shirt stretched over his muscled shoulders and the worn jeans that cupped him so intimately. Pity he wished to involve himself with her business rather than wait here for her to strip his clothes off one tender kiss at a time. Her heart twinged at what she was about to put him through. "I shall await you in my office."

She pivoted on her heel and allowed humor to blossom over the heartache when his low, appreciative whistle sounded behind her.

Fifteen minutes later, he stuck his head in the door of her office. "You ready?"

She set the book she'd been reading aside and rose from her seat on the couch, assessing his outfit. He'd tucked a white button-down shirt into dark brown slacks and carried a matching suit jacket in his hand. He'd also taken the time to run his electric razor over his lower face, leaving it smooth.

She cupped his jaw in her hands, savoring the clean line of his jaw. "I did not know you owned a tie."

"I didn't know you owned a business suit." He shrugged the jacket on and accepted her hands smoothing it over his broad shoulders, straightening the subtly striped crimson tie. "Is this ok?"

"More than," she murmured. "You surprise me each day."

"It's mutual, I promise. Where are we going?"

"You must trust me."

She ignored the disgruntled grimace in his expression and led him to the garage, drove them the short distance to the IECS. Endured the stares and whispers of the security guards at the gate and the silence that stretched between herself and Aaron as she guided the Land Rover through the IECS campus.

At last, she parked outside the Archives. After switching the ignition off, she turned to him. "Follow my lead."

"Ok." He drew the word out. "Now would be a great time to tell me what's going on."

She shook her head. Better that he see it for himself. "I may ask you to speak. Otherwise do not." She placed a single finger over his lips, forestalling his questions. "Do not react, if you can help it. This, above all, is paramount."

He nodded, though his gaze had grown cloudy with wariness and worry. She allowed her finger to slide away from the masculine beauty of his mouth.

"Anything else?" he asked.

"Is this not enough?"

She slipped out of the car and captured his hand as they made their way through the thin crowd into the mountain housing the People's most sacred artifacts and histories, using his gentle strength to fortify her own for what must be done. A security guard escorted them to a golf cart and handed over its keys. Hawthorne took the wheel and followed the winding tunnels deep into the heart of the mountain to a natural cavern that had long ago been refitted into a meeting hall, a place where the People could judge an individual's innocence or guilt and deliver justice accordingly.

They took their place along the front of the rows of bench seating placed in an arc around the natural curve of the cavern's wall, now overlain with concrete, as was the entire interior save the rock ceiling. Levi and his mother entered not long after, followed by Ruby and Levi's closest friends, among them Colin, who had suffered under Isolde's hand. They assumed positions to Hawthorne's rear, acceding to her role as the head of the family. Others crowded in behind them, beside them, around them, and Hawthorne nearly shuddered from the mass of humanity pressing into the cavern around them. Aaron's fingers squeezed hers, as if he knew the duress this event placed her under.

Mathias pushed his way through the growing crowd and halted in front of her.

She rose and held out her free hand. "Mathias."

"Hawthorne." He brushed a hesitant kiss along her cheek. His lips were cold, stiff, and no less welcome because of it. "I'm surprised you're still speaking to me."

"You hold no part in your wife's actions," she said gently. "Mathias, I would like to introduce you to Aaron Kesselman, my lover. Aaron, this is Mathias Zellinger, Isolde's husband."

Aaron dropped her hand and held his out to Mathias. "Sorry we have to meet like this."

Mathias shook Aaron's hand, a faint smile twisting his tensely set mouth. "I think that's my line."

They sat on the bench, Hawthorne between the two men, waiting for the proceedings to begin. The murmur of the people gathered as witnesses increased gradually. A few minutes after Mathias entered, two armed guards escorted Isolde into the center of the room, her posture straight and haughty, her gaze even in spite of the chains binding her hands behind her back. The six remaining council members drifted in behind her in a quiet line and assumed their places at a curved table on the other side of the room, their assistants ranged behind them along the cavern's far wall.

Rebecca Upton entered last, the click of her heels echoing in the suddenly silent room. She came to a stop facing Isolde. "Isolde Zellinger, you have been brought before the Council to stand trial for kidnapping Robert Lake Upton, the second of that name, a beloved Son; for attempting to kidnap Lali-Alice Harbin, a defenseless Daughter; for conspiring to commit treason against the People; and for collusion with outlawed members of the group calling themselves the Eternal Order, thus acting against the collective good of the People. How plead you?"

At the mention of the Order, a murmur rose among the crowd. Rebecca raised her hand, hushing the noise, though her gaze remained on Isolde.

"On the first two charges, I plead guilty and throw myself upon the mercy of the Council for judgment, with the understanding that I had no hand in the injuries dealt to young Upton after his kidnapping." Isolde waited for Rebecca's stiff nod before continuing. "As for the latter charges, I plea innocence. I have and ever have had the best interests of the People at heart. I have committed no treason, nor have I colluded with anyone against the collective good of the People."

"So sayeth you." Rebecca stepped back and took her place to the side, between the bench seating and the Council's table, next to a group of young women furiously scribbling notes. "The charges have been read. The trial now begins."

Lydia, the *de facto* head of the Council by way of her lineage through the eldest of the Seven Sisters, stood. "Isolde Zellinger, you have the right of defense. Whom do you call to your aid?"

Isolde stared straight ahead. "Respectfully, I call no one."

Lydia bowed toward Hawthorne. "As the presumed eldest in the line of Bagda and the mother of the accused one degree removed, the Council begs leave of Hawthorne the Chronicler. Should your kin be left defenseless or will you intercede?"

Aaron squeezed her hand, to encourage her or chide her for withholding her full appellation, she knew not. He had read several volumes of her extensive collection of journals. Surely he had by now pieced together that the journals from which he had drawn his characterization of Rebecca the Blade had been written by Hawthorne.

She stood and bowed toward the Council. "Let it be known that my kin and my lover have fallen harm to Isolde's treachery."

Isolde bowed solemnly. Hawthorne eyed her niece coldly, torn between that wretched mistress, duty, and the need to bring vengeance upon this woman for her hand in harming Lali and Aaron, and for the larger role she had played in fostering the Eternal Order's agenda. "If the accused has no objections, I shall endeavor to represent her fairly in spite of this harm, in remembrance of the woman who birthed her into this world."

Isolde's eyes widened a moment before she closed them,

shuttering her expression as she nodded again.

"So be it." Lydia resumed her seat. "You may begin."

Hawthorne bowed once more. "Isolde, daughter of Una Longshadow, Harbinger of Justice, and a descendant of the Sister Bagda, please repeat the words you told me on the night when you kidnapped my granddaughter, Lali-Alice Harbin."

"I explained my belief that if the Prophecy of Light is fulfilled, it will leave us all vulnerable to the Shadow Enemy's sword."

Miriam, the councilmember representing the Sister Marnan and her descendants, rose. "How so?"

"With the Prophecy's fulfillment," Isolde said, "we all become mortal, losing the one advantage the People have: The strong arms of her immortal Daughters."

And so it went, back and forth between Isolde and the Council, a civilized discussion moderated by Hawthorne that ripped and clawed at the underlying fabric of hope that had held the People together for ten millennia or more. Detractors stood and had their say, logically laying out the reasons why the Prophecy should be fulfilled, reminding the assembled crowd of the past wrongs committed by the Eternal Order, and on and on until Hawthorne's nerves stretched thin and her mind ached with fatigue.

After nearly two hours, the questions wound down. Hawthorne concluded her defense simply. "Have you anything further to say, Isolde?"

"I have laid my arguments in front of the Council with the honesty of a Daughter of Bagda."

Hawthorne nodded and resumed her place between Aaron and Mathias. Aaron's hand found hers, his warm upon her icy skin.

Lydia stood, her gaze even as she scanned the room. "Are there any here who wish a further say in this matter?" When no one spoke, she continued. "Judgment to the Council. On the charges of treason and collusion, I say innocent. How sayeth the

263

remaining Council?"

Each of the women rose and weighed in. Eleanor Shadowfell of the line of Ganenda; Gwendolyn from the Sister Lilleni and Phoebe from Lilleni's twin, Eleni; Miriam; and Anya, representing the youngest Sister, Abragni. All called innocence on the charge of treason, while Eleanor, Gwendolyn, and Anya cried guilt on the charge of collusion, leaving the Council tied on a verdict.

Hawthorne closed her eyes in a futile attempt to combat the resignation rising in her. It had come to this and she had no idea how she would call. She rose from her seat even as Lydia stood, and listened to the councilmember's words with a sinking heart.

"Hawthorne, as the eldest of the line of Bagda and in place of the absent seat on the Council, it falls upon you to decide the fate of the accused. How say you?"

Hawthorne opened her mouth, intending to render a harsh justice, and produced only silence. Aaron's hand crept to hers, his fingers firm. She glanced down and found him watching her, his chocolate eyes serious. *Think of Una*, he mouthed, and she nodded without thinking her gesture through, without considering the ramifications of taking advice from her mortal lover in front of the People and its ruling body. *Think of Una*, he had told her. Una, her beloved sister, gone these many centuries. Una who had sacrificed her own honor first in the hopes of sparing her younger sibling. Una who had led Hawthorne through the decades after as they cut down the men who had flogged their mother and brutally raped the children they had been.

Una, who had eventually found love, but not before birthing an immortal Daughter, the woman who stood in front of them all, accused of a crime so heinous, it would bring torture and certain death at the end of Hawthorne's hand.

As the eldest in their line, punishment fell to her, and she would trust no one else to deliver a swift and sure death to her niece.

*Think of Una.*

Hawthorne drew her fingers from Aaron's and stepped forward, her heels nearly silent on the hard concrete floor as she moved toward her niece. When she stood near, she cupped Isolde's face and gazed upon the near twin of her beloved sister. "Isolde," she said, her voice resolute, "I say innocent."

Hawthorne had only a moment to notice the relief on Isolde's face before a great weight drove her down. Her knees hit the floor, grinding into the rough surface through her slacks. From a distance, Aaron shouted her name and a great hew arose from the onlookers. Isolde was yanked backward by an unknown force as lights erupted behind Hawthorne's eyes. She pressed a shaky hand to her forehead, inhaled a single breath. The weight lifted, freeing her from its burden. She gasped and arched, following it upward as it escaped into the ether, and lost all sense of time and space. A wave of dizziness swept her into a swirling vortex of the shadow that had ever been her companion and she floated to the ground, no longer aware of the world around her.

# TWENTY-ONE

THE RELATIVE SPACIOUSNESS of the rural hospital outside of Tellowee surprised Aaron for the second time in two weeks, or would have if he'd had room in his mind to worry about the size of the ER or the quality of the nursing staff or the steady stream of traffic shuffling by the curtained cubicle where Hawthorne lay on a narrow bed.

Her skin was pale, cold, and her chest rose so slightly with her shallow breaths, he kept a finger on the pulse at her wrist, measuring each heartbeat with one of his own. Her slacks were torn at the knees and her hands were scraped where she'd fallen on the concrete, though no one had bothered with bandages or an IV or anything he would've expected a patient to be subjected to in a hospital. When he'd asked a passing nurse, she'd shrugged casually and told him that no one ever did anything to an immortal Daughter while they were unconscious unless their injuries were life-threatening. Apparently, they didn't appreciate the confinement and tended to wake up swinging, wreaking havoc on everything and everyone around them.

Ethan Phillips stood at the foot of the bed examining a hefty summary of Hawthorne's medical records. The doctor was about Aaron's age with eyes the color of leaves in the spring. His hair was brown, clipped military short on the sides and back, and had a distinctly reddish tint under the fluorescent lights in the ER.

Like nearly everybody Aaron had met since coming to Tellowee, Ethan was fit and athletic, and uncomfortably direct. They'd met the week before when Hawthorne had brought Aaron to the ER after Isolde bludgeoned him. He hadn't expected to see the doctor again so soon, not in the hospital, anyway. Maybe at The Omega or out in Tellowee, but not here in the ER with Hawthorne out like a light and showing no signs of waking.

"How long have you known Hawthorne again?" Ethan said.

"Since last August. We met at DragonCon."

"Hmm." Ethan flipped another page, yawned. "Mmm. Sorry. It's been busy around here lately. So, let's see. You've been dating for, what, about three months?"

Aaron rubbed his forehead with his free hand. "More like two."

"Having sex the whole time?"

"Er. Mostly."

Ethan looked up, his mouth curved into a small smile. "How do you mostly have sex with somebody?"

A hint of heat touched Aaron's cheeks. "She has trust issues." No need to add that some of those issues had been caused by him, and that it had driven what felt like an insurmountable wedge between them.

"All Daughters do." Ethan tucked the file under his arm and pierced Aaron with a no-nonsense stare. "Have those trust issues been resolved yet?"

Aaron's gaze drifted to Hawthorne, still out from whatever had happened to her at Isolde's hearing. "Not exactly."

"What about love?"

"It's there, on both sides." He hoped. Aaron dragged his gaze away from Hawthorne's still form and pinned his own glare on the doctor. "Look, shouldn't you be trying to help her instead of asking all these nosey questions?"

"These nosey questions *are* helping her. Her vitals are good, there's no sign of trauma or injury." Ethan hid another yawn behind the back of his hand. "Are you sure she doesn't trust you?"

"Think I'd know if she did."

Ethan's lips compressed into a thin line. "This looks very much like submission to me."

Aaron did a double take. "What?"

"Submission. Breaking the curse?" A vee appeared between Ethan's eyebrows. "Surely she told you."

"Yeah, she has." Still, it didn't seem very likely, all things given. "You really think so?"

Ethan shrugged. "Did she take your advice or trust you or do anything you suggested before collapsing?"

Aaron shook his head.

"Are you sure?"

"We were at Isolde's hearing. Hawthorne specifically told me not to speak or react."

"So you didn't do anything. Hold her hand, touch her back? Sway her in some way toward something you wanted her to do?"

"Well, I did sort of mouth something to her, right before she had to decide whether or not Isolde was innocent." Hawthorne's pulse skipped under Aaron's fingers. He lifted her hand and pressed a kiss there, willing her to wake up and be ok. "I told her to think of her sister, and hoped like hell she wouldn't do something she'd regret for the rest of her life."

"And she cried Isolde innocent."

"Yeah, she did."

"Because you asked her to." Ethan's brow cleared and a grin spread across his face. "Congratulations, man. You now have yourself one mortal Daughter."

Aaron's heart kicked into overdrive, hammering so hard he thought it might jump out of his chest. "Yeah?"

"Pretty sure."

She trusted him. Even after everything he'd done, she trusted him. He let that settle in for a while, tried to wrap his head around it. All he could think of was her face the day he'd told her she was crazy, the tears clouding her beautiful gray eyes, the utter hopelessness in her expression, and her hands curled into fists at her sides. "I don't think I deserve her."

"Hunh. What man deserves the woman he loves?" Ethan tapped Aaron's shoulder with Hawthorne's file. "She should wake up soon, though you can never tell with the really old ones. I'll swing by and check on her in an hour or so. If you need me before then, grab a nurse and have me paged."

"Thanks," Aaron said faintly.

Ethan step through the curtains separating the ER cubicle from the rest of the floor. Aaron barely noticed, his mind caught in the implications of Hawthorne's collapse. Had she really trusted him that much, enough to change her mind on something so important? Or was there a deeper cause that Dr. Phillips had missed?

When he turned back toward Hawthorne, her eyes were open and fixed on him.

"Hey," he said. "You're awake."

"So it seems." She grimaced and lifted her fingers to her temple. "May we leave now?"

"Not on your life." Aaron placed his hand on her shoulder, a mild encouragement for her to remain prone. "Not until Dr. Phillips gives you the all clear."

"I am fine, Aaron. Being mortal does not change that."

"So you knew?"

"Not until I overheard you and Ethan speaking on it." She shifted restlessly on the bed. "I wish to sit up."

"Forget it."

"Aaron..."

"No. I just got you here, and here is where you're staying until Dr. Phillips comes back." He cupped her hand between both of his, smoothing his fingers over hers. "You scared the ever-loving hell out of all of us. I thought your family was gonna bring the mountain down around us when you collapsed."

A slow smile bloomed across her face. "That would have been an interesting sight."

"Says you. You weren't the one arguing with Levi over who got to carry you out." He inhaled a steadying breath. In the end, Aaron had carried her and Levi had driven them here, followed by a convoy of concerned kin and friends, all waiting to hear how Hawthorne was doing. "So, you trusted me, huh?"

"I have trusted you in small ways for some time, with my body, with Lali."

He sat back in his chair and barely kept himself from gaping at her. "You trust me with Lali?"

"You saved her, did you not?"

"I did what anyone would've done."

"Not anyone," she corrected gently. "Someone who loves her deeply enough to sacrifice himself for her well-being. It is no insignificant thing, what you did."

"I love her," he said simply.

"She knows. We all do." She turned onto her side, curling her legs up on the thin sheet spread beneath her. "What happened to Isolde?"

"Her guards took her back to wherever they were keeping her."

"The Council did not punish her?"

He shook his head. "Not that I'm aware. Why?"

She blew out a small breath. "That is why I brought you there, to witness how the People treat those who betray us. She was to be whipped for her crimes, and would have been put to death if the Council had found her guilty of treason."

"Shit. Really?"

"It is so. As her elder, carrying out her punishment will fall to me."

"No." He gripped her hand hard and tugged until their eyes met. "You absolutely will not whip her, you hear? I forbid it."

Her lips tilted into a smile. "Do you truly think my submission on one occasion allows you the ability to control my actions henceforth?"

"Well, no, but still. You can't whip her. It's a heinous way to punish anybody." He shifted closer and brushed a hand over her hair, pressed a kiss to her forehead. "Besides, it would be too much like hurting Una. I saw the resemblance between Isolde and the picture you had me create of her mother, and I know how much you loved your sister. It's in your voice every time you speak of her."

She gazed at him for long, silent moments, unblinking, her expression empty. Her hand came up and her fingers trailed along his jaw. "What would you suggest?"

"Can't you confine her? Maybe make her pay a bunch of fines or something?" He turned his face into her palm and breathed in the light perfume she'd dabbed on her wrist earlier that day. Tea roses in full bloom, a breath of summer in the middle of the coldest winter. God above, he loved that. "Don't you have a work release program or chores that need doing?"

She laughed, the sound too soft to carry outside the space around them. "This is not the mortal world where good works outweigh the bad. Still, I shall approach the Council with your suggestions and plea for lenience on her behalf."

Relief filtered through him. At least Hawthorne wouldn't have to be the one wielding a whip, anyway. "Thanks. I bet Mathias will be happy to have his wife in one piece, too."

"He will. I shall implore for his sake as much as for yours, though Isolde will not escape a harsh punishment. At the very least, a significant portion of her accumulated wealth will be forfeit, paid as recompense for young Upton's kidnapping and the harm she did to you, Lali, Ruby, and your guards."

"I don't want anything of hers," he said flatly.

"You have no say." She pressed her fingers to his lips, effectively silencing his argument. "The fine will be put into a trust for your benefit and the benefit of your heirs. On this, I shall not be moved."

He nodded, though he didn't pretend to be happy about it. "So this is what it's like living with a Daughter, huh?"

"Be happy I have mellowed with age, else I would have

carried you out of here by now."

"Yeah?" He grinned and rubbed the tip of his nose against hers. "I'd like to see you try."

She lifted her mouth to his and kissed him, gently and sweetly, releasing him slowly.

Aaron stuck his head out the curtains and asked a nurse to find Dr. Phillips. It was time to take his lover home.

IT TOOK HAWTHORNE two days to convince Aaron of her complete well-being, two days in which he coddled and spoiled and loved her with the magnificence of a man who has no other in his heart. Two days after submitting her will to his on a matter so trivial it hardly bore reflection, she awoke wrapped around him, her bare legs tangled with his, her head resting on his broad chest over the steady beat of his heart.

That afternoon, she would return to the IECS, state her case for leniency before the Council and carry out whatever punishment they believed Isolde deserved. Fines and a life of confinement and service would render justice where a whipping might have killed her mortal niece. As irritated as Hawthorne was over Isolde's actions, she did not wish to lose the only link she had left to her beloved Una.

Hawthorne sighed as she slid her hand along Aaron's lower abdomen, resting it over his hip. He shifted in his sleep, turning toward her as he always did, as if he could not help being drawn to her.

After overseeing Isolde's punishment, Hawthorne would fulfill her duty to the People and assume her place on the Council, serving and representing her foremother, Bagda. The reluctance gripping her was eased by the presence of the man at her side. No longer must she face these onerous duties alone without council or comfort or love. No longer must she endure the endless centuries, haunted by the past. Aaron had brought peace into her life and helped her remember the joy of living.

Even if she had never given him her heart, she would be thankful for that.

"Good morning, lover." His voice was a rough rumble beneath her ear, his embrace a comfort she hoped never to do without again. "What's going on in that beautiful mind of yours?"

"I am considering the day ahead."

"The day ahead, huh?"

He urged her on top of him with gentle tugs and pulls. She straddled his stomach and guided his hands to her hips.

He held her there, savoring touch of skin on skin. "How about we focus on the now and let later take care of itself?"

Later, after they sated each other in a rush of heat and love, he turned her toward the nightstand and wrapped himself around her. Her gaze fell on a small white box with a red bow on top. "What is this?"

He pressed a kiss to the nape of her neck and slid his hand down her flank, resting it on her thigh. "Open it and find out."

She reached a hesitant hand toward the tiny gift, her heart thumping in her chest, abetted by the nerves fluttering in her stomach. It was light in her hand, not much more substantial than air. She sat up, drawing her legs under her, and fingered the bow.

Aaron settled behind her, surrounding her with his body, and rested his chin on her shoulder. "It won't bite."

"I know," she said, and felt silly saying so. Of course, it would not bite. It was an inanimate object, a box that might or might not hold the traditional gift of his people on such an occasion as this, when two people declared their love for one another. A slight tremor ran through her hand. Could it really be?

"You know, it kind of ruins the surprise when the giver has to open the gift."

She leaned her head against his, touching their temples together. "I am merely savoring the moment."

"I thought that was called *delaying the inevitable*." He gathered her closer, clasping his hands together over the butterflies dancing in her stomach. "You'll never know what's inside if you don't take a peek."

She inhaled deeply and tugged gently on one end of the bow. It slithered off, leaving the box unguarded in her hand. She pulled the lid off, revealing a golden ring holding a pear-shaped diamond surrounded by rubies. Her breath left her in a rush and her heart seemed to still absolutely within her.

"Marry me," he said, whispering it into her throat. "Marry me and make babies with me and live forever with my love."

"Aaron, I..."

"I know it's too soon. I know there's a lot we still need to sort out." He tugged her around, cradling her in his arms, and touched his forehead to hers. "I know you still need time to trust me, but I couldn't go another day without having this ring on your finger. I love you so much, more than I could ever show you, and I swear, I'll spend the rest of my life trying. Marry me, Hawthorne. Be my heart."

"Oh, love." She gazed up at him, at the tender-hearted skeptic who had wiggled his way under her guard the first moment she'd seen him, and not long after, had captured her completely, heart and body and soul. "I shall happily be your bride."

"Yeah?" He hugged her close and grinned. "When?"

"Soon, before the spring equinox." She fingered the ring, tracing its shape. Once upon a time, she had told him of her origins, of the hardest moments of her youth and the changes she had made to adapt, to survive. He had understood that, even as his disbelief had cut at her. "I should very much like to marry you under the name of my birth, if you would have me thus."

His chocolate eyes went soft and hot at the same time, and the smile dropped from his expression. She cupped his nape and tugged him down, close enough to whisper in his ear, and told him a name only a handful of people remembered, one none had dared call her since before her father's death nearly two millennia before.

He drew back and ran his fingers over the curve of her cheek, along the lobe of her ear, down the side of her neck. "It's beautiful. What does it mean?"

"Blessed treasure."

"Will you let me...?"

"Yes, you may, whenever you wish."

"I wish. You have no idea how much." He plucked the ring from its protective casing, slid it upon her finger, and tossed the box over his shoulder. "And now, I'm gonna make love to you until Lali comes running in with her sword to protect you from the mean ol' grumpy puppy."

She laughed and shifted with him on the bed, threading her fingers through his as he covered her. For the first time, no memories of past harms intruded between them, leaving her free to accept his touch, free to return it fully. They made love with the early morning sun shining in, blessing their union as he whispered her name and she opened her heart, giving him the love she had saved for the man who forever after would stand at her side, loving her as she had always wished to be loved.

# EPILOGUE

L ALI STARED at the window next to her bed, waiting for the pretty lady to knock, just like she always did when something 'portant happened. Nana had told Lali that Airn would be marrying them soon and that he would be her puppy forever.

Becka was gonna be so jealous. *Her* puppy didn't make up the awesomest bestest stories ever like Airn did. *Her* puppy didn't stay with her all the time and take her to the park every day and let her play on his 'puter. Lali frowned. Becka's puppy *did* help her with her bath and read a story to her every single night while she washed.

Lali decided then and there that Airn would have to do the same *or else*. He wasn't a big guy any more. He was her puppy, and that's what puppies did. They squirted stuff in their little girl's hair and swirled it into funny shapes and read stories and made everybody laugh. It was just one of those things puppies did, and since Airn was gonna be her forever puppy now, he had to do it, too.

She blinked through a yawn. Where was the pretty lady? She should've been here by now.

Before Airn had come to see them, the pretty lady had come through the window and told Lali all about him, how Airn would love her so much, he'd save her from the mean cushion.

The pretty lady had come that night, too, and reminded Lali to be brave and follow the 'structions Nana had told her. How to sneak through the walls without making a peep and how to open the vault so they would be safe, only it hadn't worked perzactly the way it was supposed to. The mean cushion had still got them, but Airn had saved Lali, just like the pretty lady said he would.

And a long, long time before that, the pretty lady had told Lali about Petey, the little boy who would be her friend forever and ever and ever, just like in the stories Airn told her.

Lali sighed happily. And now, Petey had come to her and it had all worked out the way it was s'posed to.

A rap on the window startled her out of another yawn. She jumped out of bed and raced to it, climbing up on the chair she'd pulled there earlier so she could unlock the window and open it for the pretty lady.

And there she was, the pretty lady with her long black coat and big ol' boots and the wooden mask over her face. Lali skipped out of the way and waited patiently. The pretty lady climbed through the window and closed it, then knelt in front of Lali.

"Lali-Alice," the pretty lady said. "You have done well, child."

Lali beamed at her. "You, too, pretty lady. I gots my Airn and my Petey now, and the mean cushion won't never hurt us again, not ever."

"Then all is as it should be." The pretty lady touched one finger to the end of Lali's hair. "And I shall not have to visit you again for a long, long while."

Lali slumped and held her eyes wide as the sad feelings made her eyes wet. "But I will miss you so, pretty lady."

"And I you. Never fear, child. We shall meet again."

The door creaked open behind them and Lali whirled with a gasp. Nana stood in the doorway, her sword held low in her hand. "Is that so?"

The pretty lady stood slowly. "I have no quarrel with you or yours, Hawthorne."

"Yet you do not hesitate to break into my home and discuss matters with my granddaughter that are best left to her future."

"The future is upon us. Have you not felt its heavy sting? Have you not heard its rush and sway as it pushes you toward your duty?"

Nana nodded, though her face looked all empty and mean, like it did when Lali did something she wasn't s'posed to do. "Duty is a harsh mistress."

"Spoken like a true Daughter of the People."

"I know my duty well."

"As do I. As do we all." The pretty lady held her hand out to Lali. "Should we fail, our duty falls to this one. She shall pick up the mantle of the future and bow under its unforgiving hand. Would you allow this fate to weigh upon her?"

Nana looked at Lali and her face went all sad, the way it'd done when Airn went away to visit his mama in Sampracisco. "I would not. What may I do to spare her?"

"Help the Light fulfill the Prophecy and break the curse that holds us all in its grasp."

The pretty lady pushed her hood back and untied the bows holding her mask on. She lifted it up, taking it off, and held it in her hand.

Nana gasped and fell to her knees, and her sword dropped to the floor with a loud clatter. "No. I know your face. I know that scar."

The pretty lady's hand went to the white mark around her neck. "This was given by a betraying hand, long before your birth. You know much of betrayal, do you not, Iriamina of the Iceni."

"I do."

Nana bowed her head, and when she looked up again, her face was all wet. Lali ran to her and threw her arms around Nana's neck, holding on tight so she wouldn't cry no more. Nanas were never supposed to cry. Everybody knew that.

Nana's hand held the back of Lali's head, as if *she* were the one crying. "You helped my mother avenge the ones who betrayed her."

"I did, as I rode with you and your sister when you brought justice to the ones who had robbed you of your honor. Duty takes many forms, Daughter. It is the lawmaker and the rule breaker, the jury and the witness. It is the hand that comforts a child whose heart has endured enough pain for a dozen lifetimes."

"That is love."

"Love carries its own duties, does it not?"

Nana brushed her cheek along Lali's hair. "You sound so sad."

"I have loved for far too long, child. My time is coming to an end."

"No. You must wait for..."

"I shall endure long enough for that."

Lali twisted around in Nana's arms, resting her head on Nana's shoulder, and bit her lip to keep herself awake. It wasn't time to go to sleep yet. The pretty lady always tucked her into bed and sang a song.

"Not tonight, Lali," the pretty lady said. "Tonight, you will return to bed and dream of the days yet to come."

"Okey dokey." Lali's eyes drifted shut as she yawned big. She blinked and blinked and blinked, trying to stay awake for just a little while longer. "I can do that."

The pretty lady tied her mask back on and went to the window. She stopped with her hand on the lock and looked over her shoulder at them. "I shall be watching."

Nana nodded, and then the pretty lady opened the window and was gone. A cold wind blew in and Lali shivered. Nana scooted Lali off to bed and shut the window, then tucked her in and sang a song to her.

When Nana was gone and the lights were out, Lali drifted into sleep, her mind filled by the days yet to come.

## Acknowledgments:

Many thanks to Traci Burrell and Lee Carpenter for their expertise on DragonCon. All errors in interpretation and fact are my own.

## About the Author:

Lucy Varna lives in Georgia, surrounded by her large, extended family. Visit her online at:

www.lucyvarna.com
www.daughtersofthepeople.com

## The Daughters of the People Series

Book 1: *The Prophecy*
Book 2: *Light's Bane*
Book 3: *The Enemy Within*
Book 3.5: *Tempered*
Book 4: *In All Things, Balance*

## Also by Lucy Varna, the Cullowhee Heritage Series

Book 1: *A Higher Purpose*
Book 2: *A Wicked Love*

Look for *Say Yes* (A Sons of the People Novel) coming in April 2015.

*The adventure continues...*

*Sanctuary* (Daughters of the People, Book 5)
Jerusha Mankiller and Drew Martin continue the People's
search for Sanctuary and the Bones of the Just.

*Coming soon!*

## Future books in the series:

Book 6: *The Gathering Storm*

Book 6.5: *Redemption*

Book 7: *War's Last Refuge*

*Don't miss the first Sons of the People novel!*

Single mom Sera Noland wasn't looking for love the day
Levi Ewart walked into her life, especially when her heart,
and her son's, had already endured enough hurt to last a
lifetime.

Look for *Say Yes* (A Sons of the People Novel)
coming in April 2015.

www.ingramcontent.com/pod-product-compliance
Lightning Source LLC
Chambersburg PA
CBHW070657180626
46817CB00006B/2416